OPERATION
RABBIT HOLE

IRONHAND'S WAR: VOLUME 1

MIKE LYONS

**There by
Candlelight**
Press

OPERATION RABBIT HOLE

Copyright 2014 by Mike Lyons

Cover by: Jennifer Williamson

Smashwords Edition

www.cmikelyons.wordpress.com

Published by

There By Candlelight Press

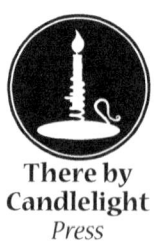

**There by
Candlelight**
Press

CONTENTS

Chapter I Operation Rabbit-Hole 1

Chapter II The Lake Of Deserters.. 18

Chapter III A Long Chase And A Small Dragon 32

Chapter IV Rabbix Tends To A Small Bill................................ 51

Chapter V Head-Trip From A Centauripede 71

Chapter VI Cat And Pepper-Spray 91

Chapter VII A Maddening Tea-Party..110

Chapter VIII The Queen's Palace Grounds.............................137

Chapter IX The Mock-General's Tent.......................................159

Chapter X The Lethal Ballet..186

Chapter XI Who Stole The Queen?...214

Chapter XII Uncle's De-Brief..240

Glossary...252

About the Author's Cat..257

To the men and women who place themselves in harm's way for the safety and security of others.

Acknowledgements

First and foremost, I want to thank my wonderful beloved Jenn, without whose love, support, and encouragement, this novel would never have moved beyond the short story level.

I would like to thank the good people at La Madeleine Duluth, my writing home-away-from-home.

And, of course, to Professor Charles Dodgson, without whom there would be no Wonderland for my poor boys to invade.

CHAPTER 1
OPERATION RABBIT-HOLE

In retrospect, we should have realized it wouldn't be that easy. We had all read the pre-mission reports. Grown up on them, so to speak. Kid's stories, we thought. Piece of cake, we thought.

We were idiots.

> -CSM Daniel "Uncle" Beckworth, official de-brief, Operation Rabbit Hole.

"GRENADE!" HALSFORD'S VOICE WAS a penetrating snarl. Something small and round 'thumped' in the meticulously trimmed grass and rolled to a halt at Command Sergeant Major Daniel Beckworth's feet. He looked down with idle curiosity. A red and white croquet ball rested against the matte black leather of his combat boot.

"Boom," Halsford snickered. "You're dead."

Beckworth rolled the ball towards Halsford with a gentle nudge of his foot. "Put that back," he ordered, glancing at the neatly racked balls and mallets of the croquet stand nearby.

"Would you care for some tea, sir?"

Beckworth turned partly around to look at the small, dignified man in a butler's uniform. What was his name again? William?

1

Walter? Something with a W. The butler was in his late forties or early fifties, with a fringe of white hair clinging to the sides and back of his skull. He was short and slender, with a ram-rod straight back that made Beckworth wonder if the man had served in the military at some point. Maybe the Falklands? Currently he was all but wringing his hands at Beckworth and his men.

"No thanks, I'm fine," Beckworth gave the butler a nod of dismissal. "We're all fine," he added before the old man could start asking the other members of AFO Spectre.

The man hesitated for just a fraction of a second, sniffed softly, turned on his heel and marched away to rejoin the cluster of VIPs at the table in the porch shade.

"Definitely in the military," Beckworth muttered to himself. He turned to survey his men, and had to concede that the old butler had a point. AFO Spectre looked as out of place as a banana mag in a wedding bouquet.

Perfectly mowed grass surrounded a low maze of a rose garden cleverly arranged so that the red flowers were always 'inside' and the white ones were 'outside' of each pathway. In the center of the maze, a white gazebo sheltered a trio of marble benches, beside one of those fountains with little cherubs pissing. At the far end of the lawn, a break in the high bushes offered a glimpse of sunlight sparkling off the water of a small stream, partly shaded by a huge, twisted old oak.

In this setting, his team looked like an abomination. This was a place for gentle repose, for reading a book by the stream under the shade of the tree, or for wandering through the rose maze and smelling the sweetly blooming flowers. It was no place for camouflage fatigues, combat boots, firearms.

"Sir, why are we here?" Jones asked, digging his toe into the grass.

"I'm sorry," Beckworth said, "Did I take a different plane here? Was I involved in high-level meetings with the President while the rest of you were bouncing around inside a C-130? No, I've been with you the whole time. How the heck should I know?"

"Because you are E-9," Fernandez, Beckworth's second-in-command, grinned. "You guys know everything."

Snickers issued from most of the team.

Fernandez chuckled, glanced at Halsford, and said, "Relax. This is the nicest place we've ever been briefed. What, you'd rather be back in Kunar?"

"I'd rather be in your mom," Halsford sneered, but he couldn't muster his usual venom. It was the nicest place the team had ever been briefed.

Beckworth couldn't blame the team for being bored. He was too. They had been cooling their heels there for over half-an-hour, ever since being dropped off by helicopter in this very nice, proper English garden. Sixteen hours before that, they had been in Kandahar, hot on the trail of a weapons shipment bound for insurgent hands. The locational whiplash left the team dizzy.

Beckworth half-expected Halsford to toss a real grenade soon if someone didn't explain why they had been pulled away from insurgent-hunting to stand idly in a garden.

Time to make that happen.

Beckworth crossed the meticulous lawn to the porch, surveying the VIPs present as he walked.

Beckworth recognized only one of them. The team had reported to Captain Michael Park as ordered when they had arrived in England. He had met them at RAF Alconbury, hustled them into the Twin Huey, and flown with them to this place.

Beckworth still wasn't sure exactly whose house they were sullying with their presence.

Captain Park was an Air Force man, but Beckworth didn't hold that against him. The Captain was an inch or so short of the six-foot mark, with shiny black hair and the tan skin of his Korean ancestry. As Beckworth approached, Park was in a three-way argument with a pair of other men.

One man, three or so inches taller than Park, was a local if his accent was any indication. He had soft brown cut long and swept back from a high forehead, crooked teeth, and the slightest bit of a slouch to his shoulders. He wore a brown department-store suit and an expensive Italian silk tie. He was handsome enough to irritate Beckworth on principle.

The other man in the argument was the shortest of the three, at around five foot eight or so. He was slender, with dignified gray hair that belied his mid-forties age. He wore an expensive navy blue suit and thousand dollar loafers. His face was red from yelling and his eyes were red from tears.

Beside the three of them, a family sat around the iron table. The woman was in her late thirties, with a round face and pink cheeks. She wore an exquisite cream silk pantsuit over a pastel rose blouse. To her right was a man Beckworth took to be her husband. He had short salt-and-pepper hair, a perfectly tailored gray silk suit, and one of those puffy ascot ties. On his lap, a little girl of no more than nine years rested her head on daddy's shoulder. She looked as if she had been crying lately. Behind them, in the shadows but ever-ready to spring forth at the faintest of gestures, lurked the butler W-something.

"Sorry to disturb, sirs." Beckworth was anything but. "The animals are getting restless. Can someone please tell me why we're here?"

"Minister, please," the shorter of the standing men said to Park. "I really don't care which of you explains it, just do it. It is

U.S. policy that our troops be briefed by one of our own people. Please, if Captain Park really wants to run the briefing, please, I beg you, just let him."

The Brit with the crooked teeth let out an aggrieved sigh, then looked at Beckworth. "Very well," he said, pinching the bridge of his nose, then looked at Park once more. "You seem to have Lord Mardling's blessing on this," he inclined his head briefly at the seated man. "Fine, have it your way."

"Thanks," Park said in a droll tone. "Sergeant, with me."

"Yes sir," Beckworth said. He nodded to the Ministry of Defense man, then turned and began walking back to his team.

Park kept up with him. For an Air Force man, the Captain could really cover ground. Crooked Teeth, who had decided to follow them, had trouble keeping up.

The team snapped to attention as the small group arrived.

"As you were," Park said.

The team relaxed into parade rest.

"I'll keep this as brief as possible, since we're up against the clock on this one," Park began. He started pacing as he talked, inspecting each of Beckworth's men in turn. "Just under forty-seven hours ago, Fiona McGinney, the daughter of U.S. Ambassador Andrew McGinney, was playing here at the home of her friend Eustice Mardling when she, Fiona, was abducted. Eustice, a handful of gardeners, and the Mardling family's nanny Patrice, all saw it happen. Their accounts are consistent with each other."

Halsford and Jones glanced briefly at each other. A kidnapped girl was sad, but it didn't explain the presence of a U.S. Special Forces team in full combat regalia.

"The girls were playing down by the river," Park continued. "Four men, very short Caucasians, dressed in strange clothes and wearing red tabards with three crossed black swords, came around that tree," he pointed at the large oak. "They grabbed Fiona, then ran into that hedge right there," he pointed again. "They never came back out."

Park took a deep breath, then let it out slowly. He looked uncomfortable saying whatever came next aloud. "No-one saw where the men came from. They were not wet, so they didn't come out of the river. No-one saw them crossing the estate grounds from any other direction. It is as if, the various eye-witnesses said, they simply appeared out of no-where, took the girl, and then vanished again after climbing into the bushes.

"Lord Mardling called the police and Ambassador McGinney. The police inspected the bushes. They found physical evidence suggesting that a large group of people had crawled part-way into the hedge. Then the evidence trail simply ended. Lord Mardling had a section of the bushes bulldozed. This exposed a hole in the ground. Initially, the hole was about a meter in width and ran mostly parallel to the surface. They found it because one of the bulldozers collapsed part of it driving over.

"After more digging, they revealed a tunnel around forty feet in length, slowly descending at about a five degree angle. The tunnel ended in a large hole, twelve or so feet in diameter, that ran straight down. Dropping glow sticks down revealed nothing. The sticks fell and fell until they could no longer be seen."

Park stopped pacing and faced the line of men. They had their 'game faces' on; expressionless and hard. The story so far made very little sense, but each man was aware that the Department of Defense would not have pulled them from an important mission and flown them halfway around the world on a lark. There would be a point eventually. They just had to let the Air Force officer get to it.

Park cleared his throat, then went on. "The police sent a

volunteer on a rope down. She descended one hundred feet, to the end of the rope, but saw no turn offs and no end to the pit. She could not see the glow sticks they had dropped either, although it was possible that the tunnel would become a slope and some point and the sticks had rolled out of sight.

"They called for longer rope. Five hundred feet, lowered by crane. Nothing. Ambassador McGinney began calling his various contacts, asking if anyone had any idea about a bottomless pit in at the edge of Lord Mardling's estate. No-one did. Not at first. Then, the entire thing came to the attention of a scholar friend of his, who offered a hypothesis.

"This land was purchased by the Mardling family in the late Fifties. Prior to that, it had been owned by the Littles."

Park waited for a response, but it never came. Beckworth wracked his brain, and could tell the others were doing the same. Little... Little... Stuart? John? Red Riding Hood? What was the Captain getting at?

Park grinned in sheepish embarrassment. They were getting to the really uncomfortable part it seemed. "This scholar friend specialized in English literature, especially Nineteenth Century stuff. He suggested that, just possibly, this was the same hole that Alice Little described falling down in Alice's Adventures in Wonderland."

"Buh-what?" Adams blurted. He blushed deeply when both Park and Beckworth looked sharply at him. "Sorry sirs," he muttered.

Park chuckled, shaking his head. "It's all right, Sergeant," he said. "I felt quite the same way. Anyways, allow me to make a very long story at least a little shorter. Somehow..." and here he covered his mouth and pretend-coughed, "*NSA*." He then resumed speaking normally is if nothing had happened, "... this entire situation came to the attention of the DOD and someone at Special Circumstances Command."

Park paused again to see if that elicited a response.

This time, it did.

Beckworth had heard of SCC. Everyone at Fort Bragg had. It was a nearly-mythical department created after the 2004 Incursion, to deal with similar situations should they ever arise again. That Park was even mentioning it meant that someone, somewhere, had decided that they had, indeed, arisen again.

"SCC got involved, but not before the Brits tried sending their cop down again, this time with a mile of line. The descent appeared steady from the top, but radio reception died part way down. When they pulled the line back up, they found the harness empty. Their officer had vanished." Park started pacing again. "The DOD contacted McGinney, had him arrange things with Whitehall to allow a team of US operators to come in and handle the situation. You, gentlemen, were JSOC's first choice. Congratulations."

He gave the team a grim, tight smile that lacked real humor. "So. Your mission is to descend the hole by whatever means you deem best. Find and effect the return of Fiona McGinney. Ascertain the situation on the other side of what we assume is a Portal event. Determine if those on the other side represent a continuing threat to the people and safety of the United States or the Earth in general. If you can find that missing cop, bring her back too. Find a way back home. If possible, and if the indigents on the other side represent a threat, attempt whatever sabotage you can safely manage but do not unduly risk yourselves. The return of Fiona McGinney and the gathering of intelligence about people and conditions on the other side, are of paramount importance. Any questions?"

"Where do I start?" Halsford muttered.

Luckily for his future promotion prospects, Park pretended not to hear him.

"I have one sir," Jones spoke up. "Do we have any intelligence on what to expect down there?"

The expression Park made was half-way between a grin and a grimace. "Well, we do have the Preliminary HUMINT Report."

"I don't suppose we have access to this PHR?" Jones asked.

"Sure," Park nodded. He reached under his dress jacket and pulled something from his back hip pocket. He tossed the object to Jones.

Beckworth glanced over to see what Jones had. It was a used copy of Lewis Carroll's Alice's Adventures in Wonderland.

"We're basing our entire mission on a children's book?" Halsford scoffed.

"Can you say 'unreliable narrator?'" Adams smirked.

"Since when are seven year old girls unreliable?" Fernandez grinned wide, showing off his perfect teeth. "I have one of those, and I have never known her to be less than perfectly accurate about everything. In fact, I loan her out to the NSA from time to time. They're usually so reluctant to give her back, I have to hire mercenaries to assault Fort Meade."

"I understand your feeling," the English man with the crooked teeth spoke up, ignoring Fernadez' attempt at wit. "Sadly, this is the only intelligence we have, the only report by anyone who has ever even claimed to have been through this particular Portal. Until twenty hours ago, we all assumed this was fiction, written by Professor Dodgson for one of his child-friends. It turns out, however, that maybe he simply wrote down what she told him, rather than making it up himself."

Jones offered the book to Beckworth, who shook his head. Jones slipped it into the left thigh pocket of his fatigues.

"Anything else you can tell us?" Beckworth asked, including both Captain Park and the Englishman in the question.

Park handed out 5x7 photographs, one to each team member.

Beckworth looked at the one he was handed. Fiona McGinney was an adorable little angel with chestnut hair, hazel eyes, and a cheerful, gap-toothed smile.

Marquez, the newest member of the team, smiled at the picture. "She looks like my little sister, when she was a girl," he said.

Halsford opened his mouth to respond, then glanced at Park. He snapped his mouth shut.

"If there are no other questions?" Park looked at each man in turn, assessing. Then he nodded. "All right then. Follow me." He walked past the group, heading towards the old oak and the river beyond.

Past the tree, Beckworth saw the torn-up hedge and a huge hole in the ground. A massive industrial crane sat idly next to it, a man in work clothes and a hard-hat reading a book in the operator's seat.

A half-dozen parachutes lay in a pile beside the hole. Six 'chutes for six soldiers: Park would not be going with them.

Beckworth nodded a chin at the parachutes, then looked at Park.

Park shrugged. "In case you want them."

"According to the PHR, the girl just jumped down, right?" Fernandez asked.

"More like fell," Jones said with a shrug. "But yeah. She wasn't exactly a paratrooper."

"It's up to you," Park said. "We can lower you like they did with the cop, you can use the parachutes, or you can just trust that the PHR is at least that accurate, and just jump." He faced the team, braced to attention, and snapped a salute.

The team followed suit.

"Go with God, gentlemen," Park said.

"Thank you, Sir," six voices rang out in unison.

Park dropped the salute, then stepped back to let Beckworth take command of his team.

Beckworth turned to survey the men. If they were nervous or scared about jumping into a possibly bottomless pit in search of a little girl who may or may not have been kidnapped by characters from a children's book, they didn't show it. He felt a momentary burst of pride in his band of killers. He cleared his throat and spoke. "All right, animals," he said, "Let's do the job."

"The things I do for my country," Halsford muttered. "Hoo-fucking-ah."

"Relax," Fernandez slapped Halsford on the back. "This is your chance to get your DD 256."

"Thanks," Halsford snarled. He stepped to the edge of the hole and looked down. "Are we really doing this?"

"Last one down, buys," Jones grinned, turned his back to the hole, and jumped. A drawn out "Woohoo!" echoed back up as he plummeted.

"Fuck," Haslford drew the word out to three syllables. He leaned forward over the edge, further and further, until gravity pulled him in.

Adams blew a bubble with his gum, shrugged, and stepped off. Fernadez looked at Beckworth, grinned, and yelled "Geronimo!" as he did a swan-dive. Marquez swallowed nervously, then did a text-book perfect plane exit. Beckworth rolled his eyes, nodded at Captain Park, and stepped off feet-first.

        *   *   *   *

            *   *   *

        *   *   *   *

The shaft was dirt lined, as expected, but that didn't last very long. He never noticed the transition point, but Beckworth found himself falling past wood paneled walls lined with shelves and cupboards. Pictures and maps hung on pegs here and there as he fell. On the shelves were all manner of things, from small jars, to tea sets, to books, to small statuettes. He looked below to see how his men were doing, but he couldn't see anyone else. He looked back up, startled to realize he also couldn't see the opening above. There was no source of light that he could find, neither from above nor below, but he could see well enough to read the titles of some of the books as he fell past. That, more than anything else, unnerved him. He should have been falling far too fast to read a book spine.

"What the hell?" he muttered to himself. He seemed to be going only a slight bit faster than a brisk walk. Yet, he had been falling for over 10 seconds: he should have been going well over a hundred miles per hour by this point. He looked at his watch, and counted off another ten seconds. Then he looked at the shelves again. He read "ORANGE MARMALADE" on a label tied to one of the jars as he fell past.

Some quick math told him that he should have fallen somewhere around half a mile, and yet he was still moving slow enough to read labels.

Experimenting, he tucked his arms and legs in and tilted himself head-down. That should have increased his fall rate by roughly 2/3rds. He craned his head to see the shelves, and had no problem at all reading the title of A Syllabus of Plane Algebraic

Geometry as he plunged by. Tucking into the dive position did not, as far as he could tell, alter his velocity in any way.

He fretted over this for another minute or so, then shrugged and decided that, since there was nothing he could do about it, he should just accept the situation. He scanned below himself, but once more was unable to spot any trace of the rest of his team. He tried to identify the source of the light by which he was able to see the shelves, but it continued to elude him. Finally, he watched the shelves go by and wondered, idly, who had built them and why.

After a time, he yawned. Looking at his watch again, he realized that he had been falling for over ten minutes. If he were traveling at terminal velocity, he would have gone well over 12 miles by this point. How deep is the Earth's core? he wondered to himself. He wracked his brain, trying to remember things he hadn't thought about since high school. Let's see, he thought, the Earth is around 8000 miles or so in diameter. That would make it 4000 miles to the center, but there's a mantle and a crust and other stuff before that. How thick is the crust? Am I going to hit lava before I land? He didn't feel particularly hot, but he was falling and the air was keeping his brow quite dry. The PHR didn't say anything about lava, he mused. Hopefully, we're safe.

Another glance at his watch. Fifteen minutes. Of course, I don't seem to be moving really all that fast, he thought. Around the speed of a normal jog. So let's see, I double-time at around 8 MPH. A quarter of that is two miles. So maybe I haven't fallen all that far yet.

Beckworth yawned again. This is new, he thought, I've never been bored during a jump before. Even that novelty soon wore off, and he remembered that the PHR mentioned falling asleep during this drop. Not gonna happen, he promised himself.

When Beckworth woke, he was still falling.

He looked around quickly in panic, and saw the ground. It was coming at him sideways, and quite fast. Somehow, during his brief nap, he had managed to turn himself around. He flailed his arms, trying to angle himself correctly before he hit the ground.

To no avail.

He landed with an audible 'thump!' on a large pile of small twigs and leaves. His men were standing around, watching. Halsford had a mocking smirk on his lips. Fernandez offered a hand and helped Beckworth stand.

"Well, that was different." Beckworth brushed leaves and twigs from his fatigues. "Knock it off," he scowled at the men, triggering a wave of snickers swiftly hidden behind cleared throats and turned backs.

The pile that softened the landing was at one end of an otherwise uninteresting hallway. The floor was once polished wood, scratched and scuffed over the course of many years. Around thirty feet from where they stood, the hallway looked as if it made a 90 degree left turn.

"Looks like a soccer team uses this place as a short-cut to the field," Adams said, indicating the wear on the floor.

"Futball," Fernandez said in a deceptively mild voice, still hiding his manic grin. "We're in England."

"Are we?" Marquez asked.

No one had a good answer for that.

The entire team had an aura of barely-suppressed mania. Beckworth understood the feeling. The long fall – a glance at his watch told him it had lasted over 2 hours – had him rattled as well. He pushed the feeling into a corner of his mind. They had a job to do.

14

"Okay," he said. "Nap time is over." He instantly regretted saying that, but it was too late now. Best to just keep going and pretend he hadn't noticed his unfortunate word choice. "We have a mission; let's get on with it. Vodka, you have point. Move out."

Jones nodded once, sharply, and began to walk up the hallway. Knees bent, taking each step slow, careful, and silent, the team advanced to the corner. Jones paused before the turn and undid the button on one of his belt pouches. He pulled out a small mirror, and crouched at the corner. He slowly extended the mirror, angled to show him what was around the turn. He withdrew the mirror and returned it to his belt before standing. "Clear," he said in a voice barely above a whisper, then stepped around the corner.

Halsford followed, fanning wide to the right and sighting along the barrel of his M249. The light machine gun was easily a third again as long, and almost three times as heavy, as the M4s most of the team sported. It might have been made of balloons for all the difficulty Halsford showed carrying it.

Once the two of them turned the corner and stepped forward, the rest of the team followed suit two-by-two. The new hallway was an extension of the first one; wood floor scuffed and worn in the center. However, unlike the first hall, this was more than just floor and blank walls.

A row of lamps hung from the ceiling and provided dim, flickering illumination. Here and there, on the wall, a small curtain provided a break in the otherwise endless parade of doors on both sides. The doors came in all sizes and shapes. Several had a large white 'X' inscribed in chalk on them, others did not. The only commonality among all of the doors was the prominent keyhole in each.

In the center of the hallway stood a little three-legged table made all of glass. On the other side of the table, facing them, stood a man.

He was short, around five feet tall, with white hair although his face was unlined and youthful. His nose was wide and flat, and his nostrils flared and twitched with nervous energy above a magnificent Imperial mustache. His ears were unusually long in the lobes, and his eyes were small and black and wide-set on his face. He wore shapeless white pants of some vaguely fuzzy material, perhaps uncombed wool. Above that, he wore a waistcoat in an archaic style, with the golden chain of a pocket-watch quite visible, and a white jacket that matched his pants. On his nose, he wore a pair of small, round, wire-framed glasses with pink lenses. He looked up, startled, as the team came around the corner. In his hand was a golden key.

"The fuck?" Halsford snapped. "Contact!"

"Oh dear!" exclaimed the strange white-haired man.

"Freeze!" Jones yelled. "Don't move, or we'll... crap!" That last was because the white-haired man turned on his heel and dove through the solitary open door in the hallway.

"You said it was clear," Halsford complained to Jones.

"It was," Jones frowned, shaking his head in confusion.

"Shut up," Beckworth said. "Did you see the key in his hand? According to the PHR, that's the one we need."

Jones and Halsford looked at each other for the briefest of moments, then ran to the door. The rest of the team followed and stacked up along the wall. Jones peered around the corner, then shook his head. "I can't see anything, sir," he said.

"No sign of our friend?" Beckworth asked.

"No sir, I mean I can't see anything. It's pitch black in there."

Beckworth nodded. "All right. NODs, and let's go."

Everyone reached up onto their helmets and pulled down their night-vision scopes. Jones did a one-two-three hand count with Halsford nodding in time with each motion. Then they darted through the door in an X pattern to clear the doorway for the others. Two by two, the rest of the team followed them through.

*   *   *   *
    *   *   *
*   *   *   *

CHAPTER 11

THE LAKE OF DESERTERS

———◆———

Whoever cleans up that hallway with all the doors, we suspect it might be Rabbix, needs to do a better job. When we shrunk, we could see the underside of the table. No one ever needs to see wads of gum that large.

No one.

-CSM Daniel "Uncle" Beckworth, official de-brief, Operation Rabbit Hole

THERE WAS A BRIEF falling sensation, and then a "Splash!" and Beckworth found himself under water. Long hours of training saved him: he clamped down on the impulse to gasp at the sudden cold. He thrashed his arms and legs for a moment before forcing himself to calm down. He needed to figure out which way was 'up' in a hurry. He ripped the Night Observation Device from his head; it did him no good underwater. The water was dark and murky, but he could see his hand in front of his face. That was good. He stilled his movements, and then slowly let out a small amount of his breath. The bubbles went that-a-way, and he kicked his legs to follow them. A moment later, his head broke the surface, and he allowed himself that long-delayed gasp.

Beckworth shook his head to clear his eyes. Treading water, he looked around.

He seemed to be in a large lake or small inland sea. The water on his lip was mildly salty, but there were no large swells. In the distance, he could see a mountain range to his left, while in all other directions there was a light woods at the shore of the water. The sun was overhead, but the day cool. A chill breeze blew from the mountains.

As he surveyed the scene, Fernandez' head broke water a few feet away. The team medic gasped and coughed. While he was doing that, four more heads emerged and did likewise.

"What the heck?" Marquez said.

Adams kicked water a bit harder, lifting himself a couple of feet above the surface before falling back in. He did this four times, turning himself ninety degrees between each lift. Scouting. "I think I see a structure over there," he said, pointing.

"Sounds good to me," Fernandez shrugged, then turned to Beckworth. "What do you say, sir? Maybe someplace we can dry off? It's a little chilly to be running around in wet clothes if we can avoid it."

Beckworth nodded. "Yeah," he said. "Sounds good." He couldn't see the man they were after, so one direction was as good as any other.

The team swam with quiet deliberation, keeping their arms and legs under the water and doing side- or breast-strokes. After a few minutes of this, Marquez spoke up. "So, what happened back there? How did we get from inside that hallway to the middle of this lake or whatever it is?"

"Magic," Fernandez said with a grin. "Sorcery. Brujería. The dark arts."

"Right," Halsford sneered. "Magic. Cuz I believe in that shit."

"You got a better explanation?" Fernandez asked between strokes. Conversation was difficult while swimming in the amount of gear each man carried.

"Hold," Adams said softly. They were nearing the shore, perhaps a hundred yards away. Immediately, everyone stopped swimming and tread water.

Beckworth whispered, "What do you have?"

Adams pointed toward the shore. A short beach, black dirt and gray pebbles, gave way to slender, white-barked trees and thick dark shrubs. "I thought I saw something moving," Adams said, "Just beyond the tree-line."

Beckworth nodded. He lifted his hand slowly from the water so that it wouldn't make splashing sounds, then gestured to the left. "Vodka and Texas, flank left." He turned his hand to the right, "Parrot and Zombie, right. Rider and I will go up the middle."

Jones and Marquez began swimming to the left, while Fernandez and Halsford went right. Adams and Beckworth swam straight ahead, eyes straining for glimpses of movement. They swam low in the water, with only their eyes and the tops of their heads showing except when the raised their noses to breathe. After a time, Beckworth felt ground beneath his feet and began to duck walk forward.

Adams raised a hand in a fist, and everyone stopped moving. He pointed two fingers at his eyes, then gestured with the blade of his hand to a spot in the woods a couple of degrees to the left of straight ahead. After a moment, Jones pointed at his eyes also. He had seen whatever it was that drew Adams' attention.

It took Beckworth a few more seconds, during which time the team began to creep forward again, before he saw it also. There was a small clearing perhaps a dozen or so yards into the woods. In the clearing stood several figures who appeared to be chatting with each other.

The team approached the clearing from three sides. As they drew near, they began to make out the sounds of conversation. They halted just outside the clearing and watched for a moment, assessing the threat.

There were seven men in the clearing, and they did not look like they posed much of a danger to the Spectres. They were an odd-looking group, but Beckworth could not see any weapons except for simple knife one of them wore thrust through his belt.

The one with the knife was doing the talking at first. He was a short, slender man with a long, pointy nose which twitched constantly, and small, beady eyes. He wore mutton-chop sideburns and a pencil-thin mustache. His hair was a mousy brown color, his skin tanned to the point of being almost walnut in color. He wore brown leather pants and a homespun shirt and the tattered, filthy remains of some sort of tabard.

To his left stood another short man. He wore a green cap upon his round, bald head, and a tattered white coat over a dark brown shirt. His face was smooth shaven, with strange, long, thin lips that protruded from his mouth in a most peculiar way. He wore boots several sizes too large for his feet, and they flopped about whenever he shifted position.

Next to him stood an even shorter man; fat, with a protruding gut. His hair was dark brown, slicked up and back in a smallish sort of Pompadour style. His nose was huge, long and bulbous at the end. His arms and legs seemed short for his size, although perhaps it was merely his girth that made it seem so.

At the mid-point in the circle, opposite the mousy-looking fellow in the brown leathers, was an equally short fellow with bright red hair worn short and neat. He had a very small nose with a decidedly sharp downward crook to it, looking almost as if it had been broken and then reset by someone who didn't like

21

him much. He wore a motley assortment of clothes in all manner of garish yellows, oranges, and greens. His eyes were bright and alert, and they darted about constantly as if he were nervous.

At his side stood a youth, in his middle-teens perhaps. He was of the age where the adult he would become warred, not always successfully, with the child he had been. He had unruly hair that stuck up in tufts here and there, and red, blotchy skin. His clothes were similarly unkempt, with patches at the knees and elbows.

Beside the boy, a very short man, of about the same size of the speaker but different in every other way, rocked back and forth on his feet. Where the speaker was all brown and nervous, this man was yellow from the hair on his head to the saffron shoes on his slender feet. He puffed his chest with self-importance and reminded Beckworth of several fresh-from-officer-training lieutenants that he had met during his years in the service.

The last of the circle was two or three hairs taller than the men on either side of him, although still quite short by American standards. He had a long, sharp nose on a proud face under a shock of black hair. His coat was also black, with long opera tails, worn open to show the white shirt underneath, and his trousers matched his shirt rather than the coat.

Beckworth frowned. All of the men present, and for that matter the one who stole the golden key also, were all no more than five feet tall and every one of them was subtly 'wrong' in some way. He couldn't put his finger on exactly what it was about each of them that struck him as disturbing, but he found himself mentally comparing them (not always favorably) to animals. The speaker was a mouse, the one with the green cap was a duck, and so on. Beckworth shook his head. He forced himself to stop idly speculating and focus on what the mouse-man was saying.

"We can't let him go," said the mousy-looking man as the Spectres paused to watch. "He still has clout with the Queen. Remember, he used to be married to her third cousin on her father's side back before the Diamond Wars. If we let him go, he will tell her about us. Do you want that? Well, do you?"

"N-n-no, of c-c-course n-not," said the man with the huge nose in a sonorous voice. "B-b-but what c-can w-we d-d-d-do? H-he has th-th-the w-watch. T-t-time is on his s-s-side."

"We must run away again," said the redhead in the outlandish attire. His voice was sharp and high-pitched, with an almost musical lilt to his words. "He can only lead her here, and we won't be here. Besides," he paused for just a second, "she has more important things to worry about than us right now."

"Why, we capture him, of course," said the man all in yellow. "Then we will have a bargaining chip to use with the Queen. Why, we could negotiate our pardons and go back to our lives. I, for one, am quite tired of this tedious existence, always skulking about in the wilderness."

"We could kill him," said the man in the black opera coat. "Do it quickly before he has a chance to—"

Whatever else he would have said was lost as a noise in the underbrush caused all of the small men to turn and look. Someone crashed through the bushes, passing less than ten feet from where Jones crouched, motionless. Beckworth let out his held breath as the newcomer showed no signs of having spotted Jones. From the way she was hustling, she had more important things on her mind than searching for commandos in the underbrush.

The new arrival was a woman, short and squat, wearing an archaic metal breastplate dented and rusty from lack of proper care. A short-sword hung at either hip.

Beckworth gave Adams a significant glance at this sign of open armament. Adams nodded; he'd seen them too.

"What are you doing here?" snapped the mousy man in anger. "We told you to keep an eye on—"

"He's gone!" yelled the armed woman. "I turned my back for just a second, and when I looked back, he had rabbited. What do we do now?"

"Flee!" cried the man in many colors.

"Catch him," said the man in the opera coat.

"Oh d-d-dear," said the man with the big nose.

"There goes our bargaining chip," said the man in yellow.

"Does this mean we have to move again?" asked the teenager.

"Look," said the man in the green hat.

"Quiet," snapped the mousy-looking man, "and let me think. Just give me a second."

"No, I mean look!" said the man in the green hat. He was gazing past the clearing, and with a start, Beckworth realized he was looking right at Fernandez.

"Crap," Beckworth said. "All right: Go! Go! Go! Try to take them alive, we may need to question them."

The six men stood and advanced, weapons at the ready. "Freeze!" Beckworth yelled. "Nobody move, and you won't get hurt."

The expected level of chaos erupted at this point. The circle of short men disintegrated, each of them turning this way or that, looking for an escape. The mousy-looking man tried to slide under a fallen tree, but Fernandez was able to grab him by the leg and haul him back out. The majority of the others took no more than a step or two before realizing that they were surrounded, and reversed direction. Some ran into each other, some fell down. The woman in the breastplate drew her two short swords and rushed towards Halsford.

"Crap," muttered Beckworth again. He didn't want to kill the locals if it could be helped.

Halsford lifted his M249 and aimed it at the woman charging him. The woman didn't seem to know what the big weapon was, however, for she continued to run, yelling a fierce battle-cry. She swung her left sword at waist level and her right one at shoulder level in a crossing pattern.

Beckworth tensed, expecting an explosion of machine gun fire.

Instead, Halsford spun the M249 counter-clockwise, deflecting both sword blows and cracking his attacker across the temple with the butt in one smooth motion. The woman slumped to the ground, out cold. Halsford kicked the swords out of reach.

Looking up, Halsford caught everyone staring at him. "What?" he snapped.

Adams blew and popped a bubble. Fernandez chuckled. Jones smirked.

"All right." Beckworth turned his attention to the milling crowd of captives. "Calm down, and you won't be hurt. We just want some information. You may have guessed that we're not from around here. We're not here to hurt you, but we need to find someone. Short guy... well, maybe not by your standards," he corrected himself with a slight, embarrassed cough. Seeing that he had everyone's attention, he lifted his hand to shoulder level. "About this tall. White hair, long ears, pink glasses, waistcoat. He might have come out of the lake," he gestured behind himself, in case there was any doubt which lake he was talking about. "He took something we need, and we just want it back, that's all."

"He's talking about the—" the teenager started to say, but the man in yellow shut him up with an elbow to the ribs.

"Hey!" Jones snapped, stepping forward and pointing his weapon at the man in yellow. "Back off!"

The man in yellow puffed out his chest and glared at Jones imperiously. The effect was ruined by the fact that the man had to tilt his head back at an awkward angle to make eye contact with Jones, who topped out well over a foot taller. Still, the man managed to do an impressive job of looking 'down' his short little nose at the soldier.

"I am quite sure," the man in yellow chirped, "that we can come to an arrangement. I am the duly elected mayor of Carnford Downs. You may negotiate with me."

The man in the green hat snorted, but subsided at an angry glare by the man in yellow. "Now," said the yellow-clad fellow, "it seems that we have something you want, to wit: information. What do you offer in exchange?"

Halsford looked at Beckworth. "Sir, do we have time for this? I can make this little bird sing; just give me five minutes alone with him."

Beckworth shook his head at his man. "No," he said, "We don't hurt anyone if we don't have to." He slung his M4 behind him and crossed his arms, looking down at the man in yellow. He gave the man a placating smile. "Let us be civil. What do I call you, your mayorship?"

"As a ruler of a municipality, you address me by the name of my holding. You may call me Carnford," stated the man in yellow, giving Beckworth a calculating once-over. "I take it you are in charge of these... ruffians?"

"'Carney,' is more like it," Adams muttered.

"All right, Mr. Carnford." Beckworth ignored Adams. "What will it take to get you to tell me what I want to know?"

"Don't," said the mousy-looking man to Carnford. "They're with Him. Look at them! They're..." he paused for dramatic effect before finishing in a whispered hiss, "humans!"

Jones and Fernandez exchanged a glance at this.

Beckworth nodded calmly. "That's right," he said. "We're humans. And we're looking for another human. A—"

"I told you!" the mousy-looking man yelled. "They're with Him! They're lost and trying to get back to his army! Don't tell them anything! Bastards! Bastards!" he spat at Adams, who adroitly side-stepped the spittle.

"I have no idea who 'He' is," Beckworth continued in a calm, reasonable tone. "We're looking for a little girl who was taken a couple of days ago and brought here. We assume that the Queen knows about it, so we need to get to her. Now, we know that the fastest way to the Queen's castle is through the small door with the golden key, so we need the key that the fellow in the waistcoat and pink glasses took. Do you see? We get the key, we get the girl. We get the girl, we leave you in peace. It's that simple."

"G-g-girl?" the man with the big nose stepped forward. "D-d-do y-you m-m-mean A-a-alice? W-w-we haven't s-s-seen her in w-w-weeks."

"Weeks?" Fernandez raised an eyebrow. "Sir, wasn't that book published back in like, eighteen-eighty something?"

"We're getting side-tracked," Beckworth said. "We're not looking for Alice, we're looking for Fiona. But first, we need the golden key. Which was taken by the man in the pink glasses. Have you seen him?"

"We still haven't determined what it is you will be offering us in exchange for this information," said Carnford as he shoved the man with the big nose out of the way. "I am the duly elected mayor, and these are my privy cabinet members," he said, gesturing at the other captives. "And as you have treated us roughly, I believe that the price for what you want just went up. Yes, yes indeed. You'll really have to pay now."

"You attacked us," Adams pointed out.

The smile faded from Beckworth's face. He shook his head slowly. "I'm sorry you feel that way," he said softly to the mayor. "All right. I didn't want to have to do this, but you leave me little choice." He straightened his shoulders and took a step back, giving the captives a cold look. "You are not the privy council of anything. You are fugitives, on the run from the Queen. From the look of some of you, I'd say you're deserters from whatever army it is she's assembled to fight against whomever it is you think we are with. Now, I don't really care about your local politics, but you are stopping me and my men from accomplishing our mission, and that I do care about. So!" he clapped his hands together loudly, causing most of the captives to startle. "You can tell me what I want to know, and I mean Right Now, or..." he drew out the pause, looking at each man in turn. "Or I start giving you to him," he pointed at a wickedly smiling Halsford. "Your choice, but you have ten seconds to decide."

"Now listen here, human," said Carnford, who puffed up his chest. "You can't talk to me like that. I'm the—"

"Five seconds," Beckworth interrupted him. "I think we'll start with you, Mr. Mayor. Three seconds. Two. One. All right, take him."

"W-w-wait!" the man with the big nose waved his short little arms about in wild, frantic haste. "W-wait! D-d-don't hurt us! I w-w-will t-t-talk!"

"Perfect," muttered Halsford. "The one guy who wants to talk is the one who stutters."

Beckworth fought the urge to agree with Halsford's assessment of the Universe's sense of humor. He turned to the man with the big nose. "Your name?" he asked.

"Ch-Ch-Charles," said the man with the big nose.

28

"Really?" Marquez raised both eyebrows in surprise.

Adams smirked at him, but shook his head and put a finger to his lips for silence.

"Sorry," Marquez blushed.

"All right, Charles," Beckworth said, "Talk to me. The man with the pink glasses. Where is he?"

"G-g-gone," said Charles. "And I-I-I'm af-f-fraid you kn-n-nocked out th-th-the woman w-w-who c-can t-t-tell you m-m-more," he pointed at the unconscious figure in the breastplate at Halsford's feet. "Th-th-the m-m-man y-you're l-looking f-f-for is c-c-called R-R-Rabbix. He use-use-used to b-be th-the Q-Q-Queen's herald. Wh-when w-w-we s-saw h-h-him, w-we c-c-caught him and w-w-were d-d-deciding wh-what t-t-to d-d-do with him wh-wh-when you f-f-found us."

"God damn it," Halsford said.

"Vodka," Beckworth said to Jones, who nodded. "On it," Jones said. He grabbed the nearest captive, the man with the black opera coat, by the arm. "Show me where you were keeping Rabbix." He pushed the man in the opera coat gently but firmly in the direction from which the guard had come.

Beckworth turned to Marquez and said, "Collect the weapons. Toss 'em in the lake."

"Sir," Marquez nodded. He gathered up the guard's two swords and took the knife from the belt of the mousy-looking man. He walked to the shore of the lake and tossed the blades, one by one, into the water.

"You can collect those once we're gone," Beckworth said to Charles. "We mean you no harm, but if you come after us, we will not hesitate to kill you. Do you understand?"

Charles nodded.

Beckworth continued, "Good. Now, once we're gone, you all may want to find a new place to hide. We have no interest in turning you in, but if doing so helps us with our mission, we will do it. So you may want to be elsewhere when we reach the Queen, just in case she thinks to ask about you."

"Ahh, y-y-yes," said Charles, nodding. "I un-n-understand. Th-th-thank you."

From the woods, Jones' voice called, "Over here."

Beckworth made a circular motion with his hand, then pointed in the direction of the call. The rest of his men picked their way through the brush. Beckworth pulled up the rear, keeping an eye on the locals just in case one of them possessed a hidden weapon and an over-developed sense of vengeance. The last he saw of most of them, they were crouching over the woman in the breastplate and arguing about where to go next.

Jones waited for the group in another clearing perhaps a hundred yards or so deeper into the woods, near a ramshackle hut that had seen better decades. As Beckworth entered the clearing, Jones pointed at the ground. "Got his tracks," Jones said.

Beckworth nodded. He looked at the man in the black opera coat and said, "Scram."

The other man cocked his head at Beckworth in confusion. Evidently, 'scram' wasn't a word he was familiar with.

Beckworth tried again. "Go. Leave. Return to your friends. Now."

The short man understood that. He scampered off so fast, his feet barely touched the ground as he fled. The brush rustled behind him.

"Am I missing something?" Halsford asked. He lifted his left hand and peeled back the Velcro tab on his wristband. Inside was the picture of Fiona McGinney that Captain Park had given him. Halsford turned his arm so everyone else could see the picture. "They mistook this girl for Alice? McGinney's a brunette, for crying out loud. They look nothing alike."

"You're thinking of the cartoon," Fernandez said with a grin.

"No," Halsford shook his head, "I'm thinking of the pictures in the PHR. Alice was blonde."

"That's never said," Jones said. "In the Report, her hair color is never mentioned. The artist could have been wrong."

"Are you sure?" Halsford frowned at him.

"Man, I reread it on the way down," Jones said. Seeing the looks Halsford and Adams directed at him, Jones shrugged. "What? It was a boring fall."

"Makes sense," Fernandez said. "You've filled out dozens of after action reviews, right? How often do you manage to work your hair color into the report? You don't, because the person you're writing the report for already knows what you look like."

Halsford continued to frown for a moment. "Yeah," he said at last, "I guess you're right."

Beckworth cleared his throat, brushing his brown hair back from his forehead. The rest of the team looked at him. "All right," he said. "We're in potentially hostile territory. There seems to be some sort of internal conflict going on which we don't care about, but might engulf us anyway. Try to avoid it. We're here for the girl, the intelligence, and the cop; not to take sides in a local spat." He saw restrained impatience on the faces of his men; they were eager to get on with it. He nodded in approval. "From here on out, call-signs only. Try not to hurt the locals if we can avoid it, but don't take chances. We're pretty far out of range for a QRF. Conserve ammo, we're not getting a resupply. All right, you know all this, I'm not telling you anything new. Let's do the job. Who Wants To Live Forever?"

"We Do!" five voices rang out in unison.

Beckworth grinned. "Roll out."

CHAPTER III
A LONG CHASE AND A SMALL DRAGON

———◆———

The first few sets of locals we met were harmless weirdos. We allowed that to lull us into a false sense of security. Even the thing with 1SG Fernandez seemed more like a faintly amusing accident than anything truly malicious. Because the locals were small, we made the mistake of assuming that they were harmless. That error would cost us dearly.

-CSM Daniel "Uncle" Beckworth, official de-brief, Operation Rabbit Hole

VODKA TOOK POINT, WITH Zombie five paces behind him. Under normal circumstances, there would have been a larger gap between point and the next man, but Vodka was tracking which meant his attention was divided between his surroundings and the footprints and other signs of passage on the ground. This, in turn, meant it was not watching for ambushes. Thus, the closer than usual spacing.

The tracks, which consisted in the main of bent branches and torn leaves, lead more or less straight through the woods for nearly half of a mile. The wood gradually thinned in that direction, the trees growing more and more sparse and the bushes between them becoming thicker and harder to push through. Here and there, Vodka found fibers torn loose from the quarry's pants or jacket. The team moved in near silence, broken only by the occasional rustle of brush against fatigues. In the branches overhead, birds both familiar and those of a sort never seen on Earth called to each other.

The woods ended abruptly as if someone had drawn a line beyond which the trees could not grow, leaving the team facing a wide, rolling plain of grass. The thick, lush grass varied between ankle- and thigh-height to most of the team members. Small hillocks limited visibility to between one and two hundred yards. It looked, Uncle thought, rather like an ocean of grass with its swells and dips, peaks and valleys. He half expected to see a ship sailing across the prairie.

"Uncle," Vodka called attention to bent and crushed blades of grass leading off to the right. "He went that way," he added.

"Really?" Rider smirked. "You don't say?"

"All right," Uncle said, looking at the rather obvious tracks. "Anyone can follow these—"

"Even the FNG," Zombie muttered.

"— so we can pick up speed. Let's see if we can't catch this guy. This is already taking way longer than I was hoping for."

"And I'm still wet," Zombie complained. "After we get the key, I may have to show my displeasure. On this guy's face."

The team turned and began following the trail through the grass. Parrot chanted under his breath, "Kandahar. Bagram. Kabul. Mojave. Sahara. Gobi. Kalahari. International Grain Futures Conferences. Tax Annuities."

"What the fuck are you doing?" Zombie glanced over his shoulder at the medic.

"Thinking dry thoughts," Parrot replied with an overly saccharine-sweet smile.

33

Zombie muttered something inarticulate under his breath as he stomped ahead just a little faster. Texas chuckled. It was rare to see anyone reduce Zombie to inarticulate muttering.

"Do you ladies mind?" Uncle let a hint of steel creep into his voice. Silence fell, and after a time the birds in the trees to their right resumed their chatter.

The team crested one of the small hills, and Rider said, "Hold." He looked off into the distance from the vantage point, using the scope of his TAC-50, but they still weren't high enough. The hills further away from the woods were higher still, and the trail they followed was skirting the edge of the trees. "Sorry," Rider said with a shrug.

Uncle nodded, shrugged. "Roll out," he said to Vodka. The team resumed the hunt.

The sun shone directly overhead, but a cool breeze kept the temperature bearable. The exertion of the walk soon dried out the last of the lake water, only to replace it somewhat later with sweat. Down this hill they tramped, and then up the next, and then again, and again. Insects droned in the distance, and the birds chirped and sang lazily to each other. Their world was limited to the field of grass, the next hill in front of them, and the woods to their right. The constant up and down, combined with the monotony of the view, had a soporific effect. Uncle found himself zoning out now and again. That was dangerous. He shook his head and resolved to concentrate harder.

That resolve lasted for a few hours, and then he found himself spacing out again. From the way the others shook their heads violently from time to time, he knew the same thing was happening to everyone. It's not uncommon. You go into a situation keyed up and expecting violence, and instead you end up with hours of boredom and monotony.

Uncle cleared his throat, preparing to say something to re-focus the team when Vodka's voice said, "Sir? You need to see this."

Uncle stepped around Texas, Parrot, Rider, and Zombie. "What is it?" he asked.

Vodka pointed at the ground. Uncle looked down and cursed. "Crap," he said.

The single, narrow trail of bent grass they had been following had become a wide, much-trampled path. Several others had joined their quarry.

"What is it?" he asked. "Reinforcements? Or others chasing our guy also?"

Vodka shook his head angrily. He looked mightily pissed. Uncle had seen that look before. Vodka wore it whenever he was annoyed with himself. He felt he had made a mistake.

"What is it?" Uncle repeated.

"Sir," Vodka sighed in disgust. "That's us. We've gone in a circle."

"All that walking and we're back where we started?" Zombie kicked a tuft of grass. "I'm definitely going to jack this bastard up when we catch him."

Uncle frowned, then looked up at the sky. The sun was directly overhead. He glanced at his watch. It had been four hours since they landed from their long fall. "God damn it," he snarled. "The sun isn't moving. What the hell? Is it always noon here?" Texas opened his mouth to say something, but Uncle cut him off with a chopping motion. "Never mind. Vodka, did Rabbix turn off at any point? Or is he now following his own trail?"

Vodka did not answer right away. He was inspecting the bushes where, some hours ago, the team had left the woods and entered what they now realized must be a large circular prairie. At length, he shook his head. "Following his own trail sir," he said.

Uncle thought for a moment. "All right," he said. "Parrot, Zombie, Texas. Go back the way we came. This guy might just be going in circles to mess with us and tire us out. Vodka, Rider, and I will keep going ahead. If you find signs he went off the circle, fire two shots into the air and then wait there. We'll do the same. If you find our man, do not, I repeat, do not kill him. He could be useful in dealing with the Queen."

"How come I gotta babysit the FNG?" Zombie asked rhetorically.

Texas shot him a hurt look, but Uncle ignored the grousing. It was just Zombie being Zombie.

"What if we run into each other?" Rider asked.

"We'll deal with that if and when it happens," Uncle said. "Let's roll."

Zombie swept his arm in an exaggerated invitation to Texas, who took point. Parrot followed him, and then Zombie brought up the rear with the big gun. Going the other way, Vodka lead, followed by Rider and then Uncle.

Vodka continued to move with cautious deliberation, scanning both sides of the trail for any signs that the man with the pink glasses had stopped following his own tracks. Uncle had to force himself to be patient; the desire to hurry was strong. If they hurried, however, they might miss a subtle sign and end up costing themselves even more time later as they had to cover the ground yet a third time.

An hour into the second loop around the prairie, Uncle reflected that in a way, their quarry had done them a favor. There was no temptation to zone out this time, even if repeated viewings failed to make the terrain any more interesting.

An hour and a half after splitting up, they heard two reports from a little left of straight ahead.

Vodka looked over his shoulder at Uncle, who nodded.

"Run," Uncle said.

They ran.

A few minutes later they crested yet another hill. They saw their quarry halfway down the slope of the next hill ahead of them. He was running towards them, and behind him Uncle could see Texas and Parrot just reaching the top of the other hill.

Vodka ran down the hill, and the others followed him. They were less than one hundred yards apart when Rabbix looked up and saw Vodka heading towards him.

"Oh dear!" Their quarry came to a halt. He looked over his shoulder and saw all three of the second team bearing down on him. "Oh dear, oh dear!" said Rabbix. He dropped an old style folding paper fan and reached for the pocket of his waist-coat.

"Gun!" Vodka yelled.

Rabbix did not draw a weapon. Instead, he pulled out his pocket-watch and looked at it. He took one step to the side and turned so he could see both groups of men rushing at him. He lifted one hand and waved, while with the other he pressed the button on top of his watch.

Rabbix vanished.

"The fuck?" Vodka skidded to a halt. In front of him, Texas slowed and then stopped also.

"Are you fucking kidding me?" Zombie stared, open-mouthed, at the spot where their target had been just a moment before.

Everyone else arrived and stood around in a loose circle.

"Uh," Texas said. "What happened? Did... did he teleport?"

Uncle had no answer to that. He stood, in shock. To have come all this way and fail was unacceptable, but he could see no way to chase an opponent who could just teleport away whenever he felt like it. "Son of a bitch," he muttered.

Parrot bent down and picked up the fan. "He dropped this," he said. "Maybe... maybe he'll come back for it?"

"Please," Zombie said, his voice dripping derision. "He's gone. He's fucking gone. Damn it!"

"No," Vodka said. All heads turned towards him sharply. He pointed at the grass. "He didn't teleport," he said. "See? Bent grass. He ran off that way," he pointed into the woods.

"Invisibility then?" Parrot asked. "Hmm. Maybe we could... Hmm."

"Dust," Zombie said.

Everyone looked at him. Uncle lifted a hand, palm up, in a gesture to continue.

"Everyone get a pocket full of dust," Zombie said. "When his tracks end, toss the dust at where he should be. The dust wasn't with him when he went invisible, it should stay visible. It covers him, and we can see him that way."

"You've done this before have you?" Rider asked drily.

Zombie chewed his lip, looking more embarrassed than Uncle had ever seen. "Of course not," he said. "I uh... saw it."

"You saw it?" Parrot cocked his head at Zombie. "Where, exactly, have you ever encountered an invisible person before?"

Zombie looked away and muttered something. When everyone continued to stare, he repeated himself in a louder voice. "The Legion of Amazing Cavaliers," he snarled.

Parrot blinked in surprise. Rider snickered. Texas snorted. Jones rolled his eyes.

"Calm down," Uncle said. "Look, it's an idea. I don't hear the rest of you coming up with any. What the hell, it can't make things worse. Grab a handful of dirt, and let's go." He turned to Vodka and nodded. "Lead on."

Vodka pocketed a handful of dirt and grass, then began following the signs of passage into the woods again. The rest followed suit, scooping up pockets full of loose particulates with which to shower Rabbix, like the world's least sanitary wedding reception.

"I can't believe you watched that shit-fest of a movie," Rider said as the rest of the team followed Vodka into the brush.

"Bite me," Zombie replied. "The tickets were free."

"You over-paid."

Vodka moved as fast as he dared. There was no point in stealth; Rabbix knew they were coming. All the same, Vodka didn't dare rush too fast for fear of missing a sign and losing the track. The others crowded on his heels. Their eagerness and fear were palpable. The feeling was understandable; AFO Spectre had never faced an enemy that could turn invisible before. It altered the balance in ways they were not comfortable with.

There were a lot of things Uncle wasn't comfortable with on this mission, he mused. The entire fairy-tale nature of the situation, the obvious existence of some sort of phenomena he couldn't explain, and the fact that they seemed to have wandered into the middle of a war they knew nothing about; these things all disturbed him. What did I expect? he thought to himself as he pushed aside some vine-like thorny plant he recognized but couldn't think of the name of. It's not like the CIA has a Wonderland desk.

The chatter of birds overhead slowly took on an eerie cadence, like hearing people talking too softly to make out words but you knew it was a conversation by the pattern of it. Uncle began to feel that the birds were watching them and comparing notes. If they start laughing at me, we're having squab for dinner, he promised himself.

Uncle was deep into a fantasy about bursting into the house of a famous raven author and blowing him away as while he sat at his writing desk penning terrorist manifestos when Zombie's voice brought him back to reality. "Cut that shit out, Parrot. It's distracting."

Uncle decided that it wasn't worth stopping or even looking up for. Just Zombie bitching again. The man loved to bitch.

"What are you talking about?" Parrot's voice sounded genuinely confused. That was unusual. Normally when Parrot messed with Zombie, he sounded like he was laughing on the inside.

Vodka stopped and turned around.

Behind him was Texas, his weapon sweeping this way and that. He might be the FNG, Uncle thought, but he does know what he's doing. Texas also halted, and looked over his shoulder.

Behind him, the line went Parrot, Zombie, Rider, and then Uncle himself pulling up the rear. Uncle saw at once what Zombie was talking about: he almost couldn't see Parrot. Only the top of his head was visible over Rider's shoulder. The medic was either walking bent-knee, or he was standing in a ditch.

"Damn it, Parrot," Zombie said. "This isn't the time for this."

"What are you... wait," Parrot said. He looked around himself in fear, and a rising note of panic entered his voice. "What the heck is going on? Why are you..."

Uncle stepped aside so he could watch, and he saw Vodka tap Texas on the shoulder, then step around the new guy to see what the hold-up was. Uncle stopped dead and stared.

"Parrot," Uncle said, his voice dark and dangerous. "Tell me you're standing in the world's smallest patch of quicksand."

As Uncle watched, he could see Parrot's head slowly lowering. The medic was only up to Texas' armpit by then. He said, "It's not me, boss. I... I'm not... I'm not..." He looked down at his own feet, squarely on the same dirt that the rest of them trod upon. It was not quicksand.

"The fuck?" Zombie took a quick step back as if worried that he might catch whatever it was that was afflicting Parrot.

"Freeze!" Uncle's voice rang with authority. The tone went straight to the lizard part of the brain and tickled that part of a soldier that never really left boot camp. Everyone froze in place.

Parrot's head was down to Texas' waist now.

"Parrot, did you eat or drink anything local?" Uncle asked.

"No," Parrot said, shaking his head. "Well, the lake water, but I imagine we all had a taste of that." His eyes were wide in fear as he watched, from his perspective, all of his teammates growing taller and taller.

Vodka frowned, one hand tapping his hip pocket.

Something nagged at the back of Uncle's mind. Something he had seen. Back in the prairie, something Parrot had done. He raked the medic with his eyes, trying to remember.

"Are you sure? A berry off a bush? A piece of grass to chew on as we walked?" Uncle's voice was urgent. Parrot was down to Texas' mid thigh.

"I'm telling you, no! I haven't!" Parrot's voice grew higher and higher pitched and, if Uncle had to be entirely honest, he sounded quite funny. The situation, however, was anything but.

Vodka snapped his fingers. He had the appearance of a man with an idea. He hustled past Texas.

Parrot wasn't much larger than a GI Joe doll by that point, and Vodka didn't have have time to be gentle. He picked Parrot up. Parrot squeaked in fear, but Vodka ignored him as he looked him over quickly. Vodka found what he was looking for sticking out of Parrot's pants pocket: a folding paper fan. Vodka snatched the fan from Parrot's pocket with his thumb and forefinger and tossed it as hard as he could into the bush.

"Vodka! What are you..." Uncle cut himself off when he realized what Vodka was doing. In his mind saw the prairie again. Rabbix was looking at them in fear, fumbling with his waist-coat pocket. He pulled out the watch... and dropped a fan. Rabbix vanished. Parrot bent over...

The team held their breath, all eyes on Parrot as he dangled from Vodka's hand.

The medic was perhaps eight inches tall.

Seconds ticked past.

He was still eight inches tall.

The rest of the team let out their breaths in gusty sighs. "Fu-uck," Zombie expressed the sentiment they were all thinking.

"Put me down!" Parrot's voice sounded like he had sucked all of the helium from a birthday balloon.

"I don't think so," Uncle shook his head. "Parrot, you're small enough to be stepped on. Someone has to carry you until we can figure out how to make you grow again."

"Not it," Zombie said. Uncle turned to him with an angry glance, but Zombie shrugged, unapologetic. "I'm already carrying more than anyone else. Besides, with the size he is, the sound of Overbite here?" Zombie patted his machine gun lovingly, "Well, that might blow his eardrums clean out."

Uncle considered for a moment, then nodded. "All right," he held out his hand. "Give him here, Vodka. I'll carry him."

Vodka handed Parrot with deliberate care to Uncle, who opened the breast pocket of his fatigues with one hand. "Here," he said, almost whispering, "you can ride here, and still see what's going on. Parrot, what the hell were you thinking, picking up that fan?"

Parrot squeaked in indignation as he was slipped into Uncle's pocket, but the assessment was correct: the pocket came to just under Parrot's armpits. He could even shoot out of his new vantage point. Whether or not there was any value in him doing so was, of course, unknown.

"It was a fan," Parrot said, "I thought, what harm could a fan do?"

Now that the immediate danger was over, the comedy value of Parrot's tiny little voice was beginning to affect the rest of the team. Texas turned his head to hide a smirk, and even Zombie had the grace to cover his snicker with a cough.

"Clearly, you need to re-read the PHR," Uncle shook his head in annoyance.

"And watch Ghostbusters," Texas said. Rider peered at him oddly until Texas shrugged. "Never ask 'what harm could X possibly do'. That's all I'm saying."

Uncle squeezed Vodka's shoulder. "Quick thinking, there. Thanks."

Vodka nodded with a faint smile tugging at one corner of his lips. "My pleasure, sir."

"Look on the bright side," Zombie said as Vodka began once more leading the group on Rabbix' trail, "worst comes to worst, he's one less person we gotta shrink to use the Golden Door."

"You're a ray of sunshine, you know that?" Rider smirked at Zombie. He turned to Parrot and smiled. "Don't worry. The PHR says changing sizes is pretty common here. We'll get you sorted."

"I dunno," Zombie said, also looking at Parrot. "I think he's kinda cute that size." Parrot flipped him off, and Zombie laughed. "Look at those tiny little indignant fingers! So cute!"

"Enough," Uncle snapped. The situation wasn't funny. "We're a man down now. And need I remind you, he's our medic. If any of you idiots gets hurt, there's not much he can do about it." He didn't say it, but he was also worried about Parrot getting hit by an enemy. Pretty much any blow would be lethal at that size. Uncle also worried about Parrot falling out of his pocket. Given his current size, that would be the equivalent of a nine or ten story fall.

Uncle worried about a lot of things.

He forced himself to stop fretting and focus on the job at hand. "Vodka, find this asshole for me. And I mean now."

"Sir!" Vodka nodded sharply. He glanced around for the tracks, then resumed the hunt once more.

The woods thinned out after about an hour, giving way to what had once been fertile cropland. The fields, bordered by small stone walls twelve or thirteen inches tall, lay abandoned and choked with wild, tall weeds that had claimed most of the land. The vista presented a lonely, vaguely haunted appearance.

Vodka paused at the tree line and waited for the rest to catch up. Uncle was moving cautiously, watching his footing with extra care lest he trip and squish Parrot. Once the team had stacked up on him, Vodka pointed to bis left where Rabbix' tracks continued, skirting the edge of the closest field.

Uncle acknowledged the direction with a nod, but before Vodka could move off Rider spoke up.

"Sir," he said, pointing the other direction. "Smoke."

Uncle turned to look and saw that yes, far off in the distance, a haze of smoke hung low over the horizon.

Texas whistled. "To make a cover like that, that's a lot of smoke." Uncle looked at him with an eyebrow raised, and Texas grinned. "Brush fires. I'm familiar with that look. Normally, you'd need at least ten thousand acres to get that kind of blanket. Of course, I'm talking about dry brush. Wet, healthy plants produce more smoke when they burn, so maybe it's less."

"It's not brush," Rider said, a grim hitch in his voice. "That's battle damage. Houses and buildings. I think we found that war they were talking about."

Everyone watched the horizon for a moment, lost in private memories of battles fought. After a minute, Uncle said, "This isn't finding our guy. Let's move."

Vodka took point, leading the group around the weed field.

That one gave way to another, and another, and then the team found themselves walking through a small, abandoned town. The houses seemed a little too short to their eyes, but otherwise everything looked disturbingly normal for a pre-industrial society. A building with the look of a tavern held pride of place in the middle of the small village. Across the weed-infested square stood a building with an open side, through which could be seen a smithy. A few pieces of metal rusted in the open air along one wall beside the cold, long-dead forge. Other houses and small shops completed the main, and only, street. Signs on the shop doors indicated a tailors, a hat maker, a chandler, and a general store. An open shutter banged mournfully against its window sill.

The team was on high alert as they entered the center of the village, weapons at ready and heads on swivels. Each door and each window was scanned for signs of ambushers, each movement caused by the flutter of tattered curtain in open window was cause for minor alarm.

Despite the team's heightened caution, nothing immediately happened.

As the team reached the tavern, Vodka indicated that the prints continued, heading out of the village.

Nothing continued to happen. The team gradually relaxed.

"How long has this war been going on?" Vodka wondered aloud.

"Yeah," Texas said. "This place has been falling apart for ages."

They crossed out of the square and passed into more outlying weed farms. The tracks lead them along a small dirt road, little more than two pairs of wagon ruts in which the overgrowth was slightly less than that on the sides next to the low stone walls.

The farmland continued for the better part of an hour, a fact which Uncle confirmed by frequent glances at his watch. At last, the bordered fields gave way to another light wood, but this time Vodka indicated that their quarry had gone around, rather than through, the underbrush.

Uncle rolled his neck from side to side to loosen his muscles. He stopped abruptly, looking up. He frowned for a moment, then chuckled. "Well," he whispered to Parrot, "the sun has begun to move again. So that's something."

Parrot, still stinging from being called 'cute' and somewhat self-conscious about his voice, nodded in silence.

They circled the woods for a few minutes, then the tracks turned sharply and entered the trees. The team followed.

The trees were less dense but taller and thicker, with bushier canopies. The growth between them was correspondingly thinner and easier to walk through. Small clearings were common, as were little streams small enough to step over without getting their boots wet. The team picked up speed.

The attack came as they were crossing one of the larger clearings.

Vodka was halfway across, his head lowered as he followed the tracks in the thin brush and fallen leaves. A large boulder squatted to the right of the team, and a small rivulet ran across the width of the clearing.

There was a brief clattering sound from atop the boulder, but Vodka must have assumed it was a branch falling on the rock, for he ignored it.

Zombie didn't. "Contact!" he yelled.

Beckworth's head snapped around to follow Zombie's gaze. There, on top of the boulder, was the largest lizard Beckworth had ever seen. It was easily half again as large as the Komodo dragons he had seen on a Nature Channel special. The hide was mottled green and brown with yellow hints here and there. The snout was long and slender, ending at a sharp point. Teeth longer than those of a crocodile jutted from its mouth. Two slitted eyes watched the team with baleful intent. The creature's hind legs were longer than those in front, and Beckworth had only enough time to wonder why, when the lizard showed him.

It leapt.

The boulder was higher than the head of a tall man, and from atop it, the lizard coiled back on those large hind legs and then sprang forward. It sailed a good ten feet, its mouth open wide. Vodka must have had an excellent look at the beast's teeth as they rushed towards him. They didn't look any more reassuring up close.

Vodka threw himself to the side and back, rolling in the leaves. The lizard crashed into the place he had just vacated. Lightning-fast, it turned its head and snapped at him. Cloth ripped as the giant lizard's teeth tore Vodka's hip pocket. He continued to roll away from the animal.

"Hey!" Zombie yelled, waved one arm to attract the lizard's attention. It was between him and Vodka. He didn't dare shoot.

Texas ran a few steps to the side, trying to get a clean line of fire. Rider un-slung his TAC-50 and carefully placed it on the ground. Uncle stepped to the side, but like Texas, he still couldn't shoot without risking hitting Vodka.

Zombie's yelling succeeded in drawing the animal's attention. It turned towards him quicker than anything that large had any right to move. Zombie barely had time to throw himself backwards. He missed being eviscerated by the sharp front teeth of the lizard by the smallest of margins. "Jesus!" he yelped, scrambling backwards on his heels and elbows. He dropped his

M249 during his leap, and the weapon fouled under the creature's front leg. Zombie fumbled for his sidearm, cursing vehemently.

Vodka took advantage of the distraction to roll to his feet. In his rolling around, he had managed to pull himself out of line with the rest of the team. As he stood, he snapped his M4 up and fired off a burst.

From the right, Texas also fired, and the noise from both weapons blended into one growl of 5.56 millimeter death. From two angles, trios of bullets slammed into the lizard; one in its right haunch and the other in its left shoulder. The lizard made a surprisingly human scream of pain, and its head whipped around towards Texas. Teeth gleamed inside its gaping mouth.

The monster exhaled a gout of fire.

Texas screamed, covered his head with his arms, fell to the ground, and rolled around in the damp leaves. The majority of the flame went over him, but he still caught a fair portion of the blast. His M4 grew too hot to hold, and he dropped it as he continued to roll until he splashed into the little rill.

Another chorus of gunfire rang out. Vodka fired two more bursts, and he was joined by Uncle's M4, while Zombie and Rider fired their M1911s as fast at they could pull the triggers. The creature screamed again and again. It thrashed its head back and forth, but there were too many targets and the pain was too great. It leapt again, away from the team, and then bounded out of the clearing. In seconds, it was lost in the trees.

In the distance, the team could hear the sound of it barging carelessly through the undergrowth.

"Parrot, tend to Texas," Uncle snapped before remembering that this was not an option. "Uh, I mean... Shit. Texas, how are you, son?" He ran over to the injured man, who had ceased to roll and now lay in the dirt, staring up at the tree canopy above him.

"What the hell?" Texas muttered.

"For once, I agree with the FNG," Zombie snarled as he changed the magazine on his sidearm. "What the FUCK was that?"

"Dragon?" Rider hazarded a guess. He also changed mags, then holstered his pistol and picked up his rifle.

"And when exactly the fuck did DRAGONS appear in the PHR?" Zombie was unwilling to be placated.

Uncle knelt and looked at Texas' injuries. The backs of both hands were burnt; Uncle guessed first-, maybe second- degree burns. In addition, Texas had a patch of burnt flesh on his left cheek near his chin. The arms of his fatigues were charred to the elbows, and some of the nylon had melded with his skin. One eyebrow was half-way singed off, but his eyes looked undamaged. Uncle thanked God for that.

Parrot leaned over the edge of his pocket and watched, then began instructing Uncle. The main med kit had shrunken along with Parrot, but each man carried some basic first-aid supplies, and Uncle worked on Texas' burns as well as he could.

"Um," Rider shrugged. "Jaberwocky?"

"Wrong book," Vodka said. With Rider and Zombie, he had formed a triangle around Texas, Uncle, and Parrot. They faced out, keeping their eyes peeled for signs of danger. The lizard might circle back, after all.

"What the hell do you mean, wrong book?" Zombie scowled, sweeping the barrel of his machine gun back and forth as he scanned the trees and bushes and rocks nervously. "It was Alice. I remember. I saw the fucking movie."

"Yeah," Vodka said, his voice soft and controlled. "But the movies usually combined the books. The Jaberwocky wasn't mentioned in Wonderland, it was mentioned in Looking-Glass."

"Same thing, isn't it?" Zombie said.

"No," Vodka said. "Wonderland was all about playing cards. Looking-glass was chess."

"Well," Zombie's voice held mocking respect, "ain't you just a fucking font of wisdom. If you know so much, what the hell WAS that?"

"No idea," Vodka said. "The only lizard the PHR mentioned talked and didn't breath fire."

"Enough chatter," Uncle said. He had managed to bandage up Texas' hands and helped the man stand. "We're down two now. God damn it. Okay. Parrot, I'm transferring you to Texas. Texas, your job is to keep yourself and Parrot from getting killed. Rider, take Texas' M4. You're on fireteam duty for now. If we need a sniper, we'll swap out gear."

Rider slung his Tac-50 over his shoulder with a nod. He picked up Texas' M4, then collected some spare magazines from Texas' belt. "Sorry man," Rider told the injured man.

Texas nodded, pain and misery etched into his features. "Not your fault," his voice was strained. The general first-aid kits contained nothing stronger than Asprin.

"Vodka, do we still have this bastard's trail?"

Vodka searched the ground for several minutes, then nodded. "Yes sir, we do," he said with some satisfaction.

"Good," Uncle said. "Let's end this."

CHAPTER IV
RABBIX TENDS TO A SMALL BILL

Two men out of action and we didn't even have a firm idea where our target was. Things were not starting out well, I'll admit. I recommend, in the strongest possible terms, that we never again use the ramblings of a scared seven-year-old girl as the sum total of our Intelligence briefing.

-CSM Daniel "Uncle" Beckworth, official de-brief, Operation Rabbit Hole

THE TRAIL LEFT THE woods again and crossed a small patch of very gently rolling grass, tall in places but not as much so as the large prairie they had crossed earlier. Rabbix' footprints were obvious in the bend and press of crushed blades. The smell of chlorophyll tickled the nose.

Vodka held up a fist, and the team stopped. He flattened his hand, parallel to the ground, and made a downward press. The team crouched, lowering their profile. Rider pivoted on his heels to face left, while Zombie faced right. Uncle looked back, but seeing that the coast behind them was clear, he duck-walked around the team.

As Uncle approached, Vodka tapped his ear twice with a finger. Uncle paused and strained to hear.

Then he heard it; a faint, rhythmic 'thunk'. At the same time, the breeze shifted and he caught a smell. Something was cooking. He tapped his nose, and Vodka nodded. He smelled it too.

Together, the two of them crept a little further forward. The high grass ended in a clean edge of cultivated lawn. Short grass covered a large expanse and, near the end of the lawn, stood a small house. It would be hard to follow the tracks across this lawn, but Uncle saw that there was no need. There, just at the door of the house, stood Rabbix.

Uncle unbuttoned his hip pocket and withdrew a small pair of binoculars.

Magnified, Rabbix looked as if he were close enough to throw a rock at. Uncle could see that the strange little man was wringing his hands in a way Uncle usually associated with P. G. Wodehouse characters. Uncle could see his lips move, and although he was too far away to hear it, Uncle imagined Rabbix repeating his favorite phrase.

Uncle scanned the rest of the area with his binoculars.

The house was a little on the small, short side, similar to those they had encountered in the abandoned village. That said, it looked like a nice, roomy place. Along the right-hand wall, a small man with jagged, pale brown hair tended a vegetable garden. The man wore a sort of cover-all type garment in a light beige color, the elbows of which were stained green. He knelt in the garden, weeding with a hand trowel.

A row of small greenhouses marched along the left-hand side of the house, some sort of leafy green plant growing inside each. Even with the binoculars, the distance was too great to identify the plants. Not that being closer would have mattered, he thought. Uncle's thumb was so un-green it bordered on the infra-red.

Uncle swung his view back to the front of the house, where a neat little trellis bordered the front door. A polished brass plaque was nailed to the door, but Uncle could not read the words at that distance. As he watched, Rabbix looked sharply to his left. Uncle followed his gaze, and saw that the gardener was approaching, mouth moving as he said something to Rabbix. Rabbix and the gardener hurried around the house, and were out of Uncle's line of sight in moments.

Uncle lowered the binoculars. He and Vodka to return to the others. "Texas," Uncle said after he had finished filling the team in on the layout, "Do you think you can spot for Rider?"

Texas thought about it for a moment. Uncle appreciated that. It meant Texas wasn't so gung-ho that he would endanger the mission just to prove he was healthier than he truly was. He wasn't letting his machismo interfere with is duty.

At last, however, Texas nodded. "I should be able to, sir. My eyes are okay, and I can close my left hand enough to hold the scope."

Uncle nodded. "All right. Parrot, I'm putting you down beside this rock over here. Keep out of sight. Texas, you spot. Rider, keep a clear line of sight on that front door. Zombie, flank left. Come in near the first of those miniature greenhouses. Vodka and I will go right. Stack up on the door. We'll make sure the place is empty before worrying about anyone outside."

He turned to make eye contact with Texas. "When the building is secure, I'll wave a green flag out a window. Before that signal, if anyone tries to enter the building behind us, Rider puts them down. After the green flag, let them come in. I'd like to try to interrogate someone, but at this point that's only a 'want.' Clear?"

"Clear," everyone chorused.

Rider set the M4 gently down in the grass nand un-slung his Tac-50. He lay on his belly and wormed his way forward until he had a clear line of sight on the entire front wall of the house. Texas crawled to Rider's left, cradling the spotting scope in his left hand. Once in place, he began estimating distance and atmospheric conditions, relaying the information to Rider in a quiet voice.

The others checked to make sure they had fresh magazines and that safeties were off, then crept to the edge of the tall grass. Zombie jogged in a wide arc to the left, keeping the entire house in his field of vision. Once he had gone about forty feet, Uncle nodded to Vodka and they likewise began to jog, circling around to the right.

Uncle swept his muzzle from window to window as he ran, half-crouched over to minimize his silhouette. They arrived at the corner of the house without incident and made their way to the door, keeping low so they wouldn't be seen by anyone who happened to look out a window at the wrong moment. Zombie was on the other side of the door. He shook his head to indicate that he had seen no-one on his way in.

Uncle put a hand on the doorknob. He pointed to Vodka, then himself, then Zombie. The men nodded. As Uncle turned the knob and pushed the door open, he noticed that the bronze plaque read "W. Rabbix, Esq." So now their enemy had a first initial.

The door swung inwards on well-oiled hinges. Vodka darted through, sliding to his left to leave the doorway clear. Uncle spun around the jamb, taking up a crouched position on the other side.

He could see Zombie's shadow in the beam of sunlight from the open door.

The room in which they found themselves would have done justice to a production of The Importance of Being Earnest performed by a troupe of jockeys. A sofa held the center of attention in the room. Ornately carved leaves and vines adorned the hardwood of the back and arms of the couch, while deeply stuffed cushions of yellow with white flower prints rested on the seat. Beside the couch, a carved wood end table squatted on three legs that twisted like vines around a central strut. An oil lamp sat atop a white lace doily on a small end table.

In front of the couch, the mantle of a brick fireplace supported several small knickknacks. Wood was laid out inside the hearth, awaiting only the touch of flame to bring crackling warmth to the room. Along the wall opposite the entrance, two bookcases flanked a door that stood half open. Leather-bound volumes of myriad topics crowded and overflowed the deep, walnut brown book cases.

Uncle wondered if maybe he had found the source of the shelves in the Rabbit Hole.

Everything was clean and neat and vaguely anachronistic, and about a quarter smaller than it should be, in Uncle's eyes.

"Clear," Vodka said softly. The rhythmic thumping sound they had heard earlier was louder inside the house, and it seemed to be coming from the partly open door in the opposite wall. Under the assumption that the noise might represent a person, Vodka kept his voice quiet.

"Clear," Uncle repeated. Zombie contented himself with a sharp nod. While Vodka and Zombie flanked and covered the interior door, Uncle crept to it and peered around the edge. He leaned back and shrugged, then made hand signs indicating a hallway going left and right. He pointed to Zombie, then left, then held his fist up. He pointed at Vodka and himself, and gestured right, his hand a vertical blade which he lifted and lowered twice. The other men nodded in understanding.

Uncle quietly opened the door fully. Vodka stepped through, glancing left briefly before turning around and facing right. He took a step forward, giving Uncle enough room to slip in behind him. Uncle kept his weapon trained on the ground. As he and Vodka moved forward, he saw Zombie out of the corner of his eye. Zombie took up a position in the doorway facing the other direction, watching their backs.

The hallway in front of Vodka was short, about five or six feet in length. A large picture window dominated the end, overlooking the garden outside. In front of the window, a small rectangular table with a cloth-of-gold runner stood, a small potted plant taking in the sunlight in the center. To the left of the window and table there was an open doorway. The thumping sounds issued from there.

Vodka looked over his shoulder to make sure Uncle had noticed, then nodded towards the door. Uncle nodded in return, and they crept forward. Vodka crouched just before the doorway and pulled out his pocket mirror. He peered around the corner for a few moments. The thumping stopped, then resumed during this time, and Uncle thought he heard a tuneless humming in the brief silence. Vodka replaced his mirror and fastened the pocket, then turned to face Uncle.

Vodka pointed his fingers at his eyes, then held up a single digit.

Uncle nodded. One visible contact.

Vodka slung his M4 behind him. Staying crouched low and moving slowly and silently on the balls of his feet, he slipped around the corner. Uncle took his place, leaning forward so he could see around the corner.

The room was a small, cozy little kitchen. Open windows overlooked the garden and let in a light, cool breeze that smelled wetly of earth and green growing things. On the wall opposite the windows, a huge fireplace operated as both oven and stove. A merry fire burned and popped inside, warming a large cast-iron pot suspended over it by a hook on a swing. The smell of stew wafted from the pot and Uncle was glad his stomach didn't rumble. Directly across from him was a long counter, above which hung a number of pots, pans, and strings of dried herbs and onions.

In the center of the room rested an island. At the island, a man stood with his back to the door. With a wooden mallet, he pounded strips of meat flat. Here, then, was the source of both the thumping and the tuneless humming. Now and again, the cook would finish with a strip and lay it aside on a plate already quite full of the same.

Vodka sneaked up behind the man, hands held outstretched and low in front of him. When he was directly behind the cook, Vodka exploded upwards. He wrapped one arm around the man's throat while the other cradled his head from behind and pushed forward. With one leg, Vodka kicked the chef's knees out from under him. The cook dropped his mallet and flailed his arms for a moment, seeking in vain for purchase on his attacker. In less than a minute, the arm across his throat rendered him unconscious.

The cook never made a sound.

Uncle stepped into the room as Vodka eased the unconscious fellow to the ground. Like everyone else so far in this place, the cook was short; a mere five feet tall, and very odd looking. His head was disproportionally large, with a nose like a shapeless mushroom squatting on his red, blotchy face. He wore simple homespun under an apron deeply stained red, brown, and green.

Uncle checked the cook for a pulse, then nodded in satisfaction.

The man lived.

Uncle stood and looked around the room. There was one other open doorway that lead to a small dining room with a table just large enough for two. Rabbix either didn't entertain often, or he had another room for guests and this was the equivalent of a breakfast nook.

Uncle poked his head into the small dining room, then came back and shrugged. "No exit," he whispered, then gestured back towards the hallway. As they crossed the kitchen, Uncle could hear, from outside, a voice saying, "Oh you poor dear! Who did this to you? Pat, fetch —" but whatever it was Pat was meant to fetch was lost as the voice moved further away and Uncle could no longer hear it.

Vodka peered around the doorway into the hall, then stepped in. In a barely audible voice he said, "Blue, blue," as he crept up behind Zombie. Zombie nodded to acknowledge that he had heard. The three stacked up at the door to the living room.

Further down, the hall sported two doors on the right side and one on the left. The one on the left would put it behind the fireplace in the living room, whereas the closer one on the right would be behind the massive kitchen hearth. No sense wondering, Uncle decided, when they would find out what the rooms represented in a moment. He indicated the closer, right-side door.

Vodka nodded and approached. Zombie turned around to cover their backs.

Unlike the others so far in the house, the three doors on half of the hall were all closed. Vodka couldn't see around the corner with his mirror.

Uncle and Vodka flanked the door Uncle had chosen to enter first. Uncle took the doorknob in a careful, gentle grip, and twisted it. It was unlocked. He nodded to Vodka, then opened and pushed. The door swung wide and Vodka rushed through right after it.

Uncle followed a second later, just in time to hear Vodka say, "Clear."

It was a bedroom. A fireplace on the right wall as they entered would share a chimney with the one in the kitchen, and kept the room nice and warm. A large four-poster bed with heavy red, white, and black curtains held back with lace stays dominated the room. In addition to the bed, the room contained an armoire, a foot chest, two tables flanking the bed, and a vanity table upon which rested a large pink diamond ring. Illumination came from a pair of skylights and, when they were lit, the four oil lamps scattered around the room.

Across from where Uncle stood, an open door showed a bathroom. A copper tub rested on four feet, two of a large cat and two of a hunting bird of some sort. A wash basin and a toilet completed the interior of that room. There was a single window, closed and curtained, on the far wall.

If Uncle had to guess, he would have said that this was most likely the master bedroom. That bed had a 'master of the house' look to it.

As there was no one present, and Zombie wasn't shooting at hypothetical hordes of angry guards pouring from the other rooms in response to the noise of the door being thrown open, Vodka and Uncle returned to the hallway.

The other room on the same side of the hall turned out to be a stand-alone bathroom.

The door on the opposite side of the hallway opened onto a smaller bedroom that shared a fireplace chimney with the living room. Uncle presumed the smaller bedroom belonged to the cook. The pile of clothes tossed into a corner were all of rough homespun or other similar poor materials. Not at all like what Rabbix wore. Also, the bed was a small cot, rather than the canopied monstrosity in the other bedroom.

"Clear," Uncle said once all the rooms had been checked and found empty of people. Together with Vodka and Zombie, he returned to the living room. Zombie knelt behind the couch, facing the front door, while Vodka took a position against the front wall. Uncle checked their placements, nodded in approval. He pulled green handkerchief from one of his belt pouches and waved it out the window for Texas and Rider. Three minutes later, they, along with Parrot riding in Texas' pocket, entered the house.

"Something's going on behind the house," Texas' voice was tight with pain as he reported. "The gardener went running off out of our line of sight, then came back a couple minutes later carrying a heavy leather satchel. He was practically dragging it, it was so full of whatever it contained. He vanished behind the house, and never came back out."

"Roger that," Uncle said. "We still need Rabbix. I'd love to trap him inside, but he seems to have something important on his hands. Recommendations?"

"We only need the key," Zombie said. "I suggest we just shoot the son-of-a-bitch, take the key, and be on our merry."

"Negative," Uncle said. "We need intelligence. He may know how to reverse the fan."

"I'm all for that!" Parrot said.

60

Rider bit his lip to keep from laughing at Parrot's tiny little voice. "I agree with Sideswipe here," he said. "Suggest we flank the building and see what he's up to. If the situation warrants, we can use flashbangs. Either way, we hit him from two sides, shock-and-awe style."

"'Sideswipe?'" Texas asked.

"Yeah, you know," Rider grinned. "The G.I. Joe medic."

Parrot offered Rider a one-fingered salute.

"Don't be silly," Jones said. "The Joes' medic was Doc."

Parrot offered him a one-fingered salute as well.

"Do you remember what happened last time we flanked this bastard?" Zombie snarled. "He turned Parrot into a goddamn action figure and then fucking went invisible on us."

"Zombie has a point," Uncle sighed. He looked at his watch, then looked out the window to check the position of the sun. "Son-of-a..." he muttered. The sun had stopped moving again. "What is with this place? So much for waiting for nightfall and sneaking up on him. Besides, that cook isn't going to sleep forever." He chewed on the cuticle of his thumb for a moment as he thought. The others gave him silence.

"All right," he said at last. "He needed that pocket-watch of his to turn invisible, remember? So. Parrot and Texas, you guys stay here. Zombie and Rider go right around the house but wait at the black/blue wall. Vodka and I will do the same with white/blue. Rider, use the M4 but hold position. The rest of toss flash bangs on three squelches, then charge in. If he reaches for that pocket-watch, Rider, try to put one in his arm. If the only way to stop him from activating it is to kill him then... fine. Do it. But only as a last resort." He grinned as a sudden thought occurred to him. He opened a pouch and fetched the remote detonator from his belt. "I'll try to bluff him also. Questions? Okay, let's roll."

Zombie and Rider slipped out of the house and circled to the right, rounding the corner where the miniature greenhouses were and vanishing from Uncle's sight. He and Vodka went the other way.

As they made their way through the garden, Uncle let out a barely audible snicker. Vodka looked over his shoulder, one eyebrow raised in question. Uncle pointed down. Vodka looked at his feet, then grinned sheepishly.

He had been walking in the furrows, careful not to tread on the vegetables.

They reached the corner and Vodka did his thing with the mirror. He blanched and shook his head at Uncle. Uncle took the mirror from him and they switched places so Uncle could see what it was that had given Vodka pause.

Behind the house, a small table and two chairs, painted wrought iron from the look of them, normally sat in the shade of a large umbrella. The table had been moved, however, and the shade was being used by Rabbix, the gardener, and another man who could have been the gardener's twin brother. They were kneeling around a large, dark shape.

It took Uncle a moment to realize what the shape was; the lizard-creature that had attacked them in the woods. The one that had injured Texas.

"F–" Uncle clamped his lips shut.

The creature was obviously injured; thick, dark blood oozed from several wounds. Rabbix and the gardener twins attempted stop the bleeding with long rolls of cloth. The lizard showed no signs of attacking them, even though the treatment must surely hurt. The damned thing is domesticated, Uncle though. He had a brief mental image of a sign he had once seen at a friend's house. 'Forget the dog,' the sign had read, 'Beware of Dragon.'

62

Awesome.

He thought for a moment, but could not see any modifications to the basic plan that would make the situation any better. Uncle hoped that Zombie had seen the lizard-creature also, and would be smart enough to stay out of fire-breathing range. Uncle shook his head in irritation. This clinched it: the universe hated him.

His sigh was only just audible, even to himself. He reached for the push-to-talk button on his tactical radio. He pressed it three times. Beside him, Vodka tossed a flash bang grenade around the corner. Both men silently counted. From the other side of the house, a tremendous explosion rang out, followed a half a second later by another. Uncle lifted his weapon and ran around the corner.

"Down! Down!" Uncle's and Zombie's voices practically merged as they stormed the group of stunned and disoriented people and their giant fire-breathing lizard pet.

"Down, down on the ground. Hands out!" Zombie continued to yell as he advanced, his weapon primarily aimed at the lizard. Uncle couldn't blame him. That damn creature made him nervous too.

Uncle held up the remote detonator and, in a loud, firm voice, commanded, "Rabbix! We have your house set to blow if you so much as make a move. Lie on the ground, arms and legs spread! Move, now!"

The problem with running operations in Wonderland, Uncle would decide later, is that no-one there knows who the U.S. Army is, or why they should be feared. Everywhere else AFO Spectre went, the locals knew to be afraid. While this had its down-sides, at least it meant that when his team burst into a situation and yelled for everyone to lie down, nine times out of ten the shock-and-awe worked and the people just fell down without anyone having to be shot.

Not so much with these people.

The gardener, or perhaps it was his twin, started to run. He was still blinded from the stun grenade, so the 'run' was more of a comedic half-circle shuffle. He tripped over one of the lawn chairs and fell down, howling in pain at his barked shin.

The other man who may or may not have been the gardener backpedaled furiously, swinging his arms blindly in front of him. One of his hands struck the flank of the lizard-creature, which bellowed in pain. The sound reminded Uncle of that movie with the dinosaurs that come to life and eat all the tourists, only slightly less ear-shatteringly loud. Evidently, real life lizard monsters don't come equipped with THX.

Vodka's weapon snapped towards the lizard, but the creature merely warbled in pain and shook its head back and forth. This knocked the retreating maybe-gardener down and he, in turn, tripped Rabbix who was walking forward slowly while rubbing his eyes.

In short, it was chaos.

Rabbix was good, Uncle had to give him that. He fell down, rolled twice, and was back on his feet as quick as you like. He fumbled at his waist-coat for his watch. Uncle's heart sank: in the confusion, Zombie had strayed into Rider's line of fire. There was no clear shot. They were going to lose Rabbix again.

Vodka sprinted forward and tackled Rabbix, knocking him to the ground again. They wrestled for a moment, but no matter how quick Rabbix might be, Vodka was far larger and stronger, and they were already in physical contact. In seconds, Vodka had his prey pinned to the ground and was holding both of the smaller man's arms down. The pocket-watch lay in the grass beside them.

Uncle darted forward and snatched up the watch. The chain was still attached to Rabbix' vest, but Uncle tore it free. As he retreated with the watch, Uncle glanced around to assess the situation.

Vodka pinned Rabbix to the grass. Zombie had his foot on the chest of one of the twins, and was pointing his machine gun at the lizard. Rider advanced quickly, his M4 aimed at the other twin who had recovered his eyesight. That worthy saw the situation and slumped to the ground without any further fuss.

Uncle took over lizard-covering detail so that Zombie, Rider, and Vodka could all secure their respective prisoners with black plastic zip-ties. Uncle almost chuckled when Vodka tied Rabbix' feet as well as his hands. Vodka was tired of tracking that guy and was taking no chances that he'd get away again.

"You," said Rabbix as he looked up at his captors. "You're the ones who hurt Bill, aren't you?"

"Who the fuck is Bill?" Zombie asked for everyone.

Rabbix gestured with his chin at the lizard-creature. "Bill. You hurt him. Why? Why are you chasing me? Why are you invading our land? What did we ever do to you people? Pat? Pat, are you all right?"

"Aye, m'lorrud," said one of the gardeners. "Ah'm quaht wayll."

"Wow," Zombie frowned, "that's the worst Irish accent I've ever heard. Don't ever do that again."

"I hardly think one rescue team qualifies as 'invading,'" Uncle said. "Besides, your people started it when you kidnapped Fiona McGinney. Now, all we need from you is—"

"Kidnapped? Kidnapped? Oh dear, oh dear, you have it all wrong. We brought Alice back because we need her, you see. We need her to help stop your invasion."

Uncle pinched the bridge of his nose between his thumb and forefinger. "First of all, her name is Fiona. Alice? The girl from the story? She's been dead for decades. Secondly, we only came here because you people kidnapped Fiona!"

"Nonsense," said Rabbix. "You've been attacking us for ages now. You think I wouldn't recognize your mechanical death contraptions?" he jerked a chin at Zombie. Or rather, Uncle realized, at Zombie's M249.

Uncle and Rider exchanged a silent look, then Uncle turned back to Rabbix. He held up his M4 and said, "You mean machines like this? Exactly like this? Or just... similar?"

"Oh, well," Rabbix blushed a faint pink color which made the white of his mustache stand out all the more. "That is to say," said he, "I never exactly got all that close, you understand..." He wiggled his nose in embarrassment. "I saw them from a distance, but they were definitely mechanical, like those. But no, they didn't look exactly the same. Not exactly, no. But a machine is a machine. You use them, Ironhand uses them. Thusly, you must work for him! You even look like his men, all... tall and funny looking."

"We're funny looking?" Zombie boggled.

Uncle waved him silent.

"Look, Rabbix, we don't know who this 'Ironhand' is, and we certainly don't work for him. We work for the President of the United States of America, and we're here to rescue a girl your people kidnapped. Nothing else. Now, no one needs to get hurt, but you do have to co-operate." Uncle loomed over Rabbix to make sure he had his attention. "When we saw you in the hallway full of doors, you had a golden key with you. We need that key. Where is it?"

"You want me to help you? Oh dear, no, no," said Rabbix. "No, I simply cannot. You say that you are not Ironhand's men, and you might well say that, but you look just like his men. That key, oh dear me, that key leads straight to the Queen's castle. If you think for a moment, for even a moment, that I will help you murder the Queen, you are very much mistaken. Yes, indeed, you are. She'd have my head in a second if I helped you. Besides," he glanced at the lizard-creature which lay still, moaning softly in pain, "you hurt Bill. Why should I help you? Why indeed? No, unthinkable."

Uncle sighed in annoyance. This wasn't going the way he had hoped. He looked at Vodka and nodded. "Search him."

Vodka knelt behind Rabbix and began patting him down, checking in his pockets, under his arms, in his shoes. The shoes revealed the prize. Rabbix had put the golden key under his left insole. Vodka held up the key in triumph.

"One more thing," Uncle said to the crestfallen prisoner. "Your fan. When one of my men picked it up, he began to shrink. He's tiny now, not much bigger than my hand. How do we reverse that?"

"Did he?" asked Rabbix, sucking on his teeth. "Did he indeed? Well well. My. How very interesting. That is unexpected. Yes, quite unexpected indeed." He rocked back and forth as he sat there on the grass. He began to hum to himself, smiling.

That ended when Zombie put a knee into the little fellow's back. "Hey, jackass! The man asked you a question. Answer, or I'm going to do more than just 'hurt' Bill. When I'm done with him, I'll start on these two," he gestured at the twins. "You feel me?"

Rabbix grunted in pain and ceased his rocking and humming. The smile, however, never went entirely away although it did shrink until it was little more than a smirk playing at the corner of his lips. "It made him small, you say? Oh my. That is good news!"

"How so?" Uncle asked.

"It means," said Rabbix, "that you may be telling the truth. You really did come here for the girl. You came from her world. Yes, yes. I believe I will help you."

"Well?"

"Oh, I can't undo what is done," said Rabbix with a short, quick shake of his head. "But! I can tell you who can. Yes indeed, I know who can help your friend."

The silence stretched, became uncomfortable, wandered past uncomfortable and into intolerable. Zombie lost his patience. "That's it," he said, "I'm killing the lizard." He drew his knife and turned to face Bill.

"No, wait," said Rabbix in fearful haste. "The Long Man. He can help your friend. He knows all about that sort of thing; the shrinking and growing and all of that."

"You seem to know a bit about it," Vodka said. "It was your fan that turned made him small."

"No, no, you don't understand," said Rabbix. "That wasn't me. No, not me at all. Or rather, it wouldn't have worked that way on me, or anyone from this land. See, it only does that on people from your world! Like Alice. You said she told stories of her adventures here? Did she mention how she kept changing size? That doesn't happen to people from this land, only her. Only her! Oh dear me, that's why the Queen wanted her back, don't you see? Her agents must have thought that his Fiona girl was Alice. That's why she wanted her. To grow tall."

"Why?" Rider blew a bubble with his gum and popped it.

"Why? Why?" sputtered Rabbix, choking on the question. "Why, it is the most obvious thing in the world," said the strange little man. "The Queen wants Alice to grow into a giant so she can win the war for us! She can crush the Metalmen, trample them underfoot, squash them quite flat. Oh dear me, yes, the

Queen is quite clever about such things, to have come up with such an admirable plan!"

"Metal men?" Vodka glanced at Uncle with a frown.

"Ironhand's soldiers," said Rabbix, nodding with firm vigor. He was very impressed with what he thought his Queen had come up with, and in his enthusiasm had quite forgotten that he was a prisoner with an injured lizard-creature pet and two captive gardeners. "They wear metal all over their bodies, you see, that's why we call them that. Quite fearsome, they are, oh dear me yes."

"Why aren't you with the Queen fighting them?" Vodka asked. His voice was soft and smooth, and Uncle knew that meant he was at his most dangerous. Vodka probably figured Rabbix for yet another deserter; only, unlike the ones by the lake, a deserter who seemed to be doing quite well for himself.

Vodka loathed deserters.

Uncle spoke up to defuse the situation. "Never mind that," he said, "tell me where we can find this Long Man of yours."

"Not mine!" said Rabbix quickly. "Oh dear me, no, he's not mine at all! He doesn't belong to anyone else but himself." He saw the look on Zombie's face and correctly assumed that he should stop arguing semantics and just answer the question. "Ah, yes, well. Dear me, you can find him, I should expect, by going that way," he gestured with his chin towards a thick little wood nearby. "When you find a clearing full of mushrooms, you will find him there. Dear me, yes, I should think that you would indeed!"

"Get Texas and Parrot," Uncle ordered Rider, who blew a bubble in reply. "And get a knife from the kitchen while you're there," Uncle called after the retreating sniper's back. He turned to Rabbix and said, "We'll leave a knife so you can cut yourself free. But if you come after us, or if you send your... pet..." he gestured at Bill, "I won't hesitate to shoot. Do you understand?"

"Bill is not my—" Zombie growled deep in his throat, and Rabbix stopped his protest. "Ah, that is," said the little man, "Yes. I understand."

"Good," Uncle said.

"Metal men, huh?" Vodka mused. "I've seen a lot of swords so far. Maybe chain mail or plate armor?"

No one else had an answer for him.

Silence reigned, broken only by Bill's soft moaning, until Rider returned with Texas and Parrot. He dropped a knife at Rabbix' feet.

The team set off in the direction Rabbix had indicated. Uncle paused and looked back. "And Rabbix?" He waited until the strange little man looked up before continuing, "If you've sent us into a trap, or if this Long Man isn't in this direction, or if you have done anything other than be totally up front and honest with us, we'll be back for you. And remember. I have your watch now." He dangled it by the chain and let it catch the light for a moment before shoving it deep in a hip pocket.

He followed his team into the thick woods. After a hundred feet or so, Vodka held up a hand to stop the group. He pointed to his left

Uncle glanced over and saw a puppy watching them and wagging its tail. He looked at Vodka. "What?"

"Puppy," Vodka replied.

"Yes, I see it," Uncle said. "What about it?"

"It's not trying to kill us," Vodka said. "I thought that was noteworthy."

Uncle tried to think of something to say in response, but couldn't. He shrugged, and the team moved on.

CHAPTER V
HEAD-TRIP FROM A CENTAURIPEDE

———◆———

Look man, I'm just telling you what I saw. No, I'm not going to explain it. It's none of your damned business.

Leave my personal shit out of it.

Why did I include it? Because you told me to.

Besides, it's all in my file already.

> -MSG James "Zombie" Halsford, official de-brief, Operation Rabbit Hole.

"I DON'T LIKE THE LOOK of this," Zombie said.

The team had pushed deeper into the woods, and with each step, it seemed, the woods had grown darker, more foreboding. The sounds of birds calling to each other had ceased. The noise of combat boots crunching on twigs and dry leaves had seemed abnormally loud in their ears.

The tree canopy utterly obscured the sun, leaving only a dim murk in which every tree became a shadowy apparition that seemed to watch them with sinister intent. The environment itself oppressed them, and Zombie had felt himself growing edgy and tense for no visible reason. Several times, he had thought he had seen something moving just at the edge of his vision. From the way the others would start and jerk now and again, he knew he wasn't alone.

In addition to darker, the forest had grown more damp as they walked along. The leaves underfoot had changed gradually from dry and brittle to damp and slippery. The tree trunks had become covered in thick, unhealthy looking moss. The air had grown moist, close, and it had smelled of decay. Footing became uncertain, and the team had had to slow down after Texas had slipped and almost fell on his ass.

Gradually, into the silence broken only by the team's harsh breathing, a soft rattling, clicking sound had made itself known. Something moved around up in the trees. Zombie imagined hordes of beetles and spiders crawling in the branches above their heads.

And then they had found the clearing, if one could call it that. The trees still came together overhead, allowing not a single beam of sunlight to reach the floor. The ground was a thick carpet of moldy leaves and pungent earth, and mushrooms grew everywhere.

They clung to every surface. They sprouted like leprous barnacles from every trunk. They soared into the gloom like misshapen white trees, some so tall that Zombie couldn't see the tops. They grew on each other, cannibalizing their fellows in an eternal struggle for supremacy.

The team stopped at the edge and stared.

"No," Zombie said, "I don't like the look of this at all. Did anyone remember to bring a flamethrower?"

Vodka prodded a nearby stalk with the barrel of his M4. When nothing immediately life-threatening happened, he kicked a small dome-capped mushroom. It exploded into several fragments. He looked at Uncle and shrugged.

Uncle considered for a moment, then nodded. "All right. Let's go."

"We are so going to regret this," Zombie said as Vodka carefully entered the clearing. The rest of the team followed, making a defensive circle around Texas and Parrot.

"Hello?" Uncle called out, peering into the gloom.

A dozen clicks from somewhere above them rewarded his hail. A muted rattling sound followed. Everyone looked up.

"Jesus fuck!" Zombie yelped as a shadow loomed, became a silhouette, then resolved into a figure. He almost fired, but Uncle's voice stopped him.

"Stand down!"

The figure had a head not entirely unlike that of a human, although the nose was little more than a double slit in the center of what would, on a human, be called the face. The eyes were huge, compound monstrosities that rested far to either side of the white, bulbous head. The mouth was a thin, lipless slash across the lower half of the face.

As if that wasn't bad enough, there was the thing's body. The upper torso could be called man-shaped if one were in a generous mood, in that it had a chest and two arms. That's where the resemblance ended. The skin was white and pulpy, and it glistened in the dim light. The arms were extremely long, slender, and multi-jointed. The hands at the end of each arm consisted of three slender, elongated fingers with sharpened talons extending from the tip of each, and an equal-sized opposing digit. The thing possessed not a single hair that Zombie could see.

At the point that would, in a human, have been the waist, the creature's flesh had several chitinous plates which grew together until, around where the hips should have been, the body became that of a giant centipede. From head to the end of the wickedly sharp stinger at the tail, the thing must have measured a good nine or ten feet in length.

It crawled around the stalks of some of the larger mushrooms until its head was only a little above and directly in front of Uncle. At that distance, Zombie saw that it carried some sort of large cylinder strapped to the upper part of the centipede body. A long, flexible hose connected the cylinder to a pipe-like handle dangling from the thing's left claw.

"Who are you?" The creature's voice was low and deceptively languid, making Zombie think of velvet and hidden knives.

Uncle didn't miss a beat. "Are you the Long Man? We met a man named Rabbix. Lives in a house back that way," he gestured over his shoulder. "He said you could help us with a problem. One my men got shrunk somehow. Can you help us?"

The creature scuttled around another couple of huge mushroom stalks, climbing atop one and looking down at the team from a substantial height. "Explain," ordered the creature.

"He, my man, he picked up a fan that Rabbix dropped. It made him shrink. He's now very small, and, you know, we want him back to his normal size."

"I do not know," said the thing.

The hairs on the back of Zombie's neck prickled. He didn't like the way the thing kept moving around. He felt like it was gauging them, deciding the best angle from which to attack. He thumbed off Overbite's safety.

"Rabbix said you know about this sort of thing. He said you can help us," Uncle said.

"You!" said the creature. It lifted the pipe handle to its mouth and sucked for a moment. Zombie could hear a bubbling sound from the cylinder on its back. Then it exhaled and blew a ring of greenish smoke. "Who are you?"

"For fuck's sake," Zombie muttered. This was going in circles.

Uncle ignored the outburst. He didn't seem upset or agitated at all. That's why, Zombie mused, the Army paid him the big bucks. Well, the slightly less-small bucks anyway.

"I'm called Uncle," Uncle said.

"Why?"

"For safety."

"Whose safety?"

"Yours," Uncle's smile was grim and sardonic.

The creature puffed away on his pipe some more. All was silent for a minute, perhaps two. Then the monster spoke again. "Why are you here?"

"I told you," Uncle said, "We need our man returned to his normal size, and Rabbix said—"

"Why are you here?" said the creature as it moved again, spiraling around another stalk and ending up to the left of the group, over near Rider.

Uncle was silent for a moment, then he shrugged. It wasn't exactly a secret. "We're here to return a girl that was kidnapped and brought here by the Queen. That's all we want. Well, that and to get our man back to his normal size. Can you help us?"

"Why did the Queen kidnap this girl?" asked the creature. It reared up, towering above everyone, but rather than attack it paused to take a long drag on its pipe. The stinger on the end of the thing's tail made a rapid clicking sound.

"She thinks the girl is Alice, another little girl from my world who came here long ago. Alice was able to change size, and the Queen thinks she can make the girl become a giant and crush the people invading this land. Alice is dead, however, and this new girl can't change size, and this battle is none of our business. We just want the girl back."

"Can your friend change his size?"

"No, that's why we need your help!" Uncle's facade of affability was beginning to crack.

Zombie was impressed. He'd have shot the creature by now.

"Yet, you say your friend is changed. If he can do it, and Alice can do it, maybe this new girl, Fiona, can do it also. Maybe the Queen isn't wrong," said the creature as it blew more smoke out of both nostrils and mouth. Whatever the monster was smoking, Zombie, decided, he didn't like it. It smelled cloying and sweet, like condensed rose water for the nose.

"It wasn't my friend," Uncle shook his head in frustration. "It was something from this place. Something Rabbix had that... that made him small. My friend, I mean. Not Rabbix. It.. we need Parrot back to his normal size. Marq— I mean Texas needs proper men. Proper medical men. Attention. Proper medical attention, men! A-ten-hut! Hut. Hut hut hunt for hutty huts."

Vodka snapped to attention. Rider began looking for huts to hunt. Zombie threw his arms out for balance as the ground quaked. Before he could do more than yell a quick warning, the ground quaked again, and then split open right under his feet.

He fell.

The ground cracked and shattered into a thousand pieces and fell into a vortex with him. A house with gingham curtains flew past, a little dog in the doorway yapping at him. A cow almost collided with him, then spun away and flew over the moon while a cat sawed madly on a violin and the cat was his sixth grade teacher Mrs. Sanchez and little Jimmy was embarrassed at how he felt every time he looked at her in that low-cut blouse while she danced a jig with a snake wrapped around her shoulders and the ground came flying up to meet him and knocked the breath from his lungs so that he lay there gasping in the hallway of the hospital and all around him doctors in red scrubs with white blood splashes ran about yelling, "Code Chartreuse! Code Chartreuse!"

Zombie sat up swiftly, gasping. He had fallen asleep in the chair in the waiting room, and his muscles were stiff and his neck hurt. A doctor was standing in front of him saying, "Mr. Zombie? Mr. Zombie, I'm Doctor Dolittle. I'm afraid your wife is dead, Mr. Zombie. She lost too much blood."

"But I'm not married," Zombie said.

"Oh, my mistake then. She's fine." The doctor turned and walked away, moving carefully to avoid slipping in the blood on the floor.

A noise drew Zombie's attention, and he saw Death leaving the gift-shop with a bouquet of Forget-Me-Nots in one hand and a teddy-bear wearing a coal miner's hard hat in the other. Death saw him looking and nodded in respect, one old colleague to another. Zombie watched the robed skeleton walk up the hallway when it hit him: a coal miner's hat! Death was here for Zombie's father!

Zombie tried to run after Death, but his feet couldn't get traction in all the blood. He grabbed the back of the chair nearest him and pulled himself along, hydroplaning until he reached the edge of the pool. "Dad!" he yelled as he began running down the long hallway. "Dad, run! Death's here for you! Dad, where are you?"

The hallway went on for over a mile, and every third light was burned out so it was hard to see ahead. Zombie couldn't remember his father's room number, so he had to stop and look inside each door as he passed it. A series of old women gazed back at him, and each of them reached out an emaciated hand to him and said, "Take me with you! Please, they're going to kill me here!" but he didn't have time to stop, he had to find his dad before Death took him. Zombie ran from door to door. Ahead, the hallway branched into a hundred identical halls. The only good thing was that Death seemed as lost as he was, for Zombie could see him there at the intersection, trying to figure out which hall to take.

Zombie ran past him down the first hallway on the left. He looked inside a door, but it was just an injured Taliban fighter laying on a bed and groaning as he tried to hold his own guts inside his body. Zombie remembered him from Shahi-Kot. "Sorry about that, buddy," he said as he turned away. He had to run, to find his dad.

He smelled cooking meat as he ran to the other side of the hall. It was a burn ward, filled with insurgents hit by artillery fire he had called in. Some were still buried under burning timbers from their houses. One clutched an AK-47 in his hands and tried to aim it at Zombie, but Zombie was already gone, on to the next room, and the next, and the next. Where was his father?

Zombie found him at last, lying in his bed at the end of the hall. Tubes ran into his nose and down his throat. There was a shadow in the door behind Zombie, and he turned to find a lady doctor there, middle-aged and stern looking. "Your father is very sick," she said. "Visiting hours are over. You need to let him rest. Come back tomorrow."

"I can't," Zombie pleaded. "Death is coming!" Over the doctor's shoulder, he could see the black-robed figure peering into a room down the hall. "He'll be dead by morning!"

"Don't be absurd," the doctor said. "We won't let him die until the money runs out, you know that. As long as you keep sending home your pay, we'll keep stringing him along instead of letting him go out with dignity like he asked. It's what you wanted, after all."

Zombie ignored her, yanking the tubes from his father. "Come on, dad," he said. "Get up. You need to get up. We have to get you out of here. We're not safe here. We're surrounded, dad. There are AQ everywhere, time to go. Get your ass up and move, soldier!"

Zombie helped his father stand, only it wasn't his father, it was the FNG, Texas. He turned around and saw his father standing in the doorway, his hat in his hands. "I'm sorry, son," he said. "They did everything they could but... there was too much damage. Punctured lung, ruptured kidneys, a piston shaft through her diaphragm. Mom's dead, Jimmy."

Zombie shook his head. "I know, dad. That's why we have to save you. Come on!" He grabbed his father's hand and pulled him into the hallway. Death was looking into the room of the little boy who had been in the house with the insurgents when the shells hit. Zombie pulled his dad the other way.

That kid was a goner anyway.

"I really must insist you come back tomorrow," the doctor said as she grew and grew. She sprouted extra arms from her back, long slender arms that ended with four-fingered talons. Her body swelled and burst, turning into a hundred legs as she loomed over him. "Visiting hours are OVER!"

Zombie ducked a slash of those wickedly sharp claws, and heard them cutting through the wall behind him as he pulled his dad forward. "Run, dad! Run!"

The patients began to stumble out of their rooms, and Zombie saw that they were all dead now, burned and rotting, with fungus growing on them and out of them. They shambled towards him, blocking the way, reaching out with decaying hands to clutch at his shirt, his arms, his face. "Zombies for Zombie," he heard the lady doctor say over the hospital PA system.

Together, they ran, Zombie and his father. At an intersection, he took the direction in which there were no zombies. An abandoned part of the hospital, the halls were filled with broken gurneys and wheel-less wheelchairs and rolling carts full of empty glass vials and beakers. The ground was wet from leaking pipes, and littered with shards of broken glass and used hypodermic needles. He had to move carefully on his bare feet lest he cut himself.

A monster stepped out of a room ahead of him. It's head was split in half, with tentacles coming out of the space between halves. It had giant ape legs and more tentacles where its arms should have been, and it wore an orderly's smock. "This part of the hospital is off-limits to patients," its voice was mushy and hard to understand, coming from two half-mouths. "But I'm not a patient," Zombie protested.

"Oh really?" the orderly pointed down and Zombie looked. He was wearing a hospital gown and nothing else, and it was flapping open in back.

He looked around for his father, but saw only Death coming slowly down the hallway towards him. Death held out a hand, and his father's voice said, "Come on, Jimmy. It's long past time, don't you think? We've been friends so long. It's time you came to me."

"No!" Zombie yelled and began running, past the orderly who grabbed at him but missed. Zombie's feet began to bleed from the glass and the needles. He ran past another doctor with a hyena's head, who threw a chart at him while laughing.

"MDR-TB!" the doctor yelled as he went by. "MDR-TB! Ha ha ha! Do you have insurance?"

"Come, Jimmy," his father's voice called from inside Death's hood. "We're such good friends, you and I. Think of all the people you have sent to me. All those people in the Middle East. Men, and women, and little children. Your mom. Did you know she came to me screaming your name? You killed her, you know. All that nagging. 'I want ice cream, I want ice cream.' She looked back to tell you to shut the fuck up. That's why she didn't see the truck coming the other way."

"No!" Zombie yelled, stumbling along on his bleeding feet. Tears blurred his vision. He tried to wipe them away, but his arms were too short. He couldn't reach his face. "No, shut up! That's not true! It was the other driver, he killed her! He was drunk... drunk..."

"But she could have avoided him," Death loomed behind Zombie. He couldn't see, but he could feel the cold of the grave emanating from the skeleton like heat from a burning insurgent building. "She could have avoided him if she hadn't been scolding you. You killed her! You killed her, and now you're going to kill me!"

Zombie's eyes cleared, and he saw his father running away from him, his hospital gown flapping open behind him.

Zombie shook his head. "No, dad! I'm trying to save you. I'm doing everything I can!" He started to run, his boots thumping on the bare linoleum as he tried to catch up to his father, to explain things.

"No, you left me! You want me to die all alone! Is this because I wouldn't let you have that cat when you were twelve? Is that why you hate me Jimmy?"

"No!" Zombie protested, stumbling forward. "I don't... I didn't leave you. You.. your insurance ran out, dad. And I had to go overseas. It's the army, dad. I don't have a say in it."

The old man looked over his shoulder as he ran. His voice was nasty, malevolent and cruel and sly, but his face was filled with stark terror. "Just like you didn't have any choice about killing all those people. But face it, Jimmy. You like it! You try to say you don't, try to pretend it's just the job, but secretly, inside, you like it."

"No! No, that's not true. I don't. I... I just..."

"You like it!" His father yelled. He poured on speed, running even faster.

Zombie tried to catch him, but it was hard to run with all those arms coming out of the ground, clutching at his legs with burned and rotting fingers. Behind him, he could hear the doctors and orderlies and horrible insect monsters catching up to him. He kicked at the arms, hearing bones crunch, but there were so many, so very many. He cried, but no tears came; only blood. "Dad, no! Please... I have to save you! I have to save someone! Please! Let me save someone!"

His father reached the stairway and went up. Zombie followed him, and now the arms came at him from the walls as well as the ground. He kicked and kicked. He ran, stomping as he went. Bones broke and Texas' wails of agony beat at his sanity from all sides. He realized he was running on top of tiny little people, and every single one of them was Parrot, and Zombie was crushing him over and over as he ran.

Then he was on the roof. His father was backing away from him, his hands upraised. "Please, don't!" the old man said, shaking his head. "Please, don't. Just let me be. Leave me alone, Jimmy!"

"Dad!" Zombie reached out a hand for his father. His hand was a skeleton, exposed bones protruding from under a tattered black robe. His father stumbled back and started to fall over the edge. "No!" Zombie dove forward onto his belly, reaching out desperately. He managed to grab his father's hand.

His father looked up at him. "Let me go," he whispered. "Stop holding on."

"I can't!" Zombie screamed. "I can't lose you too!"

"This is no way for a man to live," his father said, shaking his head slowly. It was difficult for him to talk with the tube in his mouth, the other tubes in his nose. His face was wasted and shiny from sweat, and drool trickled from the corner of his mouth. "I eat through a tube, son. I breathe through a tube. I shit my bed and they have to clean me with a sponge. This is no way for a man to live. Just let me go, Jimmy. Let me go."

"No! I can't! I can't!" Tears filled his eyes again. Zombie felt his father's hand slipping, and he tried to grab harder, but it has so difficult. After all, he was only a boy and his father was a grown man, large and heavy from his days in the mines. "Dad, please! Don't leave me!"

But his dad merely put his hat on his head and gently but firmly pried Zombie's hand free. His father fell.

"NO!" Zombie screamed, but the wind whipped away his word. He was falling, not his father. Below him, a red fire illuminated a narrow shaft full of hands, burned and bleeding, and they tore at his clothes and his hair and his face as he fell, screaming and screaming. Behind the arms, the walls of the pit were wood paneled walls lined with shelves and cupboards. There were pictures and maps hung on pegs here and there as well. On the shelves were all manner of things, from small jars to tea sets to books to small statuettes. He read "ORANGE MARMALADE" on a label tied to one of the jars as he fell past, and the pit went on and on forever and the eternal fires of Hell below waited to welcome him home while demons and doctors and insurgents sharpened their pitch-forks and watched him fall and fall and he would fall forever until his heart gave out and then his true punishment would begin.

Zombie sat up with a scream. For just a moment, he thought he heard a voice say, "The door is open. Look for the large elm past the Duchess' house."

Around him, the others were starting to stir. The clearing was just as sinister and ugly as always, but the Long Man was nowhere to be seen. Zombie reached for Overbite.

It was gone.

He swiftly inspected the dirt, leaves, and mushrooms near himself. He checked his person. He began to cuss.

"Shit-gargling, camel-fucking, skidmark-tea drinking bitchtits!" It didn't quite convey his feelings to perfection, but he was still disoriented from the drug or whatever it was the Long Man had hit him with. He wasn't at his best.

"Zombie," Uncle groaned as he sat up, holding his head with both hands. "You'd better have just found out your girlfriend left you for a rottweiler. What's your—"

"Sir, he took our weapons."

Uncle blinked at him dumbly for a moment. He, also, was clearly still recovering from the effects of what whatever was in that green smoke. Then, "Who did what now?"

"The centaur... centipede... centauripede. The fucking Long Man, sir. He took our weapons while we were out."

Vodka and Texas were semi-coherent by that time, and they joined Uncle in repeating Zombie's previous frantic search. When that turned up nothing more deadly than a combat knife, Uncle agreed with Zombie's assessment of the situation. "Mother pussbucket!"

Rider sat up, yelling, "Fine! Go! I don't care!" He blinked a couple times, then realized that everyone was staring at him. "Uh..." he looked up at the mushroom canopy. "Oh. A dream. Drugs? The green smoke?"

"That's the operating assumption," Uncle said. "It gets better. He took all our firearms."

Zombie totally understood Rider's reaction. Rider loved his Tac-50 almost as much as Zombie loved Overbite. Like Zombie,

Rider had even named his weapon, although Zombie thought 'The Truck' was a stupid name for a rifle, even if it did make long-distance deliveries on time, every time.

Once the sniper stopped kicking the heads off of mushrooms, and Uncle had checked on Parrot, the team gathered in a loose circle.

"So now what?" Rider asked.

"Well," Uncle stuck a hand in his pocket, "I guess we— GOD DAMN IT!"

Everyone jumped, just a little. Vodka was the first to figure it out. "Let me guess," he said. "He took the golden key also?"

Uncle didn't need to say anything. The sour look on his face was confirmation enough.

There was silence in the clearing for a few minutes as every man weighed options, tried to come up with a plan that didn't involve the fetal position.

Texas broke the silence. "I assume everyone had... dreams?" Nods all around met this question. "Did... did anyone hear something, right at the end? Like, just as you were waking up?"

Several heads lifted in near unison. "Yeah," Uncle said. "Something about a door."

"And a house," Rider added.

"The door is open, past the elm?" Zombie wasn't sure he remembered the exact wording. He'd been concentrating on other things at the time.

Like not pissing himself.

"'The door is in the elm, past the Duchess' house," Vodka corrected.

At this, everyone nodded. There was a chorus of 'Yeahs' and 'that's rights.'

"And a feeling," Rider said. "Like, I want to go that way," he pointed.

Zombie realized that, if he'd been asked to start walking, that's the direction he would have randomly chosen also. "Yeah," he agreed. "What the fuck?"

"A parting gift from the... what did you call him? Centipaur?" Uncle turned to Zombie.

"Centauripede," Zombie said.

"Right. That."

"Could be a trap," Vodka said.

"Why bother?" Everyone turned to look at Zombie. He shrugged. "If the centauripede wanted us dead, we were all totally stoned out of our minds and he had those long fucking claws. He could have killed us at any time. So why bother sending us into a trap?"

"Why take our weapons, and then help us?" Vodka wasn't ready to let his trap idea go that easily.

"Maybe he just didn't like the idea of us running around with automatic weapons? Maybe he's a Democrat? I don't know. But let me ask you this: do you have a better idea?" Zombie asked.

Vodka opened his mouth, then closed it again. He shook his head with a shrug.

"Okay," Uncle ran his hands through his hair, dislodging a few moldy leaves from the back of his head. "Okay. We go that way, but keep your eyes open and heads on a swivel. And since we're down to nothing but knives, I guess it's a good thing we all have some skill with those. Even so, Rider, you're right behind Vodka now, then Texas and Parrot, then Zombie. I'll pull up the rear."

"Keep your hands away from my rear," Zombie muttered, but it lacked conviction and no one was in the mood to take his invitation to banter.

Vodka cleared his throat. "Um, sir. Before we go..."

"Yeah?" Uncle looked at him.

Vodka seemed uncommonly hesitant. "Well sir, it's just that... in the PHR? The Caterpillar told Alice to use these mushrooms to get big again. 'One side makes you taller, the other side smaller,' and all like that.'"D

"You know what?" Zombie said, "Fuck the PHR. And fuck Alice, too. If that bitch wasn't already dead, I'd punch her ticket myself the moment we get out of this hell-hole. That was not a three-fucking-inch caterpillar. And Bill? Was not a 'small lizard'. So far, the only thing she's gotten right was the goddamn marmalade jar."

"I just got over a drug trip," Rider agreed. "I'm not about to start scarfing down strange 'shrooms on the say-so of a seven-year-old girl from the 19th century. They still thought leeches were a valid HMO choice back then."

"I have to agree," Uncle said. "Besides, the PHR only listed one mushroom. I see dozens of different types here. Which one is the safe one? No. We'll find another way to fix Parrot."

Rider turned to Zombie, clearly expecting him to take advantage of the slow-ball, but Zombie wasn't in the mood. He could still hear the sound of Parrot's bones crunching underfoot from his hallucination.

"Yes sir," Vodka nodded. Then he grabbed a hunk of mushroom from one of the shorter of the large ones with each hand, reaching far to each side of the cap. He stuffed the pieces into the respective pockets with a shrug. "Just in case we change our minds later," he said. "If nothing else, we can give it to some brainiac at DERPA and see what they make of it."

"Fine," Uncle said. "Let's roll."

Vodka pushed past several large 'shrooms, followed shortly by Rider. The rest of the team trailed along behind them.

It was somewhat like going backwards in time, Zombie thought. The mushrooms slowly faded, the ground and leaves grew dryer. The forest was still creepy and dark, but at least it was less fungal. This was, in Zombie's opinion, a definite improvement.

They walked for approximately half an hour when suddenly, the forest simply ended. Vodka seemed quite surprised when he burst out of the trees and into the sunlight. He started to raise a fist to call for a halt, then realized that it was too late: if anyone were around to see them, he had already blundered right into the open.

And, it turned out, someone was, although he was not in much of a position to alert anyone.

A dirt road bordered the forest. On the other side, the land became more of the ubiquitous gently rolling grassy hills Zombie was already utterly sick of. On the grassy side of the road, right in front of where Vodka had emerged from the woods, a tall wooden post protruded from the ground. From the post swung a round iron cage dangling from a chain.

In the cage was a man.

He was filthy and skinny, with a squat body and an enormous, hooked nose. He wore the grimy tatters of some sort of uniform. He sat in the cage, his temple pressed against two of the bars, staring blankly at the road. It took a moment before he realized there were people present.

"Hhhhcchh," said the man. Then he coughed and shook his head twice, and tried again. "Hchechlo. Gak." Zombie saw the man's throat convulse as he tried to swallow. He held up a short, stubby arm to his mouth and pantomimed drinking.

Vodka walked around the cage, then pointed up at where the chain connected it to the wood post. "Collaborator," he read off the sign posted there. He spat on the ground and turned his back on the prisoner.

Texas held up his canteen, but looked to Uncle for clearance. Uncle nodded, and Texas moved to the cage, handing the canteen through the bars. The prisoner took it and drank greedily, then spent a solid minute coughing. When he had recovered himself, he drank more.

"You're here for my gold, aren't you?" said the man in an irritatingly high-pitched voice. "Well, you can't have it!"

"We're not here for your gold," Uncle said.

"You most certainly are," said the prisoner. "Why, I can see it in your eyes. You want my gold. Well, you can't have it. It's mine!"

"Can I shoot him?" Zombie asked. "Sorry, I mean stab him. Can I stab him? Just a little?"

"Is that sign correct?" Uncle asked, pointing above the cage.

The prisoner craned his head, but couldn't see it from his angle. "I don't know," said he, "what does it say?"

"'Collaborator,'" Uncle replied.

"Oh, that," said the man. "General Klahb called me that when he put he in here. I don't know what it means."

"It means 'traitor,'" Vodka said over his shoulder. He refused to look at the captive. "It means you helped out your enemy. It means you sold out your own men. It means 'asshole.' It means you deserve to die in that cage."

Uncle shrugged. "More or less," he said with a nod.

"We're going to lose!" said the man in the cage. "Everyone can see it. Captain Ironhand's men are too strong, and there's too many of them. The Queen just throws us at him and we die. They chop us to bits. There's no point in resisting." The dirty little man scratched the top of his head. His arms barely reached. "So what if I told them a few things. So what if I made a little money and earned some goodwill? They'll be in charge soon. Ironhand will be the new Queen, and he'll remember me! Yes, he'll remember the help I gave him. I'll be out of this cage, you'll see. I'll have a place in his court. I'll be promoted to a Diamond, or maybe even a Heart."

He paused to draw breath, and really looked carefully at the team. "Wait," said the man, "why are you saying bad things? You're the Captain's men. Oh, is this a test? Are you testing my loyalty to Ironhand? You can trust me, I swear! I'm on your side!"

"Why the fuck does everyone assume we work for this guy?" Zombie muttered under his breath.

Uncle held up a hand for silence. "That's right," he practically purred. "You passed the first part of the test. Now for the second part. Where is the Duchess' house?"

"Oh! Yes! I can help you," said the collaborator. He thrust a tiny little arm through the bars of the cage and pointed up the road. "About three miles that way, on the left, you'll see a small path between two thorny hedges. Her house is down that path." He looked at Uncle, tears in his eyes. "Now you'll let me out, right? I passed the tests, I'm on your side!"

"We can't let you out just yet," Uncle said, "that would let the Queen know where we are. We're a covert team, you see. But you just wait here a little while longer, and we'll come get you when our mission at the Duchess' house is finished. Just a little longer."

"Oh, yes, of course," said the man. "I understand. Shh! I won't tell a soul. But when we get back, you'll tell Ironhand, right? You'll tell him that Vellen is loyal? You'll make sure he knows?"

"I guarantee that you'll get the reward you deserve," Uncle smiled his reassurance. He turned to the rest of the group and gestured the direction indicated. "Come on," he said. "Let's roll."

The team walked down the road, eyes alert for signs of trouble. After a quarter of a mile or so, Rider asked Uncle, "You're not really going to let him out, are you?"

"Hell no," Uncle said.

CHAPTER VI
CAT AND PEPPER-SPRAY

Dangerous?

Yeah, the lizard was pretty dangerous. But you know, in the end, it was just a big lizard.

That breathed fire.

No, it was nothing compared to the damned cat.

That cat was a nightmare.

-MSG Jamal "Vodka" Jones, official de-brief, Operation Rabbit Hole

A HALF A MILE FROM the caged prisoner, the road made a sharp left turn. Vodka held up his fist and then pointed into the sky.

A flock of vultures circled something a short way ahead. Uncle nodded and gestured for Vodka to continue on. They would keep an eye out for whatever it was the vultures were after.

It didn't take very long to find.

The trees on the right petered out, revealing a low-walled field. What had once been farmed there, Vodka could not say, for the fields had been torched sometime in the not too distant past. There was nothing left but charred stalks and ash.

Across the field, he saw the ruined husks of a handful of small buildings, similarly burnt and crumbling. A banner had been stretched between two of the charred timber frames, although it was facing obliquely away from him and he could not see if there was anything written upon it.

In the middle of the small farm, a solitary figure toiled, digging a deep hole with a broken-handled shovel. Behind him, a small pile of burned corpses represented the object of the vultures' attention. The digger was too close, however, and shooed away the birds with his shovel whenever any got too close.

Vodka pointed at his eyes and then at the scene.

Uncle considered, then nodded. He pointed at Rider and Zombie and signaled left, then himself and Vodka and signaled right. Texas he gestured to stay put. Parrot, of course, would go wherever Texas carried him.

The smell of ash was thick in Vodka's nostrils as he pushed his way through the scorched field. The remaining stalks and thicker bits of char crunched under his boots. For just a moment, he wondered what Sgt. Anderson, his Drill back in Boot, would have said about the state of his uniform. It almost certainly would have been racist. Anderson had enjoyed trying to get a rise out of Vodka that way.

He kept his blade in his hand as he approached. Vodka scanned the remains of the buildings, the edge of the field, and the forest line as he walked. It didn't seem like an ambush, but one never knew for sure. That was the point of an ambush.

The digger never looked up as they approached him from two sides. Closer, Vodka could see that the man was short, even by the standards of this place, no more than three and a half feet tall. He had thick sideburns, a ruddy face, and a bulbous nose. He wore a brown felt cap protected his eyes from the sun. His hair was white, but unlike Rabbix, this fellow looked old; his face creased with years and the haunted eyes of a man who thinks all his happy days are behind him.

Vodka and Uncle halted to the man's left, three seconds before Zombie and Rider arrived on the other side. Vodka spent the time looking at the bodies.

They were even smaller than the digger. Although the flesh was too badly burned to identify features, Vodka would have wagered a month's pay that they were children.

"What happened here?" Uncle's voice was soft, filled with sympathy.

The digger looked up from his task. His eyes, red and puffy from weeping, raked over Uncle from head to toe and then back up. He returned to his digging. "You happened," said he. His voice was thick and rough but flat and emotionless. The voice of a man who is dead inside. Vodka had heard its like several times in the Middle East. It never got easier to hear.

"I beg your pardon, but we've never been here before," Uncle corrected gently. He, also, recognized the tone of the digger's voice.

"Maybe not you personally," said the old man with a shrug as he tossed a shovel-full of dirt onto the mound near Rider's feet. Rider took a step away, but made no protest. "Maybe not you personally, but your kind."

Zombie clenched his fist at his side. Vodka caught his eye and shook his head. Not the time. Zombie let out his breath in a slow, silent sigh, and unclenched his hand. He nodded.

Uncle crouched beside the lip of the hole and looked across at the digger. "Sir, this was not the work of my men or anyone else from our world. We're just here to find a missing girl, that's all."

"Well, you might say that," said the old man as he scooped up more dirt. The work was difficult, as the shovel's handle was broken at the midpoint. Vodka wondered how many splinters the old man had given himself so far. "You might, but it means nothing. An enemy may not be counted upon to tell the truth."

A boot crunched burned plant behind him, and Vodka turned his head to look. Texas had approached, his entrenching tool in his hands. He crouched across the hole from the old man and began helping him dig. The man frowned in confusion. This didn't fit his expectations of how an enemy, especially a visibly injured enemy, should act.

Uncle's jaw tightened in irritation. Vodka understood: Texas had been ordered to stay put. On the other hand, this gesture of kindness might go a long way towards soothing over relations between the team and locals. After mulling it over for a moment, Uncle decided the best course of action was to ignore the situation.

"You have nothing we want," Rider said. "Why would we lie to you?"

"If I have nothing you want," said the old man, "why are you talking to me?"

"Good fucking question," Zombie muttered. He turned away, ostensibly keeping watch on the road. In reality, Vodka knew, he did it so that he would later be able to honestly say he hadn't seen the angry look Uncle shot him.

Uncle glared at Zombie's back for a moment, then turned his attention back to the old man. "Was this your farm?"

There was silence save for the scrape of shovel in dirt, the hiss of earth being piled into a mound. Vodka had just decided that the old man wasn't going to answer when he was proved wrong.

"My son's," said the old man. "And yes, mine before that. He was taken to fight in the war. I cared for his children," he gestured

94

at the pile of corpses. "We needed a new strap for the plow. I don't walk as swiftly as once I did, and our nearest neighbor is not close. Well, other than the Duchess, but she'd not have time for the likes of me. I was gone for many hours. When I returned..." he gestured again at the pile of bodies, then at the banner hanging stretched between the small farmhouse and what Vodka presumed had once been a barn.

He took the gesture as an invitation, and walked a little away until he could read the front of it. "'Surrender, Harzt,'" he read aloud. "Who is Harzt? Is that you?"

The old man turned to stare at Vodka, eyes wide with incredulity. "Do I look like a Harzt to you?" asked he. "No, I'm not but a humble peasant."

"So Harzt is...?" Uncle prompted.

The man turned again, this time to stare at him. "Your men put the banner there," said he in an angry voice. "I assume you even a common soldier would know the name of the Queen of the land he's helping to conquer."

"The Queen," Vodka muttered, nodding. "Queen Harzt." He and Uncle exchanged a glance. "It makes sense if you filter it though the mind of a little girl," Vodka said.

Uncle nodded. He retrieved his own e-tool and joined Texas and the old man in digging. There was only room for three around the hole, so the others kept watch. After a time, Rider tapped the old man on the shoulder and gently nudged him aside, taking his place. The work went faster after that.

Later, when the bodies were buried and the grave covered up once more and the vultures had flown off in search of easier meals, the old man gave the team a grudging nod of thanks. "Please," said the old man, "leave me to mourn."

Uncle licked his lips and drew a breath as if to say something, but then thought better of it. Instead, he nodded and clapped the old guy carefully on the shoulder. "Come on," he said to the rest of the team. "Let's go."

"God damn it," Zombie muttered once they were back on the road.

Uncle raised an eyebrow, but Zombie didn't elaborate at first.

They walked another half mile before Zombie spoke again. "It isn't right. They fired those houses, they had to know there were people inside. They fucking did it on purpose. Civilians. Kids. It isn't right."

"Agreed," Uncle said. "But there's nothing we can do. We have a mission, and it's not to get involved in local affairs."

"Besides," Rider said, "I'm not about to take on an enemy army with nothing but a rib-tickler." He sighed and looked off to the side of the road, staring into the distance. "I want my Truck back," he said wistfully. 'Truck' was the name of his Tac-50.

Vodka didn't understand guys who named their weapons.

Zombie snorted a short, humorless laugh. "I hear THAT!" He walked in silence for a dozen yards, then said, "I just think this Ironhand guy sounds like a real asshole. That's all. Kids, for fuck's sake." Another couple dozen yards passed before he said, "It isn't right."

No one argued with him.

Gradually, they left the burned fields behind. Wild grasses grew on the right side of the road, while on the left, bushes grew into thick, thorny hedges. After a time, Vodka spotted a small break in the hedge. He might have missed it if he hadn't been looking for it specifically, it was that small.

He halted the group and gestured at the narrow space. It was far too small for anyone but Parrot to squeeze through without getting cut up by the thorns.

Uncle came to the front of the line and stared at the tiny path. "Are you kidding me?" he sighed deeply. He tried to peer ahead, to see how deep the hedge went, but the path curved gradually, making it impossible to tell for sure. "Recommendations?"

"Burn it down," Zombie was in a bad mood. In point of fact, Zombie was always in a bad mood. This was worse than normal. The thing with the kids had really bothered him.

"Too green," Uncle said. "Anyone else?"

"Go back and go around," Rider said. "The hedges only started about a half-mile back. Assuming they don't circle the entire house, we just go around."

"And if they do surround the entire house?"

Rider shrugged. "Then we end up back here again, and we're not in any worse position than we are now."

"Agreed," Uncle inclined his head back up the road the way they had come. "Let's give it a go."

Finding the edge of the thorn hedge, Vodka attempted walking parallel to the road. The hedge slanted away from the road, however, and for a time he worried that it would, indeed, encircle the Duchess' house. After a hundred yards, however, the hedge curved back to the right once more, and Vodka felt relieved. It was a thick hedge, but not a giant circle.

Besides the hedge, there were hundreds of narrow trees clustered together. It was hard to see more than a few dozen yards in any direction. The hedge itself provided the only decent landmark, and Vodka kept it visible on his right side at all times.

At last, the trees ended and Vodka found himself on a large grassy lawn surrounded on three sides by trees and on the last by the thorny hedge. Ahead, he could see a short but sprawling house, about six feet tall and probably three or four thousand square feet in footprint. Smoke rose from a chimney. A large vegetable garden took up a sizable section of the lawn. At the edge of this, a pig rooted through a large compost pile.

The sun was now around mid-afternoon, although his watch said it was well past midnight.

"Ask her if we can rest here," Parrot's thin little helium-voice squeaked from Texas' pocket. "Texas, especially, but all of us need sleep."

Parrot must have felt this was very important, if it caused him to break his self-imposed silence. Vodka understood. If he sounded like a little girl in one of those Japanese animation movies, he would try to avoid talking as much as possible too.

"I'll try," Uncle said. "But no promises. So far, the people of this land haven't been exactly thrilled to see us."

"Under-fucking-statement of the year," Zombie said.

The team fanned out as they approached the building. Even from a distance, they could hear a ruckus from inside. It sounded like the busiest restaurant kitchen you ever heard; dozens of pans and utensils clattering against each other. The smell of something spicy drifted through an open window, and Vodka both heard and felt his stomach growl.

The team was still perhaps thirty yards from the house when the door opened. Out stepped a man wearing a butler's livery. He was perhaps five feet tall and skinny. His skin glistened with moisture, and bore just the faintest hint of green in the shadows of his round, somewhat bulbous face. His eyes were set very high and wide on his head, giving the impression that he was looking up at the sky even when his head was tilted straight forward. His nose was flat, his lips thin and wide. He wore a curly white wig like you see on judges in those dramas on BBC.

There was nowhere for the team to hide. He spotted them.

For a second, the butler sat there blinking dumbly at them. Then, as Uncle began to raise a hand in greeting, the guy in the wig turned towards the house and began screaming. "To Arms! To Arms! They're here! They're here!"

"Fuck!" Zombie said on behalf of the entire team.

"No, wait," Uncle shouted, "We're not here to—"

Six more men, dressed the same as the first one, poured out of the house. Each held a short bronze sword in his hand, and they could have all been brothers from the similarity of appearance they held to the first one. "Protect the Duchess!" one of the new ones cried.

They rushed at the team in a loose mob.

Uncle didn't even have time to tell Texas to stay back, not that he needed to. With Parrot still in his pocket, Texas wasn't about to risk taking a sword to the chest. He turned and ran, one hand clutching his pocket to try to keep Parrot from bouncing out.

Then Vodka had other things to occupy his attention. A small horde of sword-wielding members of the service staff bore down on the team, and the good-guys were outnumbered almost two to one.

Two of the enemy bore down on Uncle, Rider, and Zombie, while only one headed towards Vodka.

Vodka was insulted.

He flipped his knife into an assassin's grip, the blade held parallel to his forearm. He blocked the first hasty swing by his foe, and brought a knee up into the man's belly. As his attacker gasped and staggered back, Vodka turned to his left and launched himself at the legs of one of the guys running towards Uncle.

The wig-wearing swordsman tripped over Vodka and they rolled together in a pile for a moment. Vodka disentangled himself and stepped back, then kicked the other guy in the head as he started to rise. He heard a satisfying 'thump' as his boot connected with the foeman's temple and knocked him back down, possibly unconscious. Vodka didn't have time to see for certain, for his first opponent had recovered and was on him once more.

Vodka jumped back, leaning away from three quick slashes from the enemy's sword. His foe tended to over-extend, and Vodka used that to his advantage. He waited until the enemy began another swing, but this time Vodka only moved just barely far enough back to avoid the blow. The tip of the enemy sword whistled past his chest, missing him by less than an inch. Vodka immediately reversed his direction and stepped forward, flipping his blade back into an upright grip and slamming it into his enemy's armpit. The foe screamed and dropped his sword. Vodka drove his foot into the man's knee, shattering it and raking the calf muscle. The man collapsed. Vodka made sure he stayed down with a swift kick to the back of the head.

Finding himself with a second to call his own, Vodka snapped a quick glance about the battlefield. The man he had tripped him shook his head and started to rise, but would it would still be a few seconds before he became important again.

Vodka saw that Rider had put down two of his own foes, one with a slash across the throat and the other with a knife in the ribs. That last had been a problem, however. Rider wasn't used to fighting people this short, and had misjudged his angles. The falling enemy took Rider's knife with him, lodged into his ribs.

Uncle was putting his foe down with a pair of short, hard kicks to the ribs.

Zombie, fighting two men at once, was in a more difficult spot. He had a small cut across his forearm from an improperly blocked thrust, and both his men were still up, attempting to flank. They were, however, clear on the other side of the battle field. Vodka wouldn't get there in time.

"Rider," he yelled and tossed his knife, handle-first, halfway between the sniper and the still-raging battle. Rider sprinted forward, caught the blade, and slammed it into the neck of one of the men harassing Zombie.

Vodka turned his attention back to his own foe, who had managed to get to his feet. He lunged at Vodka blade-first. Vodka twisted aside at the last second, then grabbed the enemy's sword hand with his right and rotated, locking his foe's elbow. Vodka's left arm slammed down, breaking his enemy's arm. The man screamed and dropped his sword. Vodka kicked him between the legs, then again in the face as the man doubled over. The foe collapsed in a softly moaning heap. Vodka picked up the dropped sword and backed up, covering his opponents, but they both stayed down.

He looked around, but the fight was over. Zombie had his own man in a chokehold. The man jerked a few times then fell still as Vodka watched. Zombie dropped his captive onto the grass.

"Status!" Uncle snapped.

Vodka looked himself over for any potential wounds that might have gone unnoticed in the heat of battle, but he could find none. "Copa," he said.

The others likewise inspected themselves. Rider shrugged. "Copa."

Zombie looked at this cut on his arm, then shook his head. "A scratch." He pulled a bandage from his personal medical supply and began wrapping it around the small gash. Rider helped him cinch it tight.

Uncle inspected himself also, then nodded. "Copacetic." He looked as if he were about to say more, but at that moment, more people came out of the house.

These, Vodka decided after a glance, were not soldiers.

They were both short, perhaps four feet tall. They had enormous heads, and neither of them had missed very many, if any, meals in the recent past.

The one in front was dressed in a greasy apron thrown over a shapeless smock. Messy brown hair partially covered the woman's face; at least, Vodka assumed it was a woman. The person had faintly feminine secondary characteristics. Streams of sweat ran down her face and body, both of which were so round as to be spherical. In one hand, she held a small ceramic pot labeled, 'Pepper, Black, Ground.' In her other was a cast-iron frying pan.

The other one was similar in general outline, although she (again, Vodka assumed the gender) was even uglier of face. In addition to having a nearly square, gigantic head, she had a tiny, but sharp-looking little chin that jutted from under her sagging jowls and full, chapped lips. She had a nose that any witch would have been proud of; long and hooked and sporting the most impressive, hairy wart on the left side. Her eyes were beady little black holes under thick lids so heavily coated in red eye shadow that the word that most readily came to Vodka's mind was 'spackled.' She wore a shapeless red muumuu and an impossibly elaborate headpiece that looked like two views of Vasquez Rocks wrapped in red velvet.

The one in red, whom Vodka assumed as the Duchess, grew red in the face until she quite matched her clothes. "You DARE to lay a finger on my men?" said the Duchess. "Chop off their heads!"

"They attacked us," Uncle said. "We don't want—"

"Don't bother me," said the ugly woman in red. "I never could abide what other people want." She stepped up behind the other woman and rested her chin on the cook's shoulder. "Let them enjoy the pepper!"

The cook's lips split open in a horrible smile. Her teeth, Vodka could see, were pointed, needle-sharp, and a filthy yellow color.

"Now wait," Uncle said, still trying to salvage the situation, "We just want to find out where—"

It was not, Vodka decided later, Uncles' mission for being allowed to finish sentences. The cook ignored him and threw the ceramic pepper pot towards the team. No one reacted right away, because it was a ceramic pepper pot.

They should have known better.

The pot landed in the middle of the team and shattered. Instantly, a cloud of grayish-black smoke issued forth, engulfing Vodka. It was peppery, true, in the same way that pepper-spray is peppery. His eyes teared up until he couldn't see, and gut-wrenching sneezes wracked his body. He tried to flee the area, but tripped over one of the fallen wig-men. He sprawled in the grass, blind and sneezing so hard he found it difficult to draw breath.

Around him, he could hear others sneezing also. In addition, there was a 'thunk,' and someone yelped in pain. Later, he would find out that it was Zombie being hit by the cook's frying pan, which she had thrown. At the time, however, Vodka was too busy trying to crawl out of the pepper cloud. This, he thought, is NOT an acceptable way to die. On all fours, sneezing until his ribs ached, he scrambled in what he hoped was the right direction.

He guessed correctly, for after several feet he found the air clear of the stinging cloud. His eyes continued to water and he still sneezed another half-dozen times, but at least no more pepper was getting into his nose or eyes.

From somewhere behind him, Vodka heard a screech, suddenly cut off.

He fumbled for his canteen and splashed clean water in his eyes, then wiped at them furiously to clear them. He forced himself to his feet and looked, somewhat blearily, around.

By the door to the house, he saw that the cook was down. Above her stood Rider, holding a bloody sword he must have picked up from one of the fallen soldiers. The Duchess wailed and threw herself to her knees beside the dead servant.

Rider wiped at his eyes a few times, still clearing them out. "Sorry," he said as the Duchess looked up at him, her own eyes filling with tears. "She... she was attacking..." he stammered. Vodka wondered who he was attempting to justify the killing to; the Duchess or himself.

"You only did it to annoy," said the Duchess. "Now who will prepare me my soup? Do you know how hard it is to get good help these days? They're all gone, gone off to the war. Gone off to fight you!"

"IT'S NOT US!" Zombie yelled in frustration.

"Don't tease," said the Duchess. "So. Now you kill me, eh? You think to deprive the Queen of her staunchest ally? Well, I think not. And the moral of that is – 'you don't always get what you want.' Cat! Attack!"

With that, she leapt to her feet and ran towards the back of the house.

Rider said, "Really?" He began to run after her when he quite suddenly found his way blocked by an enormous cat.

It was huge, larger even than a lion, although it had the general head-shape of a house cat. Its coat was solid black except for a brilliant white star on the chest. Its mouth split open in what, on a person, might have been a grin, and its teeth were disturbingly long and sharp. It raised a paw, a paw from which jutted claws that would have little trouble disemboweling a bison.

It had appeared out of nowhere.

Rider yelped and threw himself forward and under the claw, rolling to his feet beside the monster cat. It leaned swiftly to the side, knocking Rider off-balance so that he stumbled and almost fell.

Uncle, Zombie, and Vodka all started running forward, snatching up swords as they rushed to the sniper's rescue. Behind them, Texas and Parrot trotted after.

The cat turned, disturbingly fast for a creature that size, and lashed out again with its paw. This time the claws hit, raking along Rider's right side and back and leaving four parallel gashes that ran crimson with blood.

Rider hissed in pain. He threw himself into a pair of shoulder rolls. The momentum carried him to his feet outside the monster cat's range.

The cat responded by rocking back on its haunches, preparing to leap. Zombie beat the creature to the punch, throwing himself through the air to stab it in the flank with his borrowed sword. The cat threw back its head and screeched. Zombie began rolling away, expecting the thing to turn on him next, but it didn't.

It vanished.

In frustrated anger, Vodka slashed through the space where the cat had been a moment ago. "I'm getting really sick of that!" he snarled.

"Contact!" yelled Uncle, pointing. Vodka followed the finger with his gaze.

There was the cat, crouched atop the Duchess' house. It licked at the wound on its flank, then turned to face the team again. It grinned once more.

"No cat should have that many goddamn teeth!" Zombie shuddered.

The cat wiggled its butt. It was about to leap again.

"Run!" Uncle yelled.

"You go," Rider said, holding up his sword in one hand and Vodka's knife in the other. "I'll cover your retreat."

"I said 'run!'" Uncle snapped. The cat leapt half the distance to the group in one bound and raced towards them. "Scatter!"

Vodka ran to the side, diving into a shoulder roll at the last moment. He felt a breeze like a passing locomotive as the giant cat rushed by. It skidded to a halt and turned back towards them.

"Fuck it's fast!" Zombie observed.

"You're not dying yet," Uncle yelled at Rider. "No heroic last stands until you're too badly hurt to run. Now: RUN!"

They ran into the trees where the big cat would have difficulty following them. At least, that was the theory.

Behind them, Vodka heard the sound of the cat crash into some bushes, but the trees did seem to stall it. At first. He sucked in breath in preparation of heaving a sigh of relief when, once again, the Universe reminded him that there ain't no justice, life sucks, and a host of other Murphy-isms.

The cat appeared in a space between trees right in front of him. The huge paw shot out, just missing Vodka as he threw himself to the side. Scrambling back, he put more narrow trees between himself and the cat.

It vanished again.

"Motherfucker!" Zombie snarled.

"Keep going!" Uncle panted.

Several more times, the cat almost caught one or more of them. They learned to avoid any space between trees that was even sort of large enough for the cat to fit into. The game of cat-and-mouse went on for a good half an hour. By the end of it, Rider was gasping for breath and having trouble keeping up. Things couldn't get worse.

Things got worse.

"Houston, we have a fucking problem!" Zombie called out. Vodka looked ahead and saw what he meant; the woods were thinning.

The small, close trees were giving way to a larger, more spaced out variety. The cat would have little problem catching them in such terrain.

As if to prove the point, the cat appeared on the branch of one of the larger trees just ahead. It grinned at them and slowly licked the paw that had tagged Rider. They couldn't move forward without giving it plenty of room to get at them, and they were too winded to continue running through the thicker woods. The cat looked perfectly content to wait them out, like Tom lurking outside Jerry's mouse hole.

When Uncle realized that both sides were at a detente, he gestured for Rider to come over. "Take off your shirt," he said, pulling bandages from his personal med kit. It didn't take long to realize that he didn't have enough, so he called, "Zombie. Give me yours too."

Zombie fumbled one-handed at his pocket until he was able to remove his kit, which he tossed to Uncle. Zombie's other hand clutched his confiscated sword, and his eyes never left the giant cat.

"Damn it," Uncle muttered. "I really wish Parrot's kit wasn't small. I'm almost certain this needs cleaning." The wounds were long and jagged, but shallow. He began unwinding the first bandage.

Rider hissed as the bandages were applied. Once the deed was done, he struggled back into his tattered shirt and jacket. The cuts limited his mobility, especially in his arm. He leaned against a tree and breathed deeply for the better part of a minute, then looked up and nodded. "I'm good to go," he said. His voice was tight with pain.

Uncle looked over the group, and Vodka could tell what he was thinking. Their firearms were gone, half the team was combat-ineffective, and they still hadn't even found the girl. They'd had less trouble with the Muj.

"I hate this place," Zombie muttered, showing that he was also thinking along the same lines.

Texas stepped forward to edge of the tree line. He looked up at the cat, which stopped grooming itself in order to watch him in return. "Hello cat," he said politely.

Zombie gaped open-mouthed at him.

Texas ignored Zombie and continued. "We're not here to hurt your Duchess. Her men attacked us first, and would not listen when we said that we mean no harm. Surely she is long gone by now. We will not pursue her. Could not, even if we wanted to. Now, you can keep us pinned here for a while, but eventually you're going to need to leave to get food. We have our own. We can wait you out. If you do catch us out in the open, you can clearly hurt us, but just as clearly, we can hurt you back. What do you say, can we declare a truce? We'll each go our separate ways and call it a draw?"

The cat crouched on his branch, grinning his evil grin, during this entire speech. When Texas stopped talking, he lifted his paw and began grooming again.

Texas let out a small, nearly inaudible sigh.

Uncle nodded. "It was worth a try." He turned to face Vodka and Zombie. "All right. Recommendations? We could try to set a trap, maybe. Or simply stick to the thin trees and see if they lead somewhere we will be at less of a disadvantage."

"Sir," Vodka inclined his head towards the tree where the cat sat.

The cat no longer sat there.

"Hotel. Alpha. Tango. Echo," Zombie snarled.

"Heads on a swivel," Uncle ordered. He picked his way to the edge of the trees, then slowly and cautiously, set one foot into the open space. When the cat failed to appear and kill him, he took another careful step, then a third. He sprinted forward five yards, spun around, and ran back.

The rest of the team kept their eyes peeled in all directions, but saw not so much as a flicker of cat. When Uncle returned to the more tightly packed trees and looked at them, Vodka shrugged. "'Looks clear,'" he said.

"Damn it," Zombie muttered. "I hate it when you say that. I can never tell if you mean it's actually clear, or if you mean you don't have a fucking clue."

"Enough," Uncle bit his lip. "All right. Staying here gets us nothing. Eyes open, keep close, watch each others' six. Vodka in front, then Texas and Parrot, then Zombie, then Rider, then me. Let's agitate some gravel." He paused for a moment, then, blushing faintly, asked, "Um. Does anyone know what an elm tree looks like?"

CHAPTER VII

A MADDENING TEA-PARTY

I tell you, Colonel... can I call you 'Aje?' No? Well anyway. I tell you, man, Zombie was...I mean Halsford. Sergeant Halsford. If we'd had our guns at that point, he'd have blown those dude's heads clean off.

Twice.

Each.

What's that? You can't shoot someone's head off twice? You don't say. I had no idea. Thanks for clarifying, sir.

They teach you that in officer's school?

   -SFC Matthew "Rider" Adams, official de-brief, Operation Rabbit Hole

WHETHER OR NOT THE trees in the immediate area were elms, not a one of them held anything that anyone could identify as a door. Heads on swivels, they moved along, keeping eyes open for the return of the cat.

Rider held his sword loosely in his left hand. His right, he tried not to move. Although not very deep, the cuts hurt quite a lot, and he feared that Uncle was right about the risk of infection.

110

Or poison, he mused. Just because cats aren't poisonous in the real world didn't mean they weren't in this absurd land.

He cursed under his breath. He hated being a drag on the team.

The thin forest continued for a while, then, as was the wont of wooded areas in this place, it simply ended. The team assembled at the edge and looked out.

It was not a pleasant vista.

A low line of hills stretched to the left, and another to the far right as the team faced. Between them lay a flat plain that may have once been pretty grass.

It wasn't pretty anymore.

The grass was trampled and crushed, ground into the mud. The mud, in turn, was a dark reddish brown. Blood soaked the earth to create that mud; the blood of hundreds of slain men.

The bodies sprawled haphazardly, some alone and others in small piles. Bodies were torn open, intestines and other vitals spilled out and trampled upon, throats slit, heads staved in or decapitated. Flocks of crows and vultures squabbled over the choicer tidbits, while a horde of flies feasted and laid eggs in open wounds. The stench was overwhelming; feces and blood and rotting meat. Behind him, Rider heard Texas retching.

Several crows screamed in protest and flapped a short distance before settling back down. Rider looked up and saw what had disturbed the birds; a small group of men picked their way among the bodies.

Looters.

Rider heard Vodka spit.

"Go easy," Uncle ordered quietly. "Maybe we can question them if we don't scare them off."

"The state we're in, we couldn't scare a Chihuahua with a nervous condition," Zombie opined, but he kept his blade held low, at his side, and moved with slow deliberation.

With Vodka in the lead, they approached the field of the dead.

The victims, Rider noted, all seemed to be on the same team. They were similar to the people the team had encountered so far, which is to say that there were few similarities between them other than a certain general amount of uncanny, and a lack of anyone over five feet in height. They did, however, all wear the same uniform; leather armor under a red tabard with three crossed black swords pointing downward. They looked, Rider decided, as if swords, spears, and/or clubs had slain them all. Not a bullet wound or arrow shaft to be seen.

There were, in fact, no weapons to be found at all. Also, no enemy soldiers. Either the enemy was very good, or they had won the day and carried off their own fallen as well as all of the weapons, leaving only the bodies of the locals.

He turned his attention to the looters as the team approached. So far, the pillagers had not seen them. There were three of them, Rider saw. They were definitely locals.

The one closest to him was of 'average' height for this place, just a hair under five feet tall. He was skinny, with long, gangly arms and big feet. His hair was a wild brown thatch sprouting every which-way from the top of his head. His big ears stuck far out, reminding Rider of certain British royals. His eyes, Rider would notice later when they were closer, were incredibly bloodshot.

The next one was shorter than the first, and more closely fit the look of the Duchess and her cook, having a head that was too large for his frame. His head wasn't quite as large as the Duchess', and he was rather skinnier all around, but all the same the general racial resemblance was clear. He wore a ridiculous stovepipe hat, like old pictures of Abraham Lincoln. At his waist swung a dull pewter or tin mug tied to his belt.

The last of the three was the shortest of them all. His head was more normally shaped than the one with the hat. In fact, he was fairly unremarkable, in comparison to his companions. He moved slowly, his head drooping. Rider wasn't sure how he saw under his long, shaggy brown bangs.

All three of them wore the same uniform as the corpses. Although the uniforms on the living men were dirty and tattered, they lacked holes in lethal places.

The looters were meticulous and thorough in searching the bodies, turning each one over and patting it down all over. Now and again, a searcher would discover a purse or a bauble or a small belt pouch. The finder would quickly look inside, then heave a sigh of disappointment.

So intent were they on their work that they didn't notice the arrival of the team until a murder of crows cawed angrily and flapped away. Less than ten yards separated the two groups by that point.

The first two looters let out nearly identical shrieks. The one with the hat thrust his hands into the air, his fingers spread wide.

"I surrender! Don't kill me!" cried the man with the big head.

The tallest one saw what his companion did, and imitated him. "Me either! Don't kill me! I surrender!"

The shortest man also put his hands up, but said nothing.

"Well," Zombie said. "That was... easy."

"Search them," Uncle ordered Vodka, who nodded and did just that.

Vodka shook his head. "No weapons," he reported.

"You won't kill us?" asked the taller man with the wild hair.

113

"Do you have any food?" begged the shorter man with the hat.

The smallest man merely watched from under heavy eyelids.

Uncle raised an eyebrow, then shrugged. He looked at the tallest man and said, "We're not going to kill you unless you try to attack us." To the middle-sized man, he said, "We'll give you food... if you answer some questions for us." To the smallest man, he cocked his head. "Deal?"

"Yes, yes, deal!" said both the tall man and the one with the hat at the same time. The small one smiled and nodded vigorously. All three men held out their hands, licking their lips. They seemed very hungry indeed.

"Not here," Uncle looked in distaste at the bodies all around them. "Come, let's find somewhere less nauseating." He turned and picked his way out of the field of corpses. The locals followed him and were followed by the rest of the team in turn.

Uncle made his way up one of the hills bordering the killing field. Rider nodded to himself in approval. That would give them a good range of vision; they could see anyone attempting to sneak up on them. Also, a light breeze at the top blew away the stench of the corpses.

Once they reached the crest, and then went ever-so slightly beyond it to get away from the sight and smell of the dead, Uncle gestured to the grass. "All right," he said. "This will do. Let's sit down here, and you can tell me what I want to know while you eat." He opened his pack and withdrew an MRE, nodding for Vodka and Zombie to do the same. He was, Rider noticed, making sure that the injured still had full rations.

"What are your names?" Uncle asked, holding up the plastic pouches.

The three locals seemed dubious about the value of a mylar bag in terms of eating, but they sat down all the same.

"I'm Hadda," said the man with the big head and the tall hat. Uncle nodded and handed him one of the MREs, and showed him how to open it and use the flameless heater. The other two watched intently, then looked up and raised their hands to Uncle.

"Name?" Uncle asked, holding up another package.

"Hayer," said the tallest of the men, he with the wild thatch on his head. He eagerly accepted his pouch, and wasted no time tearing it open.

The last man bit his lower lip, squirming in place. When Uncle asked, "And your name?" he grew visibly agitated. He opened and closed his mouth a couple of times, and made a high-pitched whining noise.

"Oh hig," said Hadda, stuffing crackers and cheese into his mouth as fast as he could. "Hou hang dog hoo hig."

"I'll just go ahead and ask the obvious," Zombie said. "What the fuck did you just say?"

Hadda swallowed twice, grimaced, and swallowed again. "I said, you can't talk to him. He has no tongue. General Klahb had it removed for 'insubordination,'" said the man at last. The little man untied the tin cup from his waist and held it out. "Water please?"

Vodka tossed his canteen, and Hadda caught it. He filled his tin mug from the canteen, then pulled a small mesh bag attached to a string from a cleverly hidden pouch in his belt. He set the cup on the FRH to heat and dunked the tea bag into it.

Uncle watched this production with a bemused smile. "All right, what's your tongueless, insubordinate friend's name?" he asked, handing the short man the last pouch.

"His name is Thormas," said Hadda. Spotting a brief pause in the conversation, he quickly stuffed a spoonful of cold mashed potatoes into his mouth.

Uncle let them eat in silence for a few minutes until the initial edge of hunger was blunted. The rest of the team settled down on the grass in a loose circle around the locals. Rider grunted as he sat. He checked himself over to make sure he hadn't torn open his injuries sitting down.

Once the frantic face stuffing began to slacken just a little, Uncle decided it was time to get some value out of the trade. "All right gentlemen. First things first. Have you seen this girl?" he showed them his picture of Fiona McGinney.

All three looked at the picture, then all three shrugged and shook their heads.

Uncle sighed. "All right then. Tell me about this war. What caused it, who are the principles, and why does everyone assume we're involved?"

Hadda checked his tea, decided it was warm enough, and took a sip. He sighed happily, then glanced up at the hard faces surrounding him. "Oh, ah... would you care for some?" he offered his mug. "It's quite a lovely jasmine."

Uncle demurred, but Zombie shrugged and accepted the tin. He peered inside, sniffed, had a sip. "Not bad," he said, handing it back.

"It needs to be hotter," said Hayer.

"I haven't a fire on me. Do you?" asked Hadda.

"Ahem," Uncle said, and both men looked up at him. Thormas continued to eat, his head nodding now and again between bites. "You were about to tell us about this war of yours," Uncle reminded them.

"Not mine!" protested Hayer.

"Most certainly not mine!" shouted Hadda.

"Why, I don't care one whit for the war," said Hayer.

"Nor I. In fact, I care not a half a whit for it!" said Hadda.

"You are a half-wit," said Hayer.

Hadda scowled at him.

"I'm armed," Zombie pointed out, twirling his combat knife in an intricate pattern which mesmerized the locals, including Thormas who looked up at the word 'armed.'

"Ah, yes," said Hadda.

"Quite," agreed Hayer. "Well. The war then."

"Yes. The war. Well, what is it you want to know?" asked Hadda.

"Let's start with the principles," Uncle said. "We've pieced together that it's between your Queen and someone called Ironhand. Who is he?"

Hayer and Hadda exchanged a glance, then both looked at Thormas, but the later was nodding off again. The two returned their gaze to Uncle.

"You know," said Hadda.

"You work for him," said Hayer.

"We fucking don't!" Zombie snapped.

"Oh," said Hayer.

"Yes, oh," said Hadda.

"How extraordinary," declared Hayer.

"Quite unanticipated," decided Hadda.

"AAARGH!" Zombie pounded a fist into the grass.

"Well," said Hadda, "the fight is with Ironhand, who, it seems, is not your boss."

"Absolutely not," agreed Hayer.

Thormas jerked his head up from his chest, then shook it emphatically.

"Pretend," Uncle said through gritted teeth, "that we're not involved, and know nothing at all about the various sides. How did it start, who are the major players, and what is it all about?"

Hayer snatched Hadda's mug and took a long drink, then handed it to Thormas. "Well, it started a few months ago, in March."

Hadda glared at Thormas. The small man had taken a long drink from the mug and then absent-mindedly handed it to Vodka who was seated near him. Hadda shook his head, then turned his attention back to Uncle. "Yes, March. It was a lovely day, full of the nicest thick fog. I remember it like it was only a few months ago."

"It was only a few months ago," said Hayer. "But yes, a nice fog that day. Only, the sun should have burned it all away. But it didn't. Part of it remained."

"The fog," said Hadda, "not the sun. The sun always remains."

"True," nodded Hayer. "Part of the fog remained. And from out of it came a man. A human, like you. He bore a white flag and he walked right up to the Queen's palace, just as calm as you please."

"Poor, silly bastard," said Hadda.

"Poor, foolish bastard," said Hayer.

"He represented, he said, someone named Captain Ironhand, and he called for the Queen to surrender," said Hadda.

"The Queen hates to lose," added Hayer.

Thormas began to snore gently.

"She cut off his head," explained Hadda. "The messenger, I mean. She chopped it right off, and had it sent back to the fog."

"Well, no," corrected Hayer, "she didn't chop his head off. She had a guard do it. She's a great one for ordering heads to be chopped off, but she never does it herself."

"No," said Hadda, "that's true. She never does it herself."

"The next day, the Metalmen began to appear out of the fog. They built a camp, and fortified it," said Hayer.

"Then Ironhand himself came out," said Hadda. "With his men."

"His men," nodded Hayer. "Not the Metalmen, but normal men like you."

"Like you," nodded Hadda until they were both nodding in perfect unison.

"It's like watching a high-speed game of ping-pong between two idiots. With ADHD," Zombie said.

Thankfully, Rider thought, the locals ignored that. He could well imagine them wasting a half an hour trying to explain what 'ping-pong' was. ADHD would take even longer.

"Then what?" Uncle prompted.

"Why, then Ironhand began attacking," said Hadda.

"He attacked some of the Queen's men," said Hayer.

"And then some of the King's men," said Hadda.

"And then more of the Queen's men," added Hayer.

"So the Queen ordered her men to attack back," said Hadda.

"Only the Metalmen killed them all," said Hayer.

Vodka sniffed the tea, shrugged, had a sip. His face wrinkled, and he passed it along to Texas.

"So the Queen raised an army," said Hadda.

"She called for every man in the land," said Hayer.

"That included us," said Hadda in a deeply sorrowful voice. "We didn't want to go, you know. It was right in the middle of tea-time."

"Right in the middle," asserted Hayer. "It wasn't fair."

"Not fair at all," agreed Hadda.

"Where is this 'Ironhand' from?" Uncle asked. "Him and his metal men? Are they from a neighboring kingdom?"

"Kingdom?" said Hayer, cocking his head to the side curiously.

"You mean a land run by a king?" asked Hadda.

"Don't be silly," scolded Hayer, shaking a finger at Hadda. "No one would ever let a king rule a country! He must have meant something else."

Uncle chose, wisely Rider thought, not to engage in a discussion about gender and politics. Instead, he limited himself to saying, "A neighboring land then?"

"There are no neighboring lands," said Hayer.

"None," nodded Hadda. "Just this land."

Texas handed the tea to Rider, who took a sip and passed it on to Uncle. Texas lay back on the ground, groaning softly.

"What's wrong with him?" asked Hadda.

"He got hurt," Uncle said.

"By 'Bill,'" Zombie added.

"Ooh," said Hadda.

"Ooh," said Hayer.

"Do you have any idea why this Ironhand is attacking then?" Uncle tried to get the conversation back on track, although Rider filed away the fact that the locals knew 'Bill' for later.

"He wants to conquer the land," said Hayer.

"Yes, all of it," said Hadda.

"Why?" Uncle asked.

"You'd have to ask him," said Hadda with a shrug.

"Only you can't," said Hayer, "since you don't work for him."

"Absolutely don't," nodded Hadda.

"If you start nodding," Zombie said, pointing at Hayer, "I'm going to put my boot so far down your mouth you'll be shitting laces for a month."

"So, you have no idea where Ironhand is from?" Uncle hounded them on the point.

"We assumed he came from your world," said Hayer with a shrug.

"After all, he's human," added Hadda.

"You keep saying that," Vodka spoke up. "Like you're not."

"Well, we aren't," Hadda blinked at Vodka in surprise as if that was the most obvious thing in the world. "You're not very smart, are you?"

"Still armed," Zombie reminded them.

"If you're not human, what are you?" Uncle asked.

"We're fairies, of course," said Hadda.

"Of course," said Hayer.

"After all, this is a fairy land," pointed out Hadda.

"Yes, all of it," said Hayer.

"Oh, of course," Vodka muttered.

"Of course," Zombie said.

"Naturally," Vodka noted.

"Obviously," Zombie agreed.

"Cut it out," Uncle ordered.

Hadda took advantage of the distraction to reclaim his mug from Uncle. He brought it to his lips and tilted it, but it was empty. He stared into it in despair, his shoulders slumped.

"We're getting side-tracked," Uncle said. "So, the Queen raised the entire land, and you people are fairies. That must have been when the war turned in your favor?"

Hadda and Hayer both stared at Uncle as if he had grown an arm on top of his head.

"In our favor?" asked Hayer.

"Who said it turned in our favor?" asked Hadda.

"We're getting creamed out there," said Hayer.

"That's why we ran away," pointed out Hadda.

"We pretended to be dead after the last battle we were in," said Hayer.

"And then once the Metalmen had left, we crawled out from under the bodies and ran away," added Hadda.

"That's why we're scavenging for food now," said Hayer.

"We can't very well go home," said Hadda.

"The Queen would catch us," said Hayer.

"And chop off our heads," added Hadda.

"That would be just as bad as dying in the war," said Hayer.

"Just exactly as bad," said Hadda.

Uncle held up a hand for silence. The two were on a roll and showed no signs of stopping on their own any time soon. "If these metal men are so unstoppable, and the war has been going on for months, why hasn't Ironhand killed every single person in the entire land by now?"

The two locals exchanged a long glance. With a sigh, Hadda shrugged. "We don't know," said he. "They... just stop. Ironhand and his main men never go very far from the fog, and the Metalmen never go anywhere without a human leader."

"They've never gotten earlier than around three-thirty," said Hayer. "Thormas once said we should just pull back before two, and let them have the rest."

"That's why General Klahb had his tongue cut out," said Hadda, giving his sleeping friend a sad glance.

"I thought it was a good idea, personally," said Hayer.

"It was a capital idea," said Hadda.

"What do you mean by 'three thirty' and 'two'?" Uncle cut them off before they could get going again.

"Why, the time, of course," said Hayer.

"What did you think we meant?" asked Hadda.

"What do you mean by 'he's never gotten earlier than 3:30?' He never gets up before then? He only attacks in the afternoon?"

The locals stared at him for a moment, then Hadda snorted. "Humans."

"Humans," agreed Hayer.

"Have you noticed," asked Hadda, "that it's always the same time wherever you are?"

"For instance," said Hayer, "We've been sitting here for a while now, but the sun hasn't moved."

"Yeah," Uncle admitted. "I've noticed. But it does move sometimes, just sort of... randomly."

Rider saw Vodka glance at his watch, and followed suit. According to his Tag Heuer, it was just short of six in the morning. The sun showed late afternoon. It had not yet been dark since they arrived.

No wonder we're tired, Rider thought. He glanced over at Texas, who was asleep, Parrot sitting in the shade beside him. At least he didn't snore.

"The Queen tried to have Time killed," said Hayer.

"Ever since then, he's been quite angry and simply refuses to perform normally," said Hadda.

"What?" Zombie asked.

"Time," said Hadda. "He's upset with the Queen, so he doesn't move. He just sits there. The hour changes when you walk, not when you sit still. You have to walk to a new hour if you want it to change."

"For instance," said Hayer, looking up at the sun, "We're currently around 4 O'Clock or so. If you go that way for an hour, it would be 5." He pointed to his right. "But," said the man, pointing left, "If you went that way for an hour, it would only be 3."

"He is behaving like quite the child, if you ask me," said Hadda.

"No one did ask you," said Hayer. "Now stop antagonizing him, or he may decide to remove 6 O'Clock entirely, and then what would we do for tea-time?"

Uncle shook his head, trying to wrap his head around the idea, but Rider got it.

"Tide-locked world," he said softly.

Uncle looked at him with raised eyebrow.

Rider shrugged. "It's like the moon, always showing only one face. But instead of one side facing the Earth, they only have one side facing the sun. So the sun never moves unless you do, walking towards or away from the equator."

Uncle nodded, picturing it in his mind. "So then, one side of the world would be always dark. And they would have 'bands' of time... circles? Like rings around the center pole?"

"Yeah," Rider nodded.

"And they think their Queen did this, but she can't handle a few dudes in metal armor?" Vodka scoffed. "Anyone who can just decide to stop the planet from rotating should have no problem with this Ironhand guy."

"The Queen didn't stop the planet," said Hadda, shaking his head so violently that his hat nearly fell off. He righted it, then continued. "I told you," said he, "she angered Time. He is the one who made the sun stop moving. He's mad at all of us."

"Well, not all," said Hayer.

"True," said Hadda, "not all."

"What do you mean?" Uncle asked.

"Well, he still gets along with a few people," said Hadda.

"A few people," said Hayer. "Like the Queen's ex-Herald."

"Time gets along just fine with him," said Hadda, and then spat to the side.

"Explain," Uncle ordered. "Who is this herald, and what does 'Time gets along with him' mean?"

"Wilford," said Hadda.

"Rabbix," added Hayer.

"And he's the ex-Herald," corrected Hadda.

"Yes, the Queen isn't happy with him anymore," said Hayer.

"No, not at all," chortled Hadda.

"Because he still gets along with Time," grinned Hayer.

"So, when she gets mad at him..." said Hadda.

"He asks Time for a favor..." said Hayer.

"And she can't chop off his head!" said both of them at the same time.

"Are you two married?" Zombie asked.

"No," said Hadda.

"No," said Hayer.

"Rabbix," Uncle's lips twisted as if he tasted something sour. "We've met him. What does it mean when 'time likes him'?"

"Rabbix can ask time for favors," said Hayer.

"Like stopping," said Hadda.

"Or going very slowly," said Hayer.

"Or very fast," said Hadda.

"He has a watch, and he can use it to do all kinds of clever things," said Hayer.

"No, he doesn't," Uncle smiled in grim satisfaction. He pulled forth the pocket-watch and spun it on the end of the chain.

Rider had never seen two men go from obsequious to avaricious quite so fast before. He half expected Hadda to call the watch his 'precious.'

"From the way you're both salivating over this," Uncle said with a small chuckle, "I assume it works for anyone who uses it, not just Rabbix?"

"Oh," said Hadda.

"Ah," said Hayer

"That is to say..." said Hadda.

"Well, um..." said Hayer.

"Yes," said both of them.

"But I wouldn't, if I were you!" said Hadda swiftly, holding up one finger.

"Why is that?" Uncle grinned. He figured the locals were hoping to keep the power for themselves. Rider couldn't blame them. If it really worked the way they said it did, this was a weapon of incalculable power.

He suspected it didn't quite work the way they said.

"You're human," said Hadda as if that explained everything.

"There's no telling what it would do to you," added Hayer.

"Explain," Uncle was no longer grinning.

The two locals glanced at each other for a moment, then shrugged in unison.

"Faerie magic doesn't always affect humans the same way it affects faeries," said Hayer.

"There's no way to know," said Hadda. "For instance, a potion that is supposed to allow one to fly might, instead, make you shrink down really small."

"Or grow really large," added Hayer.

"There was a human," said Hadda.

"A girl," said Hayer.

"Alice," said Hadda.

"She kept changing sizes the whole time she was here," said Hayer.

"Small as a doll," said Hadda.

"And then huge as a giant," said Hayer.

"It was quite disconcerting," said Hadda.

"Quite," agreed Hayer.

"The point is," said Hadda.

"Yes, the point is," said Hayer.

"You can't predict it," said Hadda.

"Only the Long Man can," added Hayer.

"But he isn't to be trusted," said Hadda.

"Not to be trusted at all," said Hayer.

"We noticed," Zombie groused. When the locals looked at him askance, he shook his head. "We met the Long Man already. He drugged us and took our weapons."

Hadda and Hayer both looked pointedly at the sword resting across Zombie's lap.

"These aren't ours," Zombie said, tapping the sword. "We took them from the Duchess' soldiers when they attacked us. Trust me, we had better weapons."

Hadda looked over his shoulder swiftly at the mention of the Duchess, while Hayer huddled down as small as he could. "She's not here, is she?" whispered Hayer in a harsh voice.

"She might try to turn us in, in order to get back on the Queen's good side," said Hadda.

"As far as we know, she's long gone," Uncle tried to sooth the strange men.

"You're wrong about one thing," Vodka spoke up. "Ironhand's men have gone 'earlier' than 3:30." Everyone turned to look at him, and Vodka shrugged. "That farm. That was around 2, by the sun position."

"That's true," Uncle nodded. He turned to deserters for an explanation.

"What farm?" asked Hadda.

Uncle explained about the farm, the burned bodies, the banner, the old man.

"Oh," said Hadda.

"Ah," said Hayer.

"Well?" Uncle prompted.

"That wasn't them," said Hayer, shaking his head.

"No, not them," said Hadda sadly, looking down at the grass.

"Then who was it?"

"The Queen," said Hayer.

"The Queen," said Hadda.

"Explain," ordered Uncle. "Why would she kill her own people? And how do you know it wasn't Ironhand?"

"The banner," said Hadda.

"The banner," added Hayer.

"Ironhand doesn't put up banners," explained Hadda. "That's something that the Reconciliationists do."

"They're people who want the war to end," added Hayer. "By putting up that banner, they were trying to tell the Metalmen that they were sympathetic, not a threat."

"Poor, silly bastards," said Hadda.

"Poor, foolish bastards," said Hayer.

"Also, Ironhand doesn't kill children," said Hadda.

"Or non-combatants," said Hayer.

"That's why we surrendered to you," said Hadda.

"We thought you were his people," added Hayer.

"The Queen tho, she hates Reconciliationists," said Hadda.

"Hates them something fierce," said Hayer.

"She probably had that farm burned as a lesson to others," said Hadda.

"And she left the banner up so people would know what the crime had been," said Hayer.

"So, you want Ironhand to win?" Vodka leaned back on the grass, propping himself up on one arm. "Is the Queen really that bad?"

"She's terrible," said Hadda.

"Horrible," said Hayer.

"Dreadful," said Hadda.

"Awful," said Hayer.

"Horrendous," said Hadda.

"Frightful," said Hayer.

"Enough with the thesaurus crap," Zombie snapped.

"Sorry," said Hayer.

"Apologies," said Hadda.

"Regrets," said Hayer.

"Amends," said Hadda.

Zombie threw himself back on the grass and looked up at the sky. "What, God? What did I do to deserve this shit? I'm a good soldier: I do my duty. Why do you torment me like this?"

"So that would be a 'yes' then?" Vodka prompted.

"Well, uh, not really," said Hadda.

"That is to say, she's monstrous," said Hayer.

"But Ironhand's not any better," said Hadda.

"He's killed thousands, trying to conquer this land," said Hayer.

"He could just leave us in peace and go away," said Hadda.

"But he won't do that," said Hayer.

"So the war goes on and on," said Hadda.

"Sometimes it feels like it will never end," said Hayer.

"He won't advance," said Hadda.

"And the Queen won't just let him have the land he's taken already," said Hayer.

"We don't really like either of them," admitted Hadda.

"Not very much," agreed Hayer.

Rider yawned, but resisted the urge to stretch. He wasn't sure his cuts could handle it.

"You indicated you know the both Long Man and the Duchess," Uncle said. "The Long Man said that there was an elm tree with a door in it, somewhere 'past the Duchess' house'. Do you know what he meant? How do we find it?"

"See that tall tree?" said Hadda, pointing into the forest at the base of the hill. "That one that sticks out like finger?"

"That's not it," said Hayer. "However, once you find that tree, the elm you want will be visible."

"You can't see it from here," said Hadda.

"It's shorter than the others," added Hayer.

"But find the big one," said Hadda.

"And you'll see it," said Hayer.

"Can't miss it," said Hadda.

"It has a door in it," said Hayer.

"Kind of distinctive," said Hadda.

"Quite," said Hayer.

"Thank you, gentlemen," Uncle nodded at the odd pair. "You've been quite... helpful."

"Not the word I would have used," Zombie muttered just loud enough for Rider to hear.

"Sir," Vodka gestured at Texas, then at Parrot who was also asleep by this time. "I recommend we take advantage of this spot to get some sleep sir. We have wounded who need it, and it's been over twenty-four hours for all of us."

"Agreed," Uncle nodded. "We'll take turns standing a two hour watch. I'll take first."

"That's okay sir," Vodka smiled. "I'm awake. I'll take first, then wake you up."

"All right," Uncle nodded. He turned to the locals and said, "You'll be safe here with us, if you want to grab some shut-eye also."

"Oh yes," said Hayer.

"Thank you," said Hadda.

Before they could launch back into their routine, Uncle laid down on the grass and closed his eyes. A moment later, Hadda and Hayer did the same.

Rider lay back with a groan and turned on his side. His cuts were burning, and he suspected he wouldn't be able to sleep, but he could at least rest.

He closed his eyes and was asleep in moments.

"Motherfucking fuckitty fuckery fuckingly fucking fuckballs!"

Rider sat bolt upright at the sound of Zombie's yelling. The tattered fragments of a dream faded even as he grasped at them with his mind. Something about that pretty Second Lieutenant at the exchange back in Germany. She'd had a cute little lopsided smile, and in his dream he was...

Wait. Why was Zombie using his favorite word as every part of a sentence?

Rider joined the rest of the team in looking at Zombie, who sat in the grass, surrounded by their backpacks, looking even more sour than normal.

"Zombie?" Uncle raised his eyebrows.

"They took our food," Zombie threw the pack he was holding down in disgust. "Those fucking little rodents, they're gone and they took all our food. Every single fucking MRE is gone." He slammed a fist into the dirt. "Our guns are gone, our FOOD is gone, we still don't have the goddamn VIP, and oh, hey, they even took three of our swords." He held up a piece of paper and waved it. "At least they left a fucking note. That was nice of them!"

Uncle clenched his jaw, then forced himself to relax. He reached out and took the note from Zombie. Rider leaned sideways to read it over Uncle's shoulder.

Fair trade.

That was all the note said.

"What the hell is that supposed to mean?" Rider asked, leaning back. "Did they leave any—" he stopped abruptly. He looked down at his side, then poked one of the bandages gently with a finger. Nothing. No pain. He yanked off his jacket, then his shirt, then tore one of the bandages free. The cut was gone, leaving only the puffy pink welt of a fresh scar.

131

"Look," Vodka said softly. Everyone turned to see him pointing at Texas.

Texas' burns were visible only as slightly shiny patches of skin. Texas touched himself in wonder. His expression said it all; he was also pain-free.

"That figures," said a tiny, high-pitched voice. Parrot was looking up at Texas and Rider. "They get cured, I'm still a freaking action figure." He stamped his little foot.

It took every ounce of Rider's self control not to laugh. Even Zombie looked marginally less pissed.

"Okay," Uncle sighed, rubbing the bridge of his nose. "Well, I'm not going to say that any price we pay to get two of our people back healthy was not worth it, but we are in a bit of a situation. No food, and I don't know about you guys, but I'm hungry." Nods all around met this, all except Parrot.

"I'm fine," he said. "They didn't take my food. Too small for them."

"Huh," Vodka said with a grin. "An unexpected benefit to being tiny."

"Recommendations?" Uncle asked.

"I say we have Vodka track those little bastards and we take back what's ours," Zombie said.

"No good," Uncle shook his head. Zombie raised an eyebrow in query, and Uncle sighed again. "They also took the watch."

That took a second to sink in. Rider remembered Rabbix pushing the button and vanishing. What would stop Hadda or Hayer from doing the exact same thing? Uncle was right; there was no sense chasing after them.

"Continue on with the mission," suggested Vodka. "The small door is supposed to lead to the Queen's castle, right? They'll have food there, and weapons." He shrugged, a little embarrassed at the suggestion. "We take what we need. The locals have proven to be dangerous despite all appearances, and not one of them has played straight with us. I say we stop pussy-footing around."

Uncle mulled it over for a moment, then nodded. "I agree. We don't start hostilities, but if someone else offers violence, put them down, hard. They took an American civilian as a gambit in their own internal war; we take what we need and no bad feelings."

"HU-fucking-AH!" Zombie muttered. "Now we're talking." He re-packed the bags he had emptied in his search for food, handing them to the respective owners as he finished with each.

Rider spent the time stretching, enjoying the freedom of movement. Funny how you take things for granted until they're gone, he thought. He saw Texas doing the same, and they shared a knowing smile.

They headed back into the woods, aiming for the large tree. Hadda and Hayer were as good as their word on one thing: the elm with the door was easy to find once they reached the tall tree. The elm was a stunted, twisted thing with but a small handful of branches coming off the very thick, squat trunk. And, of course, the door was kind of a giveaway.

They approached and made a small semi-circle around the tree. Every man exchanged uneasy glances. Strange that after fire-breathing dragons, teleporting lions, man-caterpillar hybrids, and watches that made time stop, a door in a tree truck struck everyone as being weird and sinister, but there it was.

"This mission isn't going to accomplish itself," Vodka said at last. He looked at Uncle for acknowledgment, received it, and opened the door. Inside was a small, dark space. Vodka tightened his grip on his sword and stepped inside.

After a second, Zombie said "I hate this shit!" and followed.

Rider gave them two seconds to get out of his way, and then stepped after them.

* * * *

* * *

* * * *

The darkness gave way almost instantly, and Rider found himself standing in the hall of doors. Vodka and Zombie were standing back-to-back in the middle of the hall, but there were no visible threats. Rider stepped aside to make way for the rest of the team.

Texas appeared next, stepping out of a normal-sized door, Parrot in his pocket. Last, Uncle appeared. The door shut behind them automatically.

"Status?" Uncle asked as he glanced around.

"SNAFU," Zombie replied.

Rider bit back a snicker.

The glass table was just as Rider remembered it, only now there was a small bottle sitting dead center. Tied to the bottle was a small paper label that read, "DRINK ME" in large block letters and, "first" under it in smaller, spidery handwriting.

"Any sign of the golden key?" Uncle looked around. Everyone shook their heads.

"Not sure we need it, sir," Vodka said. He pointed down low at the wall, and Rider turned to look. There was the small door.

It was open.

"Fuck me," Zombie sighed. "Are we really doing this?"

"Yes," Uncle said. He picked up the bottle, then looked at each of his men. "I'll go first. Wait. Texas, put Parrot on the ground.

I'm not sure what would happen if you shrunk while carrying him, but let's not find out. He's plenty small enough to fit through the door as it is."

Texas did this, and Parrot wandered over to look through the door, but he was careful not to step through.

"Okay," Uncle said. "I'll go first. Assuming I stop shrinking before reaching sub-atomic dimensions, the rest of you do it. We stack up on the door, but no one goes through until we're all ready. We go through together."

"Yes sir," Vodka said for all of them.

Uncle pulled the stopper from the bottle. He sniffed it, winced. "Smells like medicine," he said. He took a deep breath, closed his eyes, and took a sip. Vodka took the bottle from him. Uncle was already shrinking.

"I can't watch that shit," Zombie turned away. Rider agreed, it was disconcerting in the extreme. He made himself continue to look, all the same.

It was not unlike watching a special effect in a movie where someone starts moving rapidly away from the camera. Uncle got smaller and smaller and smaller until he was about a foot tall. He stabilized there.

"Bastard," said Parrot's tiny little voice. Uncle was a good half-again taller than him.

Uncle waved at Vodka, who took a drink and then handed the bottle to Texas, and so on it went until the entire team had drunk from the potion of incredible shrinkiness, and they were all in the vicinity of a foot tall, except for Parrot.

It hadn't smelled, or tasted, like medicine to Rider. In fact, he quite liked the flavor. It reminded him of spiced rum and hot treacle pudding on a cold winter day.

135

"Okay," Uncle nodded once Zombie, the last to drink, joined them by the door. Rider was surprised to notice that Uncle's voice wasn't high-pitched and comical. From the looks on the faces of the others, they were having similar thoughts.

"Our eardrums are smaller?" Rider wondered, and his voice also sounded normal. "Parrot, say something."

"'Polly want a cracker,'" Parrot said drily. His voice was also normal.

Vodka nodded in respect to Rider. "Good thinking."

"Enough patting ourselves on the back," Uncle said. "We go through the door on three. One. Two. Three."

Vodka stepped through the door, his sword held out crosswise in a defensive position. Rider followed him a second later.

*　　　*　　　*　　　*

　*　　　*　　　*

*　　　*　　　*　　　*

CHAPTER VIII
THE QUEEN'S PALACE GROUNDS

Even after all we'd seen, I don't think we really started to hate the Queen until we reached her palace and saw the heads. She's one sick puppy, sir. If there's ever a mission put together to go after her, sir, I'd like to volunteer.

The only good thing that came from our trip to the palace was Jack.

Jack, and some really good cheese.

   -SSG William "Texas" Marquez, official de-brief, Operation Rabbit Hole

SHRINKING HAD BEEN AN unpleasant experience for Texas, although it wasn't nearly as bad as stepping through that door. Not that there was anything intrinsically bad about the door experience. It felt no different than any other door.

The unpleasant part was going through the door and emerging in a huge garden, face-to-face with a rat the size of a donkey.

Texas froze, his hand gripping the handle of his combat knife so hard his knuckles stood out white. The rat stared at him with huge black eyes and twitched whiskers as long as Texas' arm.

"Yah!" Parrot yelled, waving his arms in the air at the rodent. The rat considered him, then remembered an important engagement elsewhere, and scurried off.

"Thanks," Texas said.

"No hay problema." Parrot grinned.

"Over here," Vodka's voice came from somewhere in the chest-high grass, behind the skyscraper sized rose bush. Texas and Parrot followed the sound and found the rest of the group. They surrounded a piece of cake.

The piece of cake was the size of a minivan, and had clearly been nibbled on by what Texas assumed were the departed rat and its cousins. Propped against the cake was a card the size of a picnic table turned on its side. In huge letters were the words, "EAT ME." In slightly smaller, far less professional writing under that command was the word, "second."

"Looks like our friend the Long Man left us a present," Vodka mused.

"I guess we should eat it," Texas said, his voice unsure, hesitant.

"Man, we can't handle the creatures in this world when we're normal sized," Vodka said. "Ain't no way we can deal like this. Besides, think how far we'd have to walk to get anywhere."

"Can it," Uncle ordered. He stepped forward and broke off a handful of the cake. "Small bites, see how I stabilize. If I need to, I'll eat again. We'll figure it out." He took a nibble from the cake.

"Hey, if this shit is supposed to make us big, how come that rat wasn't twelve fucking feet tall?" Zombie asked. No one answered however. They were all too busy watching Uncle.

He grew. And grew. And grew. One nibble and he shot up until the team had to crane their necks and step back in order to see all of him.

"Ow, fuck," Zombie spat. Parrot snapped him a glance, but the gunner was uninjured. Zombie shook his head. "I got a look up his pants leg, that's all. I never, ever want to see a cock that big again."

Texas snickered. Even at full size, the hem of Uncle's pants leg was too low for anyone to have seen up. Zombie was trying to lighten the mood in his normal, crude way.

"All right," Uncle's voice boomed, low pitched almost to the point of incomprehensibility. "Parrot, you're up."

Parrot rubbed his hands together eagerly. He was well and truly ready to stop being the shortest member of the group. That was normally Vodka's job, and Texas could tell that Parrot was excited to let Vodka resume that particular duty. He grabbed a big handful, but being careful to follow orders, only took a small bite.

Zoom! Up he shot. It was hard for Texas to tell from his angle, but he tried to compare Uncle and Parrot's heights, and it looked to him as if Parrot was back to his normal size. Parrot grinned widely and pumped his arm in victory. Rider chuckled.

"Okay," Uncle boomed. "Everyone spread out and go for it."

Texas turned to move away from the others, and saw an ant the size of a small dog clinging to the side of a bush. He waved at it, and it waves an antenna back at him. He bit his cake. It tasted like shortbread.

The experience of growing was dizzying, quite literally. Texas felt light-headed as he shot up towards the sky, a feeling that only passed after a handful of heartbeats at his normal height.

He looked over, then grinned. Parrot was taller than Vodka. Life was right once more.

Only then did Texas think to look at their surroundings.

They were in a rose garden. Or rather, it had once been a rose garden.

Now, it was an open grave.

Grass and low bushes had been trampled underfoot, hacked apart by edged weapons, and crushed by falling bodies. Small, neat rows of pretty flowers had been reduced to little more than dirt patches with the odd stem remaining in stubborn defiance of the carnage around them. Long dried sprays of blood mottled once-white roses, and the petals had wilted and fallen from lack of care. Corpses choked a series of low ridges that once would have given the garden an oddly banded look. The sun hung low on the horizon, just above a row of hills in the distance.

Vodka and Zombie poked around, turning over this corpse or that, inspecting wounds, uniform, and appearance. Parrot made a half-hearted attempt to check for living souls, but given the level of putrefaction, Texas was sure they had all been dead for at least a week.

"They're all locals," Zombie declared after several minutes of silence.

"Some are soldiers, some look like servants. Gardeners and butlers and stuff," Rider added. "They're all either wearing uniforms or livery."

"I thought that crazy dude said the enemy never went after non-combatants," Parrot said, glancing at Uncle for confirmation.

"He did," Uncle nodded. He looked at Vodka, one eyebrow raised.

Vodka gestured towards the corpse at his feet. "None of them seem to have been hit from behind. My guess? The Queen, or someone, armed the servants and sent them out here."

"No weapons," Zombie said. "Doesn't mean they didn't have any. It's just like that other battlefield we saw. All locals; no weapons. This Ironhand guy's really thorough about his clean up."

Parrot had been inspecting some of the wounds during this conversation. He stood up and announced, "Bladed weapons mostly. Swords or spears, or a combination. The occasional blunt-force, maybe a club. Again, no arrows."

"I don't trust a society that doesn't have ranged weapons," Zombie muttered. "There's something just... wrong with that."

"They even took the croquet mallets," Rider said, pointing at a half-dozen empty racks knocked over and splintered by the fighting.

"God forbid!" Zombie smirked.

Texas turned to look at the castle proper. It was more of a palace than a castle; a huge, sprawling affair that had been added to over successive generations, each of which had their own particular tastes in architecture. A cluster of towers looked over other wings of various heights. There were plenty of windows everywhere.

"Gormenghast," Texas muttered to himself.

"It looks about as defensible as a pillow fort," Parrot said, following Texas' gaze.

"No wonder they did all their fighting out here," Zombie nudged an overturned lawn table.

"We don't know that," Vodka pointed out. "Maybe there's even more dead guys inside."

Texas gulped. "I hope not."

"We're not going to find out by standing here," Uncle shrugged. "Let's go. Priority is the girl, then weapons, then food. Survivors if we can find any. Let's roll."

"HUA," Texas said. He followed Vodka, who took up the lead.

The team approached the palace and saw that there were holes in the walls in various places, and the front gates had been pulled down. Vodka inspected the damage, chewing on his lower lip. "Looks sort of like they hooked a chain around the gate and then had a four by four rip it down."

"Down!" Rider snapped. It took Texas a second to realize he wasn't just repeating Vodka's last word, but rather calling a warning. Texas dropped to a crouch.

Rider pointed. Across more rolling lawn, on a small hill about a half a mile away, figures moved. Everyone took up positions of cover. Uncle pulled out his binoculars, while Rider used his spotter scope.

"Holy shit," Uncle muttered. He handed his glasses to Parrot, who looked and whistled.

Texas pulled his own binoculars out and peered.

There were five figures on the hill, and Texas understood instantly that these were the 'Metalmen' spoken of by the various locals. They were most definitely not locals themselves.

With no recognizable person or object to use as a reference, Texas was unable to judge their heights. Each of the Metalmen had a perfectly round head mounted on a short, thin neck. The bodies were round also, with holes out of which poked two long, segmented arms that ended in pincher grips, and two skinny legs jointed at the knees and ankles. Each pincher grip held a long, pointed piece of metal not unlike a sword blade without a handle. The metal that encased, or perhaps comprised, each figure was a bright, polished copper.

They were robots.

The fifth figure was a man. He was not a local either, Texas decided. He looked like an ordinary man, albeit wearing anachronistic clothing. His long brown ponytail poked out from under a red bandana, and he sported a magnificent handlebar mustache. He wore a ruffled white shirt under a long, open coat that reminded Texas of that movie where Russell Crowe was a ship captain in the 19th century. A leather belt held up pants that matched the coat in color, if not in ostentation. On his feet he wore large floppy leather boots.

The man walked up to the robots, which stood still at his approach. He went to each one in turn and did something, but even with the binoculars, Texas couldn't make out exactly what. The man made a gesture to the left, then walked back down the hill away from the palace. The four robots set out walking the direction the man had pointed.

"Did Captain Jack Sparrow just give orders to a bunch of Cylons?" Zombie's voice held a degree of awe, as if that might have been the single coolest thing he had ever seen.

"I think they're the cast of Real Steel, but otherwise, yeah," Rider sounded equally impressed.

Texas rolled his eyes. He'd been scarred by a fire-breathing dragon, and these guys were impressed by a collection of Roombas. Heathens.

"Those things were taller than the man," Vodka said. "He looked human. If so, those are some big-ass metal dudes. I have a suggestion: let's not fight them until we get our guns back."

"Agreed," Uncle nodded. "Come on, let's see if we get lucky and our 'friend' left our stuff here."

They waited until the robots moved out of sight, then the team quietly slipped through the wreckage of the gate and into the palace.

"Dang," Texas said. Vodka's prediction had turned out to be accurate; there were more bodies inside. From the smell, they'd been here for a while.

Other than the battle damage and the rotting corpses everywhere, Texas thought that the inside of the palace looked quite grand. Cool white marble floors rang under boot heels, vaulted ceilings echoed those rings back at the team. There were tapestries and objects d'art on every wall or crowded upon every occasional table. A sweeping staircase filled the entry room, rising to a small balcony above from which the Queen could look down on her subjects and give grand speeches, if she were the grand-speech giving sort. Banisters of dark wood with gold-leaf covered posts protected guests and staff alike from long falls. A half-dozen or so doors lead out of the room on the ground floor, and a hallway beyond the speech balcony offered more doors above.

"Anyone got a map?" Parrot asked, craning his head to look at the painting on the ceiling: an intricate scene of locals and other, strange man-like figures doing battle with centauripedes while gryphons and unicorns watched from the wings.

"Damn, I knew I forgot something," Zombie rolled his eyes. "I left it in my dress blues."

"Maybe we can find a directory," Texas grinned. "I don't know about you guys, but I could really use a Jamba Juice about now."

"I jamba'd your mom's juice," Zombie offered.

"Enough," Uncle ended the banter before it got much of a chance to begin. "I can't imagine they'd drop firearms in the sitting rooms just off the foyer, but I'd also really hate it if we left without checking every possible nook and cranny. Left-hand wall formation. Let's roll."

Vodka made his way to the first door on the left, opened it, and glanced inside. When he signaled that it was clear, the rest of the group poured in.

It was a sitting room. There were no guns. There were, however, book cases that towered over their heads, crammed from top to bottom full of leather-bound volumes. Texas couldn't read any of the titles; he didn't even recognize the language that they were written in. Besides the book cases, a small handful of comfortable looking easy chairs formed a loose circle in the center of the room. Between the chairs were low, round tables.

Small oil lamps rested on each table. An open book lay beside one lamp.

"No guns," Vodka reported.

"Or food," Rider added.

"Or—" Texas started to speak, but Uncle cut him off.

"I see that. Move out."

Zombie caught Texas' gaze and rolled his eyes. Texas bit back a grin. The Old Man was getting cranky.

The next several rooms were variations on a theme, and that theme was 'rich as hell.' Texas wasn't even sure what some of the room were for, but they were all filled with beautiful artwork, probably priceless antiques, and ridiculously comfortable-looking furniture. None of them contained their weapons.

At the back of the foyer, a double set of doors under the balcony lead to a huge, long hall. An initial low area probably corresponded to the hallway above, and then the ceiling soared. Pillars set every few dozen feet supported the arched, stained glass roof above. Tapestries adorned every available vertical surface, depicting scenes of hunts, of grand balls, of tournaments, of fantastic creatures of every conceivable sort. Unicorns pranced in sunlit meadows, gryphons chased each other across cloudless skies, pixies and sprites sat on flower petals and played cards, sphinxes asked riddles of men while seaside towers burned behind them, a brunette girl with pale blue eyes pulled a thorn from the flipper of an anthropomorphic turtle.

At the far end of the hall, a four-step dais displayed a huge throne covered in red velvet cushions. Tables lined each of the long walls, but the center area was left clear for, Texas imagined, courtiers and sycophants and the occasional dance.

A handful of dead soldiers surrounded the throne, but there was no evidence that the Queen had been present when they died.

"Did these guys die trying to protect the furniture?" Zombie asked.

No one had an answer for him.

From the great hall, they were able to find the kitchens with little difficulty. It would have been even easier, but the stench of the dead bodies in the hall overpowered the smell of rotting vegetables coming from one of the several doors along the walls. The battle that caused the fall of the castle hadn't caught anyone by surprise: there was barely any food left in the pantry. What was left had gone bad days ago.

"Well, crap," muttered Vodka.

Texas understood. He was hungry too.

"Agreed," Uncle sighed. "Damn them." He was probably, Texas thought, talking about Hadda, Hayer, and Thormas.

Behind the throne, the team found a small door, nearly hidden by hanging rugs. The door opened onto a small, dark hallway. Thankfully, of all the things the team had lost by that point, their flashlights were not on the list. The beams they cast showed a stairway spiraling downward. With a shrug, Vodka began descending.

The steps wound around and around, emptying at last into another short hallway that ended at a heavy oak door banded with bronze strips. The door stood partway open, so Vodka peered inside, then opened it wider and stepped through.

It was a dungeon.

Cells lined each side of a long central corridor. A pair of lamps hung from the low ceiling, but they were cold and dark. The cells were small, cramped affairs, with dirty wet straw on the ground and the obligatory shackles bolted to the walls. Most of the cells were empty, although one contained a wasted body, a bit fresher than those upstairs.

Parrot crouched to look at the body through the bars, then turned away in disgust. "He starved," he said. "They just left him here. He's been dead maybe a day or two at most, far more recently than the others we've seen."

Uncle nodded in grim silence as he strode down the line of cells. Each one was just large enough to hold two people, and Texas counted a total of twenty, ten on each side. At the far end of the corridor, a wooden door stood shut. Uncle tried the handle, and it opened easily. He stepped inside, and Texas followed him.

He would regret that decision for a very, very long time.

The room was large, perhaps forty feet on a side. Brass sconces held unlit torches. The smoke stains on the ceiling showed that the torches were often lit for long hours at a time. In the center of the room squatted a large wooden block, stained dark on the top and sides. A semi-circular notch marred one of the top edges. A basket sat, waiting, below that gap. Hundreds of grooves scarred the top of the block. Texas frowned at the block in confusion, attempting to discern its purpose. Then he he imagined someone kneeling behind the block, their chin fitting into the notch, and an axe swinging down in the flickering torch light.

He staggered away from the headsman's block and bumped into a table. Something rattled. He looked down, then screamed.

Tables lined the walls, and each held a dozen or more skulls. There were more heaped in piles under the tables. There must have been at least four or five hundred of them, gazing empty-eyed and accusing. Texas was suddenly glad that he had not eaten in a very long while; it meant that when he heaved, nothing came up.

"¡Madre de Dios!" Parrot whispered from the doorway. He crossed himself quickly.

"'Off with their heads,'" Zombie looked over Parrot's shoulder. "I guess Alice got one thing right. This Queen of theirs is a psychopath."

"There's nothing for us here. Let's go," Uncle said, his voice tight with anger.

The team retreated back through the dungeon and the stairs, then continued on to the second floor. Bedrooms in a dizzying array of tacky décor waited there for them, but the team searched each one methodically anyway. Texas assumed that these were the quarters of the lesser royals and minor nobles. The closets were almost empty of clothes. These people expected to be wherever they went for a good while.

"Two," Rider said to Zombie, breaking the silence.

"What?" Zombie scowled.

"Two things Alice got right. The heads, and the marmalade."

Zombie glared at Rider. "Really!?"

At last, they came to what Texas assumed had to be the Queen's personal suite. The suite consisted of four rooms; a room for greeting guests and reading by the fire at night, a room for bathing, an entire room for clothes (she hadn't taken all of her clothes. Texas wasn't sure she had enough servants left to carry them all), and the master bedroom.

The bedroom was a masterpiece of opulence. A massive four-poster dominated, swathed in thick red drapes and festooned with crimson pillows that covered nearly the entirety of the scarlet comforter. Red carpet covered the floor from wall to wall, and the curtains bracing each window matched.

"She certainly has a favorite color," Parrot muttered.

Several tables rested against the walls, most of them cluttered with enough jewelry to make Harry Winston jealous. The piece-de-resistance was a huge, elaborate crown of gold and ruby, sitting on top of a white, bulbous mannequin head with large compound eyes. The head looked, Texas realized, like the Long Man.

Vodka looked under the bed, then opened an armoire, but found no weapons. Rider went into the bathroom. Texas doubted they'd put an arm-full of M4s into the tub, but better safe than sorry. He checked under the bed. Zombie went back to the walk-in closet, while Parrot looked under the cushions of the couch in the center room. Uncle poked around the tables, checking out the jewelry. He lifted the crown off of the mannequin head.

The head screamed.

Uncle jumped back, dropping the crown and yanking his knife from its sheath. Vodka spun and faced the head, his own knife extended. A clatter came from the walk-in closet as Zombie jumped in surprise. There was a muffled 'thump' from the large chest at the foot of the Queen's bed.

"What the hell?" Uncle yelled, looking at the head.

The head stopped screaming, but the mouth continued to open and close slowly. Texas could see the jaw tensing, clenching. It was impossible to say exactly where it was looking with those multifaceted eyes, or if it could even see. Maybe the scream was on the order of an alarm system.

Texas didn't believe that.

Vodka circled the bed and crouched in front of the table, looking directly at the head. He touched it gently with the point of his knife.

The head screamed again.

"For God's sake, stop doing that," Parrot said from the doorway. "It sounds like it's in incredible pain."

"It's missing a body," Vodka replied, "How much pain do you figure that causes? I'm just trying to figure out if it's actually alive or just a really messed-up alarm system."

"Why don't we ask him," Texas said.

"He's not talking, just screaming," Vodka pointed out.

"I don't mean the head," Texas grinned, pointing at the foot of the bed. "I mean the guy hiding inside the hope chest."

Uncle frowned, then nodded towards the chest. Vodka took up position to one side, Zombie to the other. Rider climbed onto the bed so he was directly behind the hinged top. Uncle nodded again, and Texas flipped open the lid.

Sure enough, there was a man inside. As the lid popped up, he tried to bolt but tripped on the side of the chest and fell, sprawling, on the carpet. Uncle grabbed him by the back of his neck and lifted him.

The man was a local, of the small body/big head variety, although his head was only slightly out of proportion to the rest of him. He was large by local standards, perhaps five and a quarter feet tall. His features were handsome, his fine, sandy hair well groomed. He wore fine clothes similar to those found in one of the other bedrooms the team had searched earlier, all in shades of red and black.

"Hello," Uncle's smile was utterly unconvincing. He gave the man a little shake, then released him with a push towards Vodka.

Vodka caught him and held him with his arm twisted up behind his back.

"Who are you then?" Uncle asked.

The man squirmed, hissing in pain. He tried to stomp Vodka's foot, but the burly soldier was ready for it. He simply shifted his weight, pushing the captive off-balance and causing him to miss. Vodka pulled a little harder on the arm in his grasp, and the local man cried out in pain.

"All right, stop!" said the stranger. "Don't hurt me! I surrender."

"This again?" Zombie sighed. He sat on the edge of the bed and twirled his knife between his fingers.

"What?" asked the local man.

"Never mind that," Uncle said. "Who are you, and what are you doing hiding in the Queen's foot chest?"

"Jack," said the man. "My name is Jack O'Hara. And I'm... well, to be honest, I'm robbing the place. I'm guessing you are also. What do you say we join forces, eh? There's more than enough treasure here for all of us. Certainly more than any of us can carry, right? We can share!"

"Well, Jack O'Hara," this time Uncle's smile was far more pleasant, "We're not robbing the Queen. In fact, we're here to retrieve some things that were stolen from us. Maybe you can help us with that, yes?"

"Uh," said Jack, "I uh... what uh... what is it you're looking for?"

"Not a 'what,'" Uncle said. "A 'who.' This girl." He showed his picture of Fiona McGinney. "Have you seen her?"

"What do I get if I say 'yes'?" asked Jack.

"I don't gut you," Zombie offered, waving his knife so it caught the light from the window.

When Uncle didn't contradict this, Jack gulped and squirmed again in Vodka's grip. "Uh," said the captive, "I... well... that is to say, yes. I have seen her. About a day, day and a half ago. It's hard to tell exactly how long, of course, without regular dinner times. But yes, I would say about a day or two ago. A group of the Queen's soldiers had her. She kept saying something about how they had the wrong girl and how her daddy was going to make them regret taking her."

"I like this girl," Parrot chuckled.

"Now Jack, here's the important part," Uncle leaned over the little man. "Did you happen to see where they went?"

"Yes," nodded Jack. "I can tell you, give you directions. Just don't hurt me."

"Did you happen to also see a... the Long Man come by here, carrying a bunch of long black staves?" Texas asked. To Rider's curious glance, he shrugged and said, "They don't even have bows, I doubt he knows that an M4 is."

"Fair enough," Rider nodded.

"The Long Ma— oh!" said Jack, his eyes growing wide. "You mean one of those?" he pointed at the head which had, thankfully, stopped screaming.

"Yes," Uncle said. "One of those, carrying a whole bunch of long black metal sticks."

"Yes, yes," said Jack, his head nodding so fast he reminded Texas of his little nephew shaking a bobble-head doll. "I saw him, just a little while ago. Not more than half a day, I'm sure of it. I didn't get close enough to see what he was carrying, but his arms were full. He seemed in an awful hurry."

"And did you happen to see which direction he went?" Uncle asked.

"Yes, yes," said Jack. "The same direction. I think they were both going to the Queen's camp, the girl and the monster both."

"Great!" Uncle clapped his hands so sharply that the severed head on the desk made a short, half-hearted cry.

"What IS that thing?" Zombie asked.

"A head," said Jack, looking curiously at Zombie. "What did you think it was?"

Parrot snickered.

Zombie raised an eyebrow. "You do realize I know 412 ways to kill you using only items within arm's reach, right?"

"I did not know that," said Jack. "But uh, 'thanks' for the information?"

"Why does it scream?" Texas asked. The conversation was in danger of wandering so far off course that they'd need a compass and a map to find their way back.

"Because it's in pain," said Jack. "Has been ever since She cut it off."

"The Queen?" Rider hazarded. "She seems to have a 'thing' for cutting off heads."

"Yes," said Jack. "This is one of her favorites. One of the only ones she's kept alive."

"How?" Zombie asked.

"Why?" Parrot asked at the same time.

"I'm not sure how," said Jack with a helpless shrug. "As for why? Why does she do anything? She felt like it. The bitch."

"You don't seem to like her very much," Uncle's voice was dry, droll.

"I hate her," spat Jack. "She killed my father, just for saying he thought he preferred peace to war. But that 'made her look bad', you see. Like a warmonger, like she wanted this war. So she had him executed."

Vodka winced. "I'm sorry man," he said, although his sympathy didn't extend to relaxing his grip on the man's arm.

"Thanks" said Jack. "So yes, I don't like her. That's why I'm taking her stuff. Then I heard you people moving around, and I thought you might be soldiers... from either side, really, it wouldn't have mattered. So I hid. And now you know the whole sordid story of Jack."

"I very highly doubt that," Uncle said, "but I also don't need to know the whole story of Jack. All I need is for you to show us where they took the girl and our metal sticks."

"And I said I would be happy to give you directions," said Jack. "Just let me go, and I'll even draw you a map. I'm sure She has some paper in one of these desks. Maybe the one with the ravens carved all over it."

"No," Uncle shook his head slowly. "I don't think so. No offense, for you seem like you might be half-way stand-up, for a thief and deserter, but since we've arrived in this place, not one person we've met other than a farmer has played straight with us. So no, no directions, no maps."

Uncle fixed Jack with a stern, no-nonsense look. "You're going to take us there in person."

"Ah, er, uh," said Jack. "That is to say, that's not a very great idea. I'm not totally liking that idea. If I take you there, that means that She will see me. And that is something I should very much like to avoid, at all costs."

"Not at all," Uncle's voice was firm. "We'll let you go the moment we see the Queen's camp. That many people, I'm sure we'll see them long before She sees you. Then you can come back here and pilfer to your little black heart's content. Or not. I won't care. But you're coming with us until then."

"I uh, I guess I don't have a choice then," said Jack. "Very well. Do you mind if we get something to eat first? I'm starving."

"Oh God, please, yes," Rider muttered.

"We've seen the kitchen," Uncle said. "There's nothing still good there."

"Well no," said Jack, "there wouldn't be. But the food in the Fresh Room will still be good. I'll show you."

Uncle considered this for a time, then nodded. "All right. But if I even think I smell a double-cross on your part, he sticks that knife of his into places you don't want it stuck," he said, nodding at Zombie, who gave Jack his most evil grin.

Jack blanched. "No, no tricks," said he, "just food."

"And no tea," Zombie said, waggling a finger.

"Uh… okay," agreed Jack, his features drawn in puzzlement. "I wasn't thinking of heating up the fire anyway, just grabbing some cold cuts and cheese."

"Sounds good," Uncle said. "Which way?"

Jack was as good as his word, although Texas noticed that Uncle and Parrot didn't eat anything. Remembering Hadda's tea, Texas didn't blame him. However, his own stomach was so empty, and he had so little left to lose, that Texas stuffed his face. The bread, cheese, and bits of cold meat were the best he had ever tasted. He noticed that Rider was just as ravenous, while Vodka and Zombie ate slower, although with no less appetite.

When they had eaten their fill, and stuffed several wheels of the delicious, hard, nutty cheese into backpacks for later, Uncle nodded to Jack. "All right, lead us to the girl."

"One thing I'm not completely clear on," said Jack as he lead them through the palace. "Who are you people? I'm guessing you're not Ironhand's men, since they know exactly where the Queen's army is. You're obviously not the Queen's men. Who are you?"

"We're here to bring that girl back to her family," Uncle said. "And no, we're not Ironhand's men either. We're not on either side of this war. We just want the girl."

"And our sticks," Zombie said.

"If we can," Uncle said, glaring at Zombie. "But they're not a priority; the girl is."

"In that case," said Jack, "we will need to avoid the Metalman patrols. Pity, that. If you were Ironhand's men, you could order them to escort us and things would go much faster."

"Avoiding Metalman patrols would be a very good idea," Uncle agreed. "Can you do it?"

Jack gave him a sour look, as if Uncle had just insulted him. "Of course I can! Who do you think you're talking to?"

"A thief named Jack O'Hara," Parrot said with a grin.

"I... Well, yes. That's right," said Jack. "Come, follow me. Stick close. Move when I move, stop when I stop. Don't ask too many questions. I'll get you there."

"Wait," Vodka raised a hand to halt him. "Before we go quiet; you seem to know a lot, so let me ask you a question. How come Ironhand's forces haven't totally over-run this entire land yet? We know he seems to be pinned down near this 'fog', but why?"

Jack opened his mouth, then closed it. He thought for a moment, tapping his lip with his finger. Finally, he said, "I'm not sure, of course, since I'm not one of his people. But here's what I've seen, and what I think.

"The Metalmen are very powerful, but not very smart. They don't think well on their feet. Ironhand needs humans, like you, to direct groups of Metalmen. The human lieutenants are the reason they can't go very far from the fog. That much is observable fact. Now, this is where we move on to conjecture.

"The humans can't stay here for more than a day or two at a time. No, I don't know why, nor do I know if the same is true of you. All I know is that they're always rotating out through the fog. That, and I suspect it won't be true for much longer."

"Why?" Uncle asked.

"They have been bringing crates through," said Jack. "Many, many crates. They stack them up near the fog, in the middle of their camp. Why would they bring crates here unless they held something important? But they don't open them, just count them over and over, and keep a tally that is delivered to Ironhand. I think that they need some amount of whatever is in the crates before they can stay here for very long. Maybe some sort of magic? Do you need any particular magic to be here?"

"No magic," Parrot said.

"Except my magic personality," Zombie argued.

"Well, I don't know then," said Jack. "But they have a lot of those crates by now. I imagine that whatever it is they are stockpiling, they'll do something with it before much longer."

"That sounds reasonable," Uncle nodded.

Vodka slapped Jack on the shoulder. "You know, you're the least crazy person we've met so far. If you weren't a deserter and a thief, I could almost like you."

"I... uh, thanks," said Jack with a worried frown. "I think." He gestured towards the front doors of the palace. "Shall we?"

They did. It was tense and nerve-wracking, but Jack was good at what he did. They sneaked out of the palace, then used a tall hedge for cover until they reached the first hill. Jack led them to an orchard, which provided them some more cover, and they darted from apple tree to apple tree. On the other side of the hill, they took a gully between peaks and were able to stay below the ridge line and out of sight.

They continued on in this way for a couple hours, the sun always to their left, then ever so slightly ahead. The sun began to rise slowly in the sky as they walked until it seemed like early evening. Jack turned hard to the right at some arbitrary point. They walked for another half hour until they reached a culvert between two high, cliff-like hills. Jack lead them through this for a time until the hill to the left began to slope down. He paused there.

"We're here," said Jack. "Just over that hill, you'll see a vast army. That's the Queen's. Now, I held up my end of the bargain, time for you to do the same, yes?"

"One moment," Uncle held up a hand.

He nodded to Rider, who climbed the hill, taking the last few feet on his belly. Texas could see Rider pull out his spotting scope and look around, then slink backward until he was far enough down that he could stand up.

"He's right, sir," Rider said. "Big army of locals wearing the uniform."

"And you're sure the girl is here?" Uncle asked Jack.

"Not at all!" protested Jack. "I merely know that this is where they were taking her. I heard the soldiers talking about it. If they moved her after getting here, I wouldn't know about it, would I?"

Uncle chewed on his lip for a moment, then nodded with a sigh. "Fair enough," he said. "You can go."

"Thank you!" said Jack. He turned to depart, then stopped abruptly. "Well, shit."

Texas and Vodka turned to face the same way, and saw Jack's escape blocked by a troop of local soldiers, led by what looked like the Duchess, riding on great flying gryphons.

"Well, shit," Vodka said.

CHAPTER IX
THE MOCK-GENERAL'S TENT

As near as we could tell, Ironhand's people were afraid to eat the local food. After reading the PHR, I wouldn't blame them. But we ate the local food, and we were fine.

There's no other explanation for why they hadn't conquered the entire place yet. God only knows it wasn't the skilled leadership of local brass.

Honestly, all Ironhand really needed to do was just stay put for a while and let the Queen's army destroy itself. It wouldn't take long with those idiots in charge.

   -CSM Daniel "Uncle" Beckworth, official de-brief, Operation Rabbit Hole

"I'M SO VERY HAPPY to see you once more, you dear old things," said the Duchess, dispelling the lingering hope that Uncle had that perhaps the leader of the gryphon riders was merely another incredibly ugly local with a huge head and a sharp chin. But no, she obviously remembered them.

Uncle's stomach tightened.

"Oh my," said the Duchess, looking at Jack, "and you brought me a present. However can I repay you? Oh, I know. I shall take

159

you see the Queen straight away. She'll know what to do with you, oh yes." Her voice positively dripped with gleeful malice. "And the moral of that is – 'What goes around, comes around.' Get them!" That last was addressed to the soldiers with her, who wasted no time in dropping off the backs of their gryphons and moving to surround the team, pointing swords threateningly at them.

Uncle could see Vodka's hand flexing. Uncle understood. His hand also itched for the feel of his M4.

"Why Duchess, how lovely to see you again," said Jack, smiling broadly and spreading his arms wide in invitation of a hug. "See what I captured? A gift, for you. No no, it's okay, I don't need credit. You go ahead and take them to the Queen and claim you found them on your own. Leave me out of it entirely, that's quite all right with me. I'll just be on my way. Ta!"

"I don't think so," said the Duchess. She made an imperious motion with her hand, and one of the soldiers took Jack into custody while the others approached and disarmed the team.

"Damn it," Zombie muttered as they took away his sword. "I was just getting used to the weight of that thing. Who the hell makes bronze swords in this day and age?"

"Which 'day and age' is that, exactly?" Parrot asked.

Zombie opened his mouth, but had no answer, so he settled for a shrug.

"Move along, my dears," said the Duchess. "We mustn't keep the Queen waiting... even if she has no idea what it is she is waiting for. And the moral of that is – 'The best surprises as the ones you didn't even realize you were expecting.'"

"That doesn't even make sense," Parrot frowned. "How can you be expecting a surprise?"

At a gesture from the Duchess, a soldier persuaded the team to move forward by digging his sharp little sword into Uncle's back.

160

They began walking, covered by the weapons of the swordsmen and the watchful eyes of the gryphons who padded along behind them.

Cresting the rise, Uncle saw the Queen's army spread out before him in all its shabby glory. A thousand or more tents covered the ground as far as the eye could see, arranged haphazardly with no regard to lines of movement or safety. Gear was stacked or simply discarded next to tent entrances, adding to the obstacle course of ropes and stakes. The smell was atrocious; the odor of unwashed bodies, old blood, smoke, food, mold, vomit, urine, and feces all blended into a nausea-inducing mélange.

Uncle saw many soldiers sitting around on small camp stools or squatting in the mud. Many appeared to be conscripts, none of them looked happy to be there. Signs of injury, bandages and splints and slings, were ubiquitous. The soldiers gazed up at the team with lackluster eyes. Seldom had Uncle ever seen an army so broken.

They passed a medical tent, and Parrot almost lost his shit.

The tent was one of the larger ones Uncle could see, although not the largest by a couple of degrees. The flaps were pulled back to allow light in, and stench and screams out. Next to the flap was a wheelbarrow full of severed limbs, and inside Uncle saw surgeons working methodically to add to that collection. There appeared to be very little in the way of hygiene or cleanliness involved in the operation, and the line of groaning wounded lying outside in the mud waiting their turn wrapped all the way around the side of the tent. Uncle could see no attempt at triage; those who held a chance often waited in line behind those who were clearly not long for the world, or, in a few instances, behind those who had already left it. Every now and again, a pair of soldiers would come and drag the deceased away, and Uncle saw the bodies being tossed onto a steadily growing pile a few yards from the medical tent.

The soldiers escorting them had to nudge Parrot several times with their sword tips before he stumbled away from the scene of malpractice run rampant.

Zombie caught Uncle's eye and nodded his head towards a small group of soldiers listlessly 'practicing' in a muddy opening between several tents. Of the six men making half-hearted swings at each other, three of them wore obvious bandages. One of them was missing his right arm below the elbow and was practicing, awkwardly, with his left.

Uncle shook his head in disgust.

They passed the gryphon pens, a crudely fenced-off area near the center of camp. Uncle wasn't sure why they bothered with the fence, since the creatures could simply fly away any time they felt like it. The animals turned to watch the parade, and the Duchess' own gryphons walked over to rub beaks with their companions. By that point, the team was so deep in the army camp that there was no thought of escape, even without the extra scrutiny of the gryphons.

Vodka nearly got the entire team killed.

He yelled, "Bastards!" and tensed to run out of the line.

Rider reacted first, tripping Vodka. Zombie sat on the fallen soldier while Vodka kicked helplessly beneath him. Uncle looked around to see what had sparked Vodka's ire.

When he saw it, Uncle nearly got the entire team killed.

Uncle understood why the medics had merely been piling the dead instead of burying them. He understood the large pile of corpses and body parts. He understood Vodka's reaction.

The gryphons needed to be fed.

Uncle turned to the Duchess, fury burning in his eyes. "You feed your own dead to your animals?" he snarled, towering over the small woman while soldiers poked at him with swords, trying to push him away. "This is how you treat your own fallen? What is wrong with you people?"

The Duchess looked genuinely surprised by the outburst. "Why, you dear thing, the poor gryphons need to eat something you know. And those men aren't useful for anything else anymore. The moral of that is – 'Waste not, want not,'" she said.

Uncle punched her. He put his weight into it, landing the blow square in the middle of her ugly face. It had felt like punching a rock wrapped in a thin layer of velvet. "Damn it!" he said, shaking his hand in pain.

The Duchess patted Uncle on the shoulder. She hadn't even reacted when he hit her. "There there, old thing. One shouldn't assume old women are weak simply because we look like it. And the moral there is – 'Always look before you leap.' Or put more simply – 'Just because the cover of a book displays a topic one is uninterested in, one should not assume that the contents follow the conventions set by the art work on the external cover, lest one miss out on a pleasurable reading experience because one pre-judged the contents based on erroneous assumptions,'" said she.

Uncle turned his back on the Duchess. He saw that Rider and Zombie had helped Vodka to his feet. Vodka made an attempt to brush some of the mud from his fatigue jacket, but he continued to glare daggers at the Duchess.

"Come on," Uncle said. "Let's get this over with."

They resumed walking. Sullen eyes watched them from the faces of exhausted soldiers. Vodka shook his head from time to time, but his momentary loss of control was behind him.

The Queen's was one of the few tents larger than the infirmary, a monstrous red and black affair with five poles supporting an acre of canvas. It was so large, it even had skylights: patches of thin mesh that kept out flies but let in light. On either side of the flap, two large (by local standards) soldiers stood blank-faced but attentive. The Duchess brought the team to a halt before these two grim sentinels and clapped twice.

The flap opened, and out stepped Rabbix, dressed in the livery of the queen. His eyes widened when he saw Uncle and his men, but he forced himself to address the Duchess as if he didn't know them. "Who has business before the Queen?" demanded the little man.

"Duchess Dimoen offers her respects to the Queen, and would the Queen be interested in some captives from the Enemy for Her amusement?" said the Duchess.

"One moment," said Rabbix. He ducked back inside the tent, and Uncle could hear talking somewhere inside although he could not make out the words.

"Well," said Jack, "we've brought them. I'll let you handle it from here, if you don't mind? I think I saw an old friend on the way here, and really should pay my respects."

"You're going nowhere," said the Duchess, taking Jack's arm and squeezing it firmly. She dug her chin into his shoulder, smiling. "I'm quite sure the Queen will want to see you as well, dearie. And the moral there is – 'Two birds in the hand are worth one in the hand and one that is is not in your hand.'"

The flap opened, and Rabbix emerged. He bowed his head deeply to the Duchess. "The Queen's respects, and would you do Her the honor of bringing your prisoners before Her person."

"I'd be delighted to, old thing," said the Duchess. To Uncle, she gestured towards the tent. "In you go."

The inside of the tent was every bit as lavish as Uncle had expected. Carpets lay piled on the ground, one atop another in a soft, plush heap. Tables and chairs sat here and there. They were not 'camp' tables and chairs, but real, honest-to-God furniture. Uncle suspected some of it was antique. The over-stuffed easy chair by a table with an oil lamp on it must have weighed a good three hundred pounds. Uncle wondered how many soldiers it took to carry the thing when they marched.

The tent was divided into 'rooms' with hanging curtains, and Rabbix stopped at one of these and clapped. "The Duchess Dimoen offers Greetings and Gifts of Esteem to Her Most Royal Majesty Queen Harzt , Protector of the Land, Grand Pontifex of All," called Rabbix in a loud voice.

"Oh, she's in a hurry to see us," whispered the Duchess. "How very lovely."

"Come," said a harsh female voice from the other side of the curtain.

Rabbix pulled aside the curtain and gestured for them to enter. The Duchess went first, then her soldiers prodded Uncle and the rest of the team in after her.

Seated on a throne that was only slightly smaller and less ostentatious than the one in the palace was a short woman with an enormous head. She wore a red and black dress so elaborate and layered that Uncle could not determine if she was naturally fat, or merely looked that way because of all the fabric. Her white hair was piled high on her head, adding an extra foot to her stature, and woven throughout with strands of rubies. She wore a near-duplicate of the crown back at the palace on her brow, and a permanent-looking scowl on her face.

The Duchess bowed deeply and opened her mouth to speak, but the Queen was looking past her, at the team. Or rather, Uncle realized, at Jack.

"YOU!" bellowed the Queen. For such a tiny body, she had quite a pair of lungs.

Uncle suspected she had refined the science of yelling to an art form.

"You are working with... with THEM?" shrieked the Queen. Her voice kept getting higher and higher pitched with each word until by 'them' she bordered on the infrasonic. If there had been dogs in the camp, Uncle would have expected them to be howling. He wondered how the gryphons handled it.

"Don't be silly," said Jack, offering an affable smile. "I brought them to you, didn't I? Besides, they're not who you think. They don't work for Ironhand."

"We. Are. Not. SILLY," said the Queen, her voice so soft and dangerous that Uncle wondered if it was possible to get audio-whiplash. "They're humans, just like Ironhand and his lieutenants."

"So is Fiona McGinney," Uncle took the opportunity to jump into the conversation.

"Who?" snapped the Queen, giving him an irritated glance.

"The girl you kidnapped from my world," Uncle said. He fished Fiona's picture out of his pocket and held it up. "You know," he said, "the one you thought was Alice."

"We did nothing of the sort," said the Queen. She didn't even glance at the photo, but turned her attention once more to Jack. "Our men made that mistake, it's true, but We knew right away she was the wrong girl. Her hair is entirely the wrong color."

"Told you," Zombie whispered.

"Shush," Parrot whispered back.

"Excellent," Uncle smiled. "In that case, you won't miss her if we take her back home with us."

The Queen peered at Uncle, then at the others one by one. Her left eye widened in delighted surprise. "You are the ones the Long Man mentioned," said she.

"Possible," Uncle said. "We did have a bit of a run in with him earlier. He took some stuff of ours. We'd like it back, if you happen to know where it is."

"Oh yes, We do indeed," said the Queen. "We know right where they are, your weapons. The problem is, Our men can't make them work." She sniffed in contempt at the incompetence of her men. "You will make them work."

"Give us Fiona," Uncle countered.

"You dare negotiate with Us?" bellowed the Queen. "Off with his head!"

"You want the weapons to work?" Uncle yelled before anyone could get the bright idea of actually following that order. "You need us alive. They only work for us. Biometric locks," he lied.

"What does that mean?" asked the Queen.

"It means, they only work for us," Uncle said. "As you seem to have noticed."

"The Long Man said nothing about that," muttered the Queen softly, speaking to herself. "He may not have known. Or maybe he did, and this is his idea of a joke on Us. Yes, that is just the sort of thing he might well do." She focused her gaze on Uncle once more. "Then you will fight for Us."

"No," Uncle said. Before the Queen could order his execution again, he hurried to add, "We're at an impasse, your Majesty. We want Fiona McGinney back, and you clearly need our help. If you kill us, you get nothing. But we have no intention of fighting your war for you. So, I propose a trade."

"We are listening." Suspicion filled the Queen's voice.

"We'll do one mission for you," Uncle said. "One objective, and then you give us Fiona and let us go."

The Queen considered for a while. As she thought, she talked aloud. Uncle wondered if she realized she was doing it.

"The Long Man said those weapons could turn the tide for Us. Kill at a distance, he said. Much more powerful than even the Metalmen. The girl is useless, can't grow like Alice could. We don't need her. But the weapons, those could be valuable. We could keep these people, these humans, and their weapons. Agree to their terms, yes, but then trick them and keep them to operate the weapons when We need them. Yes, yes, that is a good plan."

Nope, Uncle thought. She has no idea.

"Wow," Zombie said.

"Very well," said the Queen. "We accept your deal. You will do one mission for Us, of Our choosing. Upon completion, We will let you have the girl, Fiona."

"I want to see her first," Uncle said. "To make sure she's okay. No offense, but you have a bit of a reputation for cutting off people's heads when they disappoint you."

The Queen grimaced in genuine disgust at the prospect. "She's a child," snapped the Queen. "We wouldn't kill her unless We needed to.

"We've seen how you treat children," Vodka said. "We saw a farm you had burned down. It was full of kids."

The Queen rolled her eyes, looking for all the world like an irritated teenager in that moment. "She's a human girl," said the Queen, as if that explained everything.

"Right," Uncle had no idea what the Queen was talking about, and didn't care enough to get side-tracked. "I still want to see her."

"Oh, very well," said the Queen. She snapped her fingers, and Rabbix jumped to attention. "Fetch the human girl," ordered the Queen.

"Yes, your Majesty," said Rabbix. He hurried out.

"While We wait," said the Queen, turning her gaze on Jack once more, "Let Us consider what exactly We should do with you."

"Off with his head?" Parrot guessed quietly.

The Queen turned out to have very good hearing.

"Silence! Or it will be your head We have cut off." She glared briefly at Parrot before turning back to Jack. Her features melted into what was perhaps the least sincere smile Uncle had ever been lucky enough to witness. "Jack, Our dear Jack. We can't very well have you roaming about making Us look bad, now can We? No, We think you must go into the cage."

"But—" said Jack, but his protest was cut short.

"The cage!" bellowed the Queen. She gestured curtly to some soldiers. "Put him in the cage. And Jack?" she turned back to him one last time. "Let this be a lesson to you. You really should have learned from your father's example. Take him away!"

The guards dragged Jack away. He went quietly, putting up no resistance. As he passed by the team, Uncle could see the hate burning in the young man's eyes.

"Pity," Zombie said after Jack was pulled from the tent. "I liked him. I mean, for a deserter, a coward, and a thief, he was okay."

"What are you babbling about?" asked the Queen. "Jack isn't a deserter."

"No?" Zombie pursed his lips in surprise. "I thought you drafted all able-bodied males. If he's not a deserter, what is he?"

"He's Our son," said the Queen in a soft, almost gentle voice. She looked at the carpet in sorrow, took a deep breath, and let it out slowly. "But he must learn not to disobey or talk back to Us. A lesson his father never learned." She shrugged. "It is ever so difficult raising a child when one has a country to govern. Perhaps We weren't always there for him as a child. Still, there is no excuse for this kind of behavior. Simply none."

169

"He only does it to annoy," said the Duchess.

Uncle blinked in surprise; he had quite forgotten that the Duchess was still in the room.

"Yes, We are sure you're right," agreed the Queen. "Still, children are such a trial. You're lucky, old friend, that you turned all of yours into pigs before they learned to speak."

"Oh yes, your Majesty," nodded the Duchess. "I consider myself quite fortunate."

A double hand-clap interrupted the reminiscing, and Rabbix's voice called out, "The human girl Fiona offers Greetings and Punctual Arrival to Her Most Royal Majesty Queen Harzt , Protector of the Land, Grand Pontifex of All."

"Does he say that every time?" Parrot asked.

"Only when We are in a hurry," said the Queen. Then, louder, "Enter."

Rabbix pulled back the curtain and held it. Into the room stepped a small girl in a dirty flower-print dress. Chestnut hair struggled to escape twin pigtails, and she wore a smudge of dirt on her cheek just beside her nose. Her eyes were red; she had been crying.

Parrot knelt down and smiled at the girl to reassure her. "Hello, Fiona," he said softly, holding out his hand and making a 'come here' gesture. "Your father sent us to rescue you."

Fiona McGinney took a hesitant step towards him, her eyes wide with hope. Then she caught sight of the Queen, and her face fell. She stared down at the carpet and mumbled something.

"Speak up, girl," ordered the Queen. "It is not proper for young girls to mumble."

"I said, 'Your Majesty,'" Fiona said, a little more clearly. "You called for me? I'm afraid I still can't grow any faster than I already am doing."

Parrot looked up at the Queen. "I'd like to check to make sure she's healthy?"

The Queen nodded. Parrot moved to Fiona and began looking her over, all the while murmuring reassurances to the frightened little girl.

"As you can see," said the Queen after a minute or two of this, "she is quite unharmed. Now, you have seen her. Time to honor your side of the agreement." She made a flicking gesture with her hand, and Rabbix took Fiona by the arm and drew her back out of the room.

Just before the curtain fell shut, Parrot called out, "Don't worry, Fiona. We're going to get you home. I promise."

"What do you need us to do?" Uncle asked.

"Our enemy, this man who styles himself 'Captain Ironhand,' has been bringing supplies through his portal from another place," said the Queen. "You are to destroy those supplies, and, if you can, the portal itself."

"By ourselves?" Texas blurted.

"You may have some of Our resources for this mission, for it is of the utmost importance for the survival of Our land." The Queen turned to one of the soldiers and waved. "Take them to General Klahb."

The soldier bowed, then gestured for the team to follow him. Wordlessly, he lead them from the Queen's tent and across a small patch of mud to another tent that was only slightly smaller and less ornate. There, the escort spoke to a pair of guards, saying, "With the Queen's compliments, some prisoners to see General Klahb."

The sentry nodded sharply and opened the tent. "The General is waiting for them," said the other guard.

The escort soldier lead them inside the General's command center.

Where the Queen's tent had been red with black trim, and dedicated to obvious displays of wealth and power, the General's was black with brown trim, and dedicated to obvious displays of wealth and power.

More carpets on the ground, more improbable furniture, more elaborate decorations. Again, Uncle could not help but wonder how many actual supplies had been left behind to make room for the ridiculous décor.

The soldier guided them into a room dominated by a huge oak table large enough to seat twenty. Golden candlesticks held down the corners of several papers spread out across the table. Wavy lines covered most of the papers, and Uncle assumed that they were maps although he had no way of reading them. Before he could spend much time trying to figure it out, the General arrived.

The General was of average height for a local, with a head slightly larger than normal. He sported massive mutton-chop sideburns, a curly Imperial mustache, and a potbelly that would have done Santa Claus proud. He dressed in the most elaborate uniform Uncle had ever seen, with so many decorations and medals and gewgaws that Uncle wondered if it doubled as body armor. The only thing lacking was a monocle.

The General produced a monocle from his breast pocket and placed it in his left eye. "I say," said he, "What do we have here then, eh?"

Zombie bit his own lip, hard. Texas coughed to cover a laugh. Rider stared in disbelief. Parrot whispered, "If he breaks into a Gilbert and Sullivan number, I may lose it."

"Keep it together," Uncle muttered. Clearing his throat, he addressed the General. "Sir, the Queen wants us to—"

"Yes yes, I know all about it," said the General. "You're to

172

destroy the supplies that dastard Ironhand has been assembling. I'm to talk to you about reinforcements and tactics. Quite right, quite right. Well!" he clapped his hands and rubbed them together. "Let's be about it, shall we? What's first?"

There was a pregnant silence as the team waited for him to go on. After a while of staring at each other, Uncle started. "Oh, were you actually asking me?" Uncle asked.

"Who else would I be asking?" huffed the General. He withdrew his monocle, rubbed it with a black silk handkerchief, and put it back in his eye.

"I just... That is... Right," Uncle shook his head. "Okay uh. What's first. Well, why don't you show us what resources you have? Intelligence, that sort of thing?"

"Very well," said the General. He gazed off into the distance for a moment, crossed his hands in front of him, and began to speak. "'Now suppose you were assured, with regard to two finite Lines placed before you, that, when produced in a certain direction, one of them approached the other, that is, contained two points, of which the second was nearer, to the other Line, than the first, would you not think it probable— if not absolutely certain—that they would meet at last?'"

The team stared at him for a few heartbeats. Then, "What?" Zombie asked.

"You said you wanted me to show you my intelligence," said the General. "I was obliging your request. Oh, would you prefer something from literature instead? I can repeat 'You Are Old, Father William,' if you would like."

Uncle rubbed his temples. He felt he beginnings of a headache coming on. "What do you know about the ene—no, wait!" he cut himself off. "Do you have any maps that show the enemy camp?"

"Yes," said the General, puffing up his chest with pride.

173

Long seconds crawled away to die.

"May I see it?" Uncle prodded.

"Of course," said the General. He waddled to the table with all the maps on it, and pointed at one. "There we are, old chap."

Uncle looked at the map. It reminded him of the pictures Parrot's kids would draw, and Parrot's wife would pin to the refrigerator with magnets. "I am not familiar with your particular notation system," Uncle said, picking his words slowly. "Would you mind tell—That is, tell me what I'm looking at."

"A map," said the General. He cocked his head in confusion. "That's what you asked for."

"Saw that coming," Zombie said.

Uncle ground his teeth. "What do these curved lines represent?" he asked.

"Half-hours," said the General with a firm nod. "See, they start here at 6:30 and end here at 8 O' Clock."

"All right," Uncle nodded. "And these small black circles?"

"Those are where our scouts last saw the Metalmen."

"And then the circles with Xs through them are...?"

"Well," said the General, rubbing his chin, "those WERE where the scouts had seen the Metalmen the LAST time, or the time before that. They move around, you see."

Uncle stared at the General. Vodka snorted. Zombie shook his head.

Rider asked, "General, did you, by any chance, inherit your position from your father?"

"Yes, of course," smiled the General. "Why, a Klahb has been in charge of the Queen's Army for four generations now, going all the way back to the founding of this land. Why do you ask?"

"No particular reason," Rider said. He pointed at the map. "What are those blue squiggles?"

"Those are the river," said the General. He seemed particularly proud as he gazed at the blue squiggles. "They represent the ripples on the surface, you see, caused by wind or sometimes by fish swimming quickly by."

"This big squiggly thing here?" Uncle asked.

"That's the Fog," said the General. "Right in the middle of their camp."

"Right. And these little squares?"

"Those are the supplies you're going to destroy," smiled the General. "I add a new one every time the scouts tell me the Enemy has brought more crates through the Fog."

"There sure are a lot of them," Vodka said.

"Yes," said the General. "That's why we need you to destroy them. Whatever they are, the Enemy is devoting considerable attention to them. Their loss will almost certainly be a blow against that dastard Ironhand."

"What are these big brown rings that looks like a tea stains?" Parrot asked.

"Those are tea stains," said the General. "I need at least two cups in the morning, and sometimes the scouts report while I'm still having my second one."

"Okay, I've seen enough," Uncle said. "What resources do you have?"

"Well, there's my tent, obviously," said the General "And my tea. I have a couple servants, a butler and —"

"Are you doing this on purpose?" Uncle growled. His headache was getting worse. He searched for his aspirin before remembering that he had given all of his to Texas earlier.

"Helping you, do you mean?" asked the General. "Of course, old chap, of course. I mean, well yes, the Queen ordered it, but you seem like a right smart group of troops. Right smart indeed."

175

"Compared to some people," Zombie said.

"A pleasure to work with you," nodded the General. "Yes, indeed."

"Show us your soldiers," Uncle said through clenched teeth. "And anything else you have around there that might be useful in a military sense. I do not want to see your butler unless your butler is a hardened commando who only pretends to be your butler in order to covertly provide you with constant protection while lulling your enemies into a false sense of security on the subject."

"Is he?" Zombie couldn't help but ask. "Because that would be bad-ass."

"Not that I know of," said the General. "What is a 'commando'? Is that higher than a commander?"

"For God's sake," Uncle muttered. He turned to Parrot. "I need some aspirin. Or morphine. Morphine would be good. Do you have any morphine?"

"Nope," Parrot said, shaking his head. "This place is enough of a drug-trip by itself; can't have you getting stoned on top of it. Here's some aspirin though."

"Thanks," Uncle popped the pills into his mouth, then dry swallowed them. Turning his attention back to the General, Uncle sighed. "Lead on, General."

The General did so, guiding them out of his tent and into the bright late-afternoon sun. He strolled among the tents, nodding distantly to any soldier who made eye contact. There were very few who would. Most turned their backs when they saw the General approaching.

"As you can see," narrated the General as he walked, "We have a number of soldiers. Some of them even have some training. I'm afraid that the dastard, Ironhand, is murder on our experienced veterans."

"Those he doesn't kill, your medics take care of," Parrot's voice was dark. He remembered the medical tent.

"Or the gryphons," Vodka muttered. He, also, had memories of their first trip through the camp.

"Oh yes, the gryphons," beamed the General. "Quite magnificent, aren't they? They allow us to fly troops to wherever the fighting is and drop them off. They can also carry supplies from the outer farms and villages and aren't bothered by things like muddy roads or washed-out bridges. Of course, they do have a tendency to go chasing off after any turkeys or dodos they spot, but otherwise they're quite useful."

"For ferrying troops and supplies?" Uncle asked. "I just want to clarify; you don't use them for anything else?"

"What else could we use them for?" asked the General. "They're really not all that bright you know. I doubt they'd be much good at hunting on their own. They would probably just eat whatever they found instead of bringing it back for the men."

Uncle pursed his lips, then shrugged. "All right. We met a fire-breathing lizard on the way here. Do you have any of those?"

"Oh yes, of course," said the General, nodding so hard Uncle worried that his oversized head might snap right off. "They are protection for the Queen. Far too valuable to be allowed anywhere near the front, of course. They stay here by the Queen's tent and destroy any of that dastard, Ironhand's, men who may approach."

"Right," Uncle nodded. "Makes perfect sense." He glanced at the others, but they sported blank looks also; no-one had noticed any giant lizards guarding the Queen.

The General turned between two tents, stepping gingerly over or ducking under the ropes, as appropriate. "Come, this way," said he. "I'll show you our Special Troops section."

The team followed. Zombie muttered something about doing

the limbo, but Uncle didn't catch all of it. Once back in the open, he saw that the General was a dozen yards to the right, gesturing around with grand, sweeping waves of his arms.

"We could probably leave," Rider said. "It might be a good half hour before he notices we're gone."

"Yeah, but the Queen still has Fiona," Uncle said.

Rider nodded.

The team caught up with the General. "... because of a treaty signed in my grand-father's time, don't you know, but all the same, I think it worked out quite well. Wouldn't you say?"

"Absolutely," Uncle nodded. He hadn't the faintest idea what the General was talking about, but didn't really want him to start over from the beginning. "What is that for?" Uncle pointed to a large wooden enclosure beside a wide, sluggish river.

"Hmm? Oh my, that," said the General. "Yes. That's the mog turei pen."

"What's a mog turei?" Uncle clenched his hands. He just knew, somehow, that he wasn't going to like the answer, but he couldn't stop himself from asking.

"They are what mog turei soup is made from," said the General. His tone of voice indicated the thought maybe Uncle was a touch on the slow side. "I would have thought that was fairly obvious."

"Quite," Uncle said.

"This is why I'm a pessimist," Zombie said. "We're never unpleasantly surprised."

"So, what, you ate them all?" Texas asked, looking at the rather large pen. "That enclosure must have held quite a lot of proto-soup."

"No, don't be silly," said the General. "Mog turei soup is far too complicated to make in the field. We only eat them during peace time."

"Then where are they right now?" Rider's voice suggested that he suspected he would regret asking.

"I'm quite sure I don't know where they are right now. Somewhere in the river, I should think. We use them to ferry goods via the river, you see," said the General. "Capital swimmers, they are. You stretch a net between four of them, and you can haul quite a parcel of goods up or down the stream. Look, there's one now," he pointed.

A nightmare emerged from the water. Easily nine feet tall, it had a hard shell and flippers in back like a turtle, a vaguely porcine head with sharp tusks protruding from the lower jaw, and nasty claws on the ends of its long, powerful arms. It raised its head to look at the team and the General. Uncle read intelligence and malice in those dark eyes.

"River transport," Uncle said, swallowing and turning away. "Got it."

"What about ranged—ow!" Texas grunted as Vodka dug an elbow into his side.

Vodka shook his head quickly, a finger to his lips.

"The what now?" asked the General.

"The... rations," Texas amended. "You know, food. We're hungry. We have only eaten once in over a day. If we're going to do this mission, we need food. Can you take us to the DFAC, or the mess hall? Or whatever you use instead?"

"Most of the tents are pretty messy," said the General with a disdainful sniff. "What does that have to do with food?"

"Just take us to food," Uncle ordered. When the General turned his back, Uncle gave Vodka an approving nod and silently mouthed, 'good job.' He didn't want the locals thinking very much about ranged weapons.

It might give them ideas.

The General lead them back to his own tent, then called for a servant to bring food.

"Would you mind giving us some privacy, General?" Uncle asked. "We need to discuss how we're going to handle this mission, and some of what we talk about might be state secrets. You understand." He placed a hand on the little man's back and gently but inexorably pushed him towards the exit as he spoke. "We'll call for you when we're ready to begin. Thank you so much for your hospitality. Good-bye for now."

The General looked very confused as the tent flaps closed behind him.

"You just kicked him out of his own tent," Zombie's eyes widened with awe and respect. "Nice."

"We have two options, as I see it," Uncle said, dragging one of the over-stuffed chairs to the map table and sitting down. He looked comical, a big man in a small chair, but it was comfortable and he wasn't about to move just because Rider was grinning like an idiot. "We can utilize the resources here: gryphons, mog turei, fire lizards, that sort of thing. The problem with that is that we would introduce new tactics to these people, and I'm not entirely comfortable with that. This isn't our war, and to be honest, I don't like either side very much. I mean yes, I feel bad for the civilians, but would introducing new tactics help or hurt them in the long run? We might drag on a battle that is on the verge of ending any day now, if we do that."

He stopped talking as servants came in with platters of food. He almost laughed when he counted seven settings. It seemed that the General had expected to eat with them. The extra helping would not go to waste.

The servants departed. The team fell like wolves upon the food. The one meal at the palace had only taken the edge off their hunger, and hours of walking and being captured had put that edge right back on it.

The food was delicious. Hot cuts of beef roasted in a dark wine with capers and mushrooms, small chickens stuffed with several cheeses and onions, lightly steamed green beans in a garlic sauce, small, purple things that tasted like yams, fresh bread rolls, butter, and a rich, nutty dark beer to wash it all down with.

The team ate in silence. As each man reached the point of being sated, he leaned back and relaxed. Texas burped, blushed, and apologized. Zombie whacked him on the back. Rider picked his teeth with the tip of his knife.

"Good beer," Parrot said.

"Good roast," Vodka said.

"You were saying?" Zombie turned to Uncle.

"Introducing new tactics," Parrot said, nodding. "I remember. And you're right: it could go either way. It could give the Queen new hope and drag on a war that was on the verge of ending, or it could give them a decisive victory in a battle that might otherwise go on for years yet. Is there any way for us to tell which is the situation?"

"No," Vodka said so decisively that everyone looked at him. He shrugged. "Yeah, their tactics suck. Their medical sucks. Their Queen sucks. But we don't know the enemy's relative strength. There is no way to know without spending far longer spying on each side than I want to be in this crap-fest land."

"Another point," Rider spoke up. "Even just destroying the supplies as asked puts us in the same situation. We might be preventing Ironhand from winning quickly, but not hurt him so badly that he retreats. Or, we might do the opposite. We don't know."

"That was what I was thinking too," Uncle nodded. "No way to know for sure what's right. So what do we do? Thoughts?"

"Can we double-cross the Queen?" Zombie asked. "Say we're going to do it so she gives us our weapons back, then use them to get the girl?"

"Risky," Parrot said. "One: we don't know where Fiona is. Two: even having guns doesn't make us immune to harm. Three: the General said that they have more of those dragon-things guarding the Queen... I didn't see them. Did you? Where are they? Invisible?"

Zombie nodded glumly.

Uncle understood how he felt. It would have been so cathartic to get their weapons back and use them, but Parrot was right; it was risky to start throwing their dicks around. Too much they didn't know, too much they didn't control.

Texas lifted a hand briefly, and spoke. "How about we take the mission, but when we get to Ironhand's camp, we tell them whats going on and then fake destroying the supplies, without actually doing it?"

"No good," Zombie shook his head. "First, we don't know how Ironhand or his men would react to us. Maybe they'd just assume we're enemies. Failing that, they might capture us, and then we're right fucking back to problem 'A.'"

"How do we know the Queen is going to play straight with us anyway?" Rider asked. "Maybe we do the deed, and then she says, 'Tough titty, I'm not letting you go.' She seems the sort. I mean shit, if I understood that right, she killed her own husband because he said, 'Give peace a chance.'"

"That, and she flat-out said she was planning to double-cross us," Texas pointed out.

"We worry about us, and our mission," Vodka said. "None of the rest of this is our concern. Yeah, I feel bad for the civilians, and the soldiers too, for that matter. But this isn't our war. It isn't our problem. I say we do the mission. If the Queen deals in good faith, we go home. If not, we take the bitch hostage. Hell, maybe she'll give us an excuse to put her kid on the throne. He seemed at least half-way sane."

Everyone was quiet for a moment, looking for holes in Vodka's plan. Uncle broke the silence. "I agree. Which brings us back to my first point: do we use their help, and deal with the tactics change, or do we go on our own? I'm leaning towards going it alone, but I'm open to thoughts."

Rider stood up and looked at child's scribble/map. "We use their resources, but don't teach them anything," he suggested. "Have gryphons drop us off over here," he pointed at a spot roughly on the other side of the camp. "Then, at a pre-determined time, the Queen's soldiers attack from the other side, or at least cause a big ruckus. Draw Ironhand's soldiers and stuff that way. We sneak in here, plant charges, sneak back out. Blow the whole thing once we're airborn again."

"What about this river right here," Zombie tapped the blue squiggles. "We'll have to cross that somehow, and we don't know how wide or deep it is."

"Mog turei," Vodka suggested. "We have them swim out there ahead of time, and wait under the surface. When we arrive at the river, they rise up and we cross on their backs. Repeat on the way out."

"Can we trust them?" Parrot asked. "That one we saw looked less than happy, although I couldn't tell if it was us he was mad at, or just his lot in life."

183

"I think it was the General," Texas said. "I'm starting to get the feeling that... well, never mind."

"Go on," Uncle ordered.

Texas shifted his weight from one foot to the other, blushing. He wasn't used to everyone staring at him. "Well," he said, licking his lips, "it's like this. The General said that there has been one of his family in the military 'since the founding of this land,' four generations ago. The ceiling in the main hall of the palace showed the locals fighting centauripedes. I'm thinking that the weirder things around here, the Long Man, the mog turei, maybe the gryphons, that those are the true 'natives.' I'm thinking that the people-shaped people around here, the Queen and her kind, invaded a while back and took over. And the locals aren't too happy about it.

"Remember, the Queen thought that the Long Man not telling her how the guns worked was just the sort of thing he might do. For that matter, the Long Man took our guns, but then lead us straight here. He left the small door open, the drink and cake out for us. He made it relatively easy for us to get here. Why do that? Why not just take our stuff and then leave us to fend for ourselves? I think he wanted us here, and he wanted us mad."

"Assassination by proxy?" Parrot asked. He thought for a moment, then nodded. "I can see it. This also explains the screaming head in the Queen's room. Given how many heads she's cut off, why keep that particular one 'alive'? Unless maybe he was a resistance leader or something, part of a rebellion against the invaders."

"How does this help us?" Uncle asked. "So the mog turei are mad at the Queen. We're not exactly working against her best interests here. Why would they support us?"

"Two reasons," Texas said. "First, 'better the devil you know,' right? The mog turei and the centauripedes are at least familiar with the Queen and her ways. Not so with Ironhand. Second, the longer this war goes on, the more of the Queen's people get killed. If her eventual victory is pyrrhic enough, they might be able to overthrow her."

"Do we want to base an entire plan on a fucking 'maybe'?" Zombie asked.

"If the turtle-people won't do it, we get our feet wet," Vodka said. "When did you become such a baby? Did you transfer to the Air Force when I wasn't looking?"

"Blow me," Zombie said. "Your mom transferred to the Air Force."

"Weak," Parrot said.

"Very," Rider nodded. "I expected better of you," he said to Zombie.

"Yeah, well," Zombie burped. "Food coma. My brain's not working."

"Does it ever?" Parrot grinned.

"Ladies," Uncle rumbled a warning. "Vodka's right. If the mog turei don't play nice, we get the job done another way. It's a solid plan. Thank God the Long Man didn't take our C4. Okay. We fly in via gryphon, wait for the distraction, cross the mog turei bridge or get our feet wet, plant the explosives, detonate once we're safely back in the air. If anything gets in our way, we shoot it, but we try to stay silent until the big boom." He nodded firmly, then looked at Texas. "Go tell the General he can come back in."

C H A P T E R   X
THE LETHAL BALLET

Why didn't we just fly over and drop the C4?

Well, sir, we didn't want to give the locals any ideas. See, their idea of tactics was pretty much 'line up and march straight at the enemy.' And given that they'd already kidnapped someone from our world at least once, we didn't feel it was incumbent upon us to start giving them good ideas they might use against us some day.

What do I mean by 'at least' once?

Well, I mean sir, do we really know why Alice went there in the first place?

   -CSM Daniel "Uncle" Beckworth, official de-brief, Operation Rabbit Hole

THE QUEEN WAS NOT amused.

"Off with—" began the Queen, only to cut herself off with an angry shake of her head. "You want Us to waste Our own men so that you can do the task for which We have set you? If We wanted to accomplish this task Ourselves, We wouldn't have told you to do it!"

"Just a diversion," Uncle tried, with limited success, to hide a sigh as he explained, for the third time, the plan. "A timed diversion. You do have some way of telling time, right?" Sundials were out, for obvious reasons.

"We have," sniffed the Queen. She sat in her camp throne in silence as she considered.

General Klahb had brought the team back to the Queen when they announced that they were ready. The Queen had surrounded herself with courtiers, including the Duchess and handfuls of people Uncle had not seen before. Many of them wore cloaks or brooches with various devices which he assumed represented their various house symbols. All of them had the big heads that Uncle was starting to associate with the upper class of this crazy land. In addition to the courtiers, a small army of servants stood by, led by the redoubtable Mr. Rabbix.

Uncle had explained the plan, and then explained it again because Klahb didn't seem to understand the finer points, such as: the entire thing. It was during this second explanation that the Queen expressed her displeasure.

Uncle gave her a minute to digest the plan, then spoke up. "You see, if we go in and they see us, we will be forced to fight, which will draw more attention, and more of them will attack us. It is quite likely that we would be unable to complete the mission. However," Uncle smiled, "if your forces make a small sortie, it will draw the enemy forces towards this side of the camp, and their attention away from the supplies. Then we can get in, destroy them, and get out without being overwhelmed." He paused to give the Queen a long, conspiratorial look. "You do want us to destroy those supplies, right? This really is the best strategy. Just ask the General."

"Oh er, well yes, quite right," said the General, polishing his monocle. "Best thing for it, all things considered."

"We don't like it," said the Queen. She raised a hand before anyone could protest. "We don't like it, but We do not see any other alternative. However, as this will place Our men in danger, and provide you with a chance to sneak about, what guarantee do We have that you will not simply sneak away entirely while Our men are otherwise occupied?" She pointed a finger at Rider. "You will leave that one here, to ensure your cooperation."

"Can't do that," Uncle said quickly. "The plan is delicate, and requires all six of us. We simply don't have time to train one of your people to perform the tasks we need done; it takes over a year of training to do what we need Rider to do. Do you really want to spend a year while we train someone new? Who knows what Ironhand could do with all those crates in that time."

The rest of the team maintained their war faces. These were men one did not want to play poker with, a fact for which Uncle was incredibly happy at the moment. His bluff relied entirely on them not giving it away with incredulous or confused looks.

They did him proud.

The Queen slammed her hand against the arm rest of her throne. She chewed her lip. She scowled and frowned. In the end, however, she gave in. "Very well," said she, "all six of you may go. But We will impose this limitation: if you do not return in six hours, and if Our scouts do not tell Us that the supplies are destroyed in that time, We will kill the girl, Fiona. And you, when Our men catch you, of course."

Uncle thought about the map in the General's tent, and the lines that delineated half-hour intervals. He did some quick mental calculations. While he didn't know exactly how fast a gryphon could fly, the distances involved were short enough that his team could cover them on the ground in just over six hours. If the gryphons cut down on travel time at all, six hours would be plenty of time.

No need to let the Queen know this, of course.

"All right," Uncle nodded. "We need to hurry. If we only have six hours, you'd better send your mog turei now and give us back our weapons."

The Queen raised a finger towards Klahb, who in turn nodded to one of his soldiers. That man hurried out of the tent. The Queen then snapped her fingers at Rabbix and pointed at a long cabinet to one side of the tent room.

Rabbix hurried over. As he passed the team, Zombie nodded and smirked, "Wilford? Really?"

Rabbis blinked at Zombie, but with the Queen watching, he dared not waste time. He fetched a box from the cabinet and returned it to the Queen. She waved to dismiss him, and he took up his position by her side. He shot eye-daggers at Zombie.

The Queen opened the box and withdrew a large, ornately carved and stained hour glass. She set it on the arm of her throne and turned it so that the sand began falling. "Six hours," said the Queen.

Ten minutes of that time was spent waiting. When the soldier returned, staggering under the burden of four carbines, a machine gun, a sniper rifle, and six side-arms, the team descended upon him like ravenous vultures.

"Lest you think to betray Us," said the Queen as the men checked their weapons for any obvious signs of tampering, "know that the girl will be killed if We do not give the order NOT to. Now, you have your weapons, the mog turei are on their way. General Klahb, take them to their gryphons."

"Yes, Your Majesty," said Klahb, bowing low to her. He then turned to the team and gestured for them to precede him out of the tent. "Let's be about it then, shall we, chaps?"

The team stepped out into the sunlight, still checking their weapons and stowing them on their persons. "General," Rider said, "I have to ask. You have a very particular accent and way of speaking. Where are you from?"

"Oh, right here, right here," said the General. "Well, not right here where we're standing, you understand, but here in this land. You see, my father died when I was very young, and the Queen and King raised me. This is how the King spoke, and now I speak this way to remind the Queen of her dearly departed husband."

"Didn't she have her husband executed?" Texas asked.

"Well, ah, yes," hemmed the General. "But I'm quite sure she felt simply terrible about it."

"Sure," Zombie said, "that sounds like her."

The General lead them to the gryphon pens, where Uncle saw ten gryphons saddled, and four of the Queen's soldiers already mounted up.

"What's this?" Uncle asked, pointing at one of the soldiers who waiting for them.

"That's a soldier," said the General.

Uncle sighed. "I mean, what is he – No wait. Why is he –. Hang on. Let me think." He plotted his next question in his mind, playing over all the obvious, literal answers, until he was satisfied he had one that couldn't be misinterpreted. "The plan involves only my team. These men are clearly waiting for us. Since the plan doesn't involve any of your men, what are these men here to do?"

"They are the gryphon handlers," said the General. "Gryphons, you see, are quite flighty creatures. It comes from having wings, don't you know. So these men will wait at the drop-off location and make sure that your gryphons don't fly away."

"That... actually makes sense," Parrot said.

"Color me surprised," Zombie said.

"Well, good luck, chaps," said the General. "I'll see you when you return." With that, he strolled off in the general direction of the Queen's tent, pausing now and again to greet a soldier as he passed.

"Do you think he has any idea that his men hate him?" Parrot asked. Vodka's expression said it all. "No, you're right," Parrot nodded. "No clue."

"So, uh, how do we ride these things?" Uncle asked, inspecting one of the gryphons.

"Just climb aboard," said the mounted soldier nearest him. "Feet in the stirrups, hands on the pommel grip. Tell me the course you want. I'll take lead, and the others will follow. They're all from the same flock, so they do that."

"Handy, that," Rider said. He walked to an open gryphon, patted it on the shoulder and climbed smoothly into the saddle.

"You know how to ride?" Zombie stared at Rider in surprise.

"I did steeplechase for a few years when I was a kid," Rider nodded. "It's like riding a bike."

"A half-ton bike with claws and a razor-sharp beak," Zombie said, licking his lip. He eyed the gryphon closest to him warily. While he debated the merits of just walking to the rendezvous point, the rest of the team mounted up.

"Come on," Parrot grinned. "We're waiting on you."

"No no," Rider shook his head, "You can't say that now because we really are waiting on him. You have to say it when you are the one holding us up."

"Oh, sorry," Parrot chuckled.

"Blow me," Zombie spat, but he did grab the pommel and swing himself, awkwardly, onto the saddle. No sooner did he have his feet in the stirrups than his gryphon bounded twice and launched itself into air. "FUUUCK !" Zombie yelled, his hands clutching in wild desperation at the saddle.

The ride wasn't so bad, Uncle decided, once you got used to it. It reminded him of hang-gliding, soaring off the cliffs of La Jolla or along the fjords of Norway. The differences were the lack of canvas above and behind him, the swooping up-and-down motion of the flight, and the feel of the tawny animal beneath him.

Oh, yes, and the fact that he totally and utterly lacked any form of control whatsoever.

The longer he thought about it, the more he concluded that, in fact, the ride really was 'that bad.' It was not something he was looking forward to repeating on the way back.

The view was impressive, however. The gryphons climbed to about three hundred feet or so, then made a long, lazy curve away from the camp. Grass- and wildflower-covered hills rolled by below, with the occasional little stream winding its way along the valleys between. Many of the streams fed into the larger river that the gryphons kept just in sight on the left.

Uncle spotted the enemy camp in the distance, and used his binoculars to get a better view. The camp sprawled out over the tops of three hills, commanding a clear view all around. He could see only a few tents, and those were spaced far apart. Several Metalmen worked at stacking large wooden crates, while a hundred or so more robots stood, motionless, near the center of each hilltop.

The central valley lay shrouded in fog despite the perpetual mid-evening sun.

The gryphons turned away from the enemy camp, then dropped down until they skimmed the terrain. Once out of sight of the enemy units, the flock banked into a gradual curve back towards the enemy location.

They landed with a bone-shuddering jolt in a small valley between a few low, lichen-encrusted hills. Uncle slid off his gryphon and almost collapsed. Concealing how much his legs wanted to shake required an act of will. The gryphons' body was far wider than that of a normal riding horse, and Uncle's thigh muscles ached in a way he hadn't experienced since SFQC.

His gryphon turned to look at him, the sharp beak inches from his face. He patted it on the shoulder, then stumbled away.

The leader of the Queen's soldiers smiled at him in sympathy. "We'll wait here for you, sir," said the man, a short fellow with a flat, wide nose and a blond Fu Manchu mustache that dangled a good eight inches below his jaw. "Good luck."

"Thanks," Uncle nodded. He surveyed the team, and had to hide a grin. To a man, every one of them was stretching his legs. "What's wrong?" Uncle smirked at his team. "Never rode a gryphon before?"

"I rode your mom before," Zombie retorted with a faint groan. He bent over and massaged his thighs with both hands, then stood and lifted each knee to his chest.

Uncle turned his back to hide his grin. It wouldn't do for his reputation to be seen smiling as he teased his men. He glanced at his watch. 4 hours and 51 minutes remaining. "Come on," he said. "Clock's ticking."

Vodka took point, staying in the valleys between the hills to avoid being silhouetted against the sky. After a thirty-foot interval, Texas followed, then Zombie, Parrot, and Rider. Uncle pulled up the rear.

The going was slow. Loose scree left the ground slippery and the footing treacherous. Despite this, each man had to watch his feet not just to avoid slipping while also to remaining as quiet as possible. Careful, deliberate steps were the order of the hour, at least until they reached the river, a process that took half an hour. Uncle rubbed sweat from his hand on the leg of his pants.

This was taking too long.

The river, easily eighty feet in width, filled the valley between tall hills. Uncle could not tell how deep it was, but judging by the ripples on the surface, he guessed it to be moving quite fast. Somewhere in there, in theory, the mog turei waited for the team.

Vodka held his hand flat, parallel to the ground, and lowered it. As one, the team crouched on their haunches. Uncle hurried forward, bent over at the waist to lower his profile.

At the edge of the river he stopped and let out a low, soft whistle. Nothing happened. He tossed a small pebble into the water. Nothing continued to happen. He looked over his shoulder at Vodka, who shrugged. "Damn it," Uncle muttered under his breath. It looked like the mog turei had betrayed them. Getting across the river was going to be a huge pain in the ass.

He turned to face the team.

Vodka's eyes widened and he pointed behind Uncle.

Uncle spun back around in time to see the water roiling in a half-dozen places. Shells broke the surface, followed by the heads and arms of the mog turei. Uncle's shoulders slumped in relief.

The feeling was, perhaps, premature.

The largest of the mog turei, a mammoth beast with dark green shell and pale green flesh, held out one long, clawed hand. "Why do you help the Queen, humans?" The voice was unexpected, a basso rumble with a wet, slurring quality to the 'H'es.

194

Uncle chewed on his lower lip for a moment. Should he tell the truth or not? Was Texas' assessment correct? And even if it were, did that mean that the mog turei were, or were not, fully under the Queen's control.

Too many unknowns.

He took a deep breath and decided to try the truth. "She has one of our people hostage," he said. "Otherwise, we would not. We want no part of this war, we just want to get our person and then leave."

"And never come back," Zombie murmured.

The mog turei fanned out, approaching the shore. They surveyed the team in silence while the largest one, the one Uncle assumed to be their leader, considered his words.

"We want the Queen to lose this war," said the monster into the nervous silence. "Then maybe she and her people will go away and leave us free."

"You don't serve the Queen willingly?" Uncle asked.

"No. She came here with her people many years ago. There was a great war. My people did not fight," said the mog turei. "We thought we could just wait under the water until the chaos was over. We thought that the ofyo taris would defeat the invaders or, if not, that it would matter little to us, living under the surface. We were naive."

"'Ofyo taris?'" Uncle scratched his chin. "You mean the Long Men? Centipede bodies with humanoid heads?"

"'Long Men'. Yes. That is what the Queen's people call them," said the mog turei leader. He, for the voice made Uncle assume the creature was male, scratched his head with one long, wicked claw. "She slew all of them but the son of their leader, whom she allowed to live in disgrace. We, she discovered after the main battle was over. Using her foul magic, she found our hatching grounds and stole all of our eggs. We serve her lest she crush them and destroy our species."

"Why not just lay new eggs somewhere else?" Texas asked.

The massive green head swung towards him. "We cannot," said the creature. "Each of our females is given but only two eggs, which she will lay at the same time. If the Queen will not return our eggs to us, this will be the last generation of the mog turei people."

"You want Ironhand to win, in hopes that he will be kinder to your people than the Queen is." Sympathy infused Uncle's voice.

"Yes," said the leader.

"Yes," said all of the other mog turei. It is hard to judge emotion on a big pig-like monster face, but it was clear in their voices. The mog turei were desperate.

Uncle wondered how many of them were left, and how long they lived under normal circumstances.

"We don't know for sure that he will be any more friendly to you than she is," Uncle looked up into the leader's eyes. "But if we slow him down, if we do this task for the Queen, the war will drag on. That is a good thing for you. This General Klahb fellow is far too stupid to realize what a valuable battle force you are, so you are mostly safe from the war. Meanwhile, the longer the fighting drags on, the weaker the Queen's forces become. If this situation lasts long enough, win or lose, she may be weak enough when it is over for you to rebel."

"We cannot risk that," said the mog turei leader. "She might destroy our eggs at any moment if she feels week. She is temperamental. Or, she might order Klahb to use us to fight. Our shells would provide some protection from the claws of the Metalmen, but they would still kill us in numbers. Even now, our people teeter on the brink of annihilation; we cannot spare any to die fighting a foe whom we do not hate."

196

Uncle considered the problem in silence. He felt for the mog turei who, despite appearances, seemed more 'human' than many of the more normal looking inhabitants of this world. He had a job to do, however, and his sympathy needed to take second-place to his duty.

Vodka came to his rescue. "The Queen's focused all her attention here, right?" he asked. Without waiting for a response, he went on, "I mean, we've seen deserters and refugees from the war all over the place. So most, if not all, of her forces and attention are here. Your people can hide under the water, which means you can leave undetected. Leave some of your people here to continue running errands for the Queen. Meanwhile, send some of your people away, up or down river until you're a goodly ways away. Then have them come out and look for your eggs. If she really has them somewhere, you can try to find them. If you find them, spirit them off to safety somewhere she won't think to look. Then, have all your people sneak off and leave her without river transport, or join Ironhand's men, or rise up in rebellion yourselves, or whatever. Live your lives. But you need to keep the Queen's attention here, now, which means we need to accomplish our mission for now."

Uncle raised an eyebrow. That was the longest speech he had heard Vodka give in weeks. He turned again to face the leader of the mog turei. "That is a good idea. And I'll throw in something else. It is possible, based on his actions so far, that the Lon — that the ofyo taris would be willing to help you."

"Ofyo tari," said a different mog turei. "The singular is 'tari.'"

"Oh, thanks," Uncle inclined his head in respect to the speaker. He looked up at the leader again. "What say you? Will you help us?"

The leader let out a sigh like the working of an industrial bellows. "Yes," said he. "We will help you." He swung ponderously away and slipped back into the river. One by one, the others also sank beneath the water.

"Uh," Zombie said, "I'm confused. Where are they going? Didn't he just say 'yes'?"

The river grew rough and choppy as the creatures rose again. The mog turei were laying flat, creating a concourse of shell, edges almost touching. Uncle's shoulders relaxed. He hadn't even realized they had tensed. He waved Vodka across.

So close were the shells to each other that Uncle barely wet his boots when he crossed last. On the other side, he leaned over and patted the shell closest to the shore twice.

"I don't think they're trucks, boss," Rider drawled.

Uncle felt his cheeks warm as he blushed. "Shush, you," Uncle said. He looked at his watch again. "We have just over four hours, and only just a few minutes until the distraction is supposed to start," he said. "We need to do this, and do it fast. Roll out."

Vodka pivoted on his foot. Crouching, he walked swiftly and silently towards the enemy camp. The rest followed him like a string of pearls. Lethal, camouflaged pearls.

Uncle checked the sun, then shook his head in annoyance. Of course it hadn't moved. Tide locked worlds, he decided, suck for commando work. He'd have loved to have done this mission under cover of dark, but the sun stubbornly refused to drop below the horizon. The hills cast deep shadows, but that would be for naught once they climbed to the tops.

They weren't quite in place when, from a great distance, came the sounds of yells and the ringing of brass on copper. On the other side of the camp, the battle was joined.

Vodka didn't need to be told. He picked up even more speed, running in a bent-over posture. He tracked his weapon back and forth across the hill top nearest him. Zombie did the same for the

198

hill on the other side of them. They rounded an outcropping of rock, and Zombie skidded to a stop, his hand up in a fist, then held flat and lowered towards the ground. Texas, Parrot, and Rider crouched and held position. Uncle slowed, then passed them to see what had caused the halt.

Looking past Zombie, Uncle saw the area in front of them was filled with fog. It roiled and swirled, but otherwise held its shape, as if contained by an invisible bubble. Curious, he tossed a pebble in, but the pebble just vanished like expected instead of bouncing off any sort of force-field. Uncle shrugged.

That would have been pretty cool.

Uncle met Vodka's eyes, and pointed at the top of the hill to their left. If General Klahb's maps were right (and what were the odds, really?) then the supply cache would be on that hill top.

Vodka gave a sharp nod. He worked his way up the side of the hill, keeping low. As he neared the top, Vodka slung his M4 behind him and dropped to his belly. He covered the last dozen feet at a crawl. He surveyed the situation, then rolled onto his back and gave Uncle a thumbs-up gesture.

The rest of the team ascended the hill. While not overly tall, the side they climbed sloped at roughly sixty degree. Each man panted for breath before he reached the top.

Vodka's scouting was solid. There were no troops visible from where Uncle squatted. Ahead and on his right, stacks of wooden crates formed a wall a good nine feet tall. To the left, he saw a bit of a tent partially occluded by a tall boulder and beyond that, a slice of sky. The sound of battle came from ahead and a little ways to the left.

Uncle gestured with the blade of his hand towards the boxes. Texas and Zombie took up positions at the edge of the wall, using the crates for cover. Parrot and Rider held position at the edge of the hill, Parrot facing back the way they came lest unexpected enemy forces surprise them from behind. Uncle and Vodka scuttled to the wall, using the bulk of the crates to shield them from sight of the rest of the hill.

Vodka squeezed a brick of C4 in between two boxes at about chest height, then reached in to insert the detonator. He moved forward four columns and repeated the procedure. Uncle handed him another brick, and in this manner they continued.

Vodka placed a total of six bricks which would account for roughly seventy-five percent destruction of the supplies, unless they were incredibly dense. Given that none of the boxes were crushing under their own weight, Uncle assumed that this was not the case.

Uncle turned to go, but Vodka put a hand on his shoulder to stop him. Vodka held up his combat knife. He pointed at the crate nearest him, then waggled the knife. He raised an eyebrow. He wanted to see what all the fuss was about.

Uncle glanced at his watch again, then nodded. They had a few minutes. He held his finger to his lips.

Vodka slipped the blade of his knife into the seam of one of the crates and twisted, widening the gap a half an inch. He repeated the technique a few inches higher, then again, and still again, until he had pried open the back of the crate. Then, he did the same thing on the bottom. With Uncle pulling the loose corner away from the body of the crate, Vodka wormed his knife hand inside. He made a short, sharp motion with his arm.

Grain hissed as it spilled out.

Vodka pulled his hand out of the crate, then put his knife away. He caught some of the grain in the palm of his hand. He held it out to Uncle but Uncle didn't recognize it either. They both shrugged at each other. Vodka slipped the handful into his pocket.

Between the mushrooms and the grain, Uncle thought, the man was going to be bringing an all-you-can-eat buffet back to the boys at INSCOM.

The two men hurried back to the rest of the team. Uncle checked his watch. He held up three fingers, then four, then held his hand in a round '0'.

Vodka started towards the edge of the hill when a hiss from Rider caught his attention. Vodka froze and turned.

Four Metalmen walked along the 'inner' wall of crates, heading right for the team. Long, wicked-looking blades protruded from the grippers that passed as hands on the robots. They walked jerkily, but swiftly.

Uncle judged them maybe twenty or so feet away. He assumed they had come from around the boulder he had spotted earlier, or Rider would have seen them sooner. There was no way the Metalmen hadn't seen Vodka and Texas standing out there in the open.

Weapons were raised, fingers found triggers.

"Wait," Zombie said.

Uncle froze. His heart hammered in his chest. The robots were ten feet away. Nine. Eight. Any second, they would be in sword range. He looked at Zombie. "What?"

"Look at them," Zombie said. "Weapons are down. I'm not sure they—"

The Metalmen came to a halt right in front of Vodka and Texas. No one moved. The tension ate at Uncle as the seconds stretched to the snapping point.

Vodka cocked his head. When the Metalmen didn't respond, he lowered his weapon. Still no response. Vodka stepped aside a few paces.

Two of the Metalmen lurched into motion, walking through the space Vodka had created when he moved. Texas moved aside. The other two followed their companions. They rounded the 'edge' of the crate wall and walked along the 'back' side, where Uncle and Vodka had been just moments before.

"Jesus!" Rider's breath left him all at once in a blasphemous sigh.

"So," Parrot drawled, "That happened."

"They clearly saw us," Texas watched the retreating copper backs. The Metalmen showed no interest in turning around and running back towards the team.

"Worry about it later," Zombie snapped. "Like, back at Bragg."

"Right," Uncle shook his head, re-focusing on the task. "Let's roll."

Vodka half walked, half slid down the hill. The others followed him.

The mog turei rose up to form the shell bridge as the team approached the river. No enemy patrols stumbled across them as they made their way back to the landing zone. The exfiltration was proceeding smoothly at first.

Uncle later thought that this should have been his first clue.

Vodka stopped, followed shortly by Zombie.

"Are you fucking kidding me?" Zombie snarled. "Mother fucker!"

Uncle double-timed it to the front of the line to see what the problem was.

That turned out to be unduly optimistic. There wasn't a problem.

There were two.

The first was that the soldiers left behind to watch the gryphons were dead. The four corpses lay sprawled on the trampled grass, half submerged in dirt churned to mud by their life blood. They all sported defensive wounds; they hadn't gone down without a fight. Their swords were missing.

The second problem was the gryphons. Or more specifically, the lack of same. In the absence of soldiers to make them behave, the beasts had simply flown away. Other than a single long eagle feather, Uncle saw no sign whatsoever of their air transport.

"God damn it," Uncle kicked a tuft of grass. "Can nothing go right on this mission?"

"Those Metalmen didn't attack us," Rider pointed out. "I consider that a 'win.'"

Uncle ground his teeth. He sucked in a deep breath and then let it out in a long, aggravated sigh. "All right. Clock's ticking. No time to sit around feeling sorry for ourselves. We need to hump it back out of here." He checked his watch again. "Three hours and twenty-five minutes. We can do this."

"So much for blowing the C4 once we're in the air," Parrot said. "What now?"

Uncle patted his pocket. Inside, the remote detonator waited to bring ruin to Ironhand's food crates. "I'll just save this for when we need a diversion," Uncle said. He jerked his chin at Vodka. "Let's roll."

Vodka set a brisk walking pace. Every few minutes, he would shift into a jog, then drop back to a walk for twice the length of the run. Speed was essential, but none of the team were exactly sure how far from the Queen's camp they were. Exhausting themselves too soon would delay them even more. The pace Vodka set was a good one for covering large distances as swiftly as possible.

They circled wide around the enemy camp, then turned towards the Queen's forces.

What the stationary sun lacked in terms of concealing darkness, it made up for when it came to navigating. Like a big, giant North Star, Uncle thought.

Somewhere around forty minutes after discovering the dead escort, they ran, almost literally, into a troop of Metalmen. Unlike the one at the camp, this patrol had a human with it.

The man seemed short next to the robots, but in reality he nearly matched Texas' height: a breath over six feet. He wore his mousy brown hair pulled back in a ponytail. He bore several scars on his face, one of which curled his lips into a perpetual sneer. He wore a white poet's blouse, stained with dirt and sweat. His trousers were blue, faded and much patched. His leather shoes were cracked and stained by weather and long service. One sole flopped as he walked.

Vodka skidded to a halt as he saw the man. There was just a moment of confusion; did he attack? The non-violence of the Metalmen back at the enemy camp cast doubt on the ill intentions of the invaders, at least vis-a-vis the team.

The other man made the decision easy. "Kill them!"

The Metalmen raised blades and began swinging them back and forth. They advanced.

"Crap," Vodka threw himself to the side as a copper blade sliced through the air. The blade just missed him, and Vodka rolled several times.

The rest of the team fanned out swiftly, creating an arc.

Uncle raised his M4 and fired a burst into the Metalman closest to him. The robot jerked under the impact as the bullets tore through it. It did not, however, stop.

Beside him, Uncle heard the others firing also. Rider, ever the diva, placed a single shot from his fifty-cal directly in the center of a metal head. This, also, failed to slow the enemy.

Then Overbite spoke. Zombie placed a dozen or so rounds into the chest of one of the robots, then walked his fire down to the thing's right leg. The strut connecting the leg to the body disintegrated. The robot's arms pinwheeled almost comically. The weight of the Metalman's big, round body pulled it sideways, and it fell.

"Aim for the legs!" Zombie yelled.

Vodka scrambled to his feet and leapt backwards, again narrowly avoiding a sweeping blade. He took a slightly different tactic, and put two quick bursts into the arm strut. While it didn't shred quite as spectacularly as Zombie's autofire had done, it did the job. The arm dangled, held on only by a thin wire of copper. The robot could not raise the blade on that side.

It began to turn laboriously in order to get at Vodka with the other arm, but Vodka wanted none of that. He put three bursts into a leg.

The robot joined its comrade on the ground.

The rest of the team, except for Rider, followed Zombie's advice. They backed up, firing at legs until, one by one, the robots fell.

Even then, they weren't entirely out of the fight. Several of them attempted to pull themselves forward with their arms, or push themselves with their one working leg. Not an effective means of transportation, that, and the team had plenty of time to shoot out arms.

The human leader, seeing his platoon incapacitated in a matter of minutes, opted for that better part of valor.

It didn't save him.

A single shot rang out, and the running man's head exploded in a spray of gray and crimson gore.

Rider lowered his rifle, a satisfied smirk twisting his lips. "Delivery complete," he said.

"No time for gloating," Uncle tapped his watch meaningfully. "We still have to get back to the Queen before she kills the girl. Let's move, gentlemen!"

Everyone changed magazines first, then Vodka broke into a jog.

Run and walk, run and walk. The monotony of endless valleys and gulleys wore on Uncle after a time. He wondered if they were still going in the right direction.

"Hold," he called. The team stopped on command, all of them bending forward at the hip and panting. Once he had enough breath to talk, Uncle said, "Let's see where we are."

Vodka nodded. He found the nearest, gentlest rise to a hill, and scrambled up. The rest of the team followed. From the top, they had a decent view of the surrounding terrain. Over their left shoulder, the three hills of the enemy camp lay a ways behind them, but not quite as far as Uncle would have guessed. Having to follow the valleys made going in a straight line impossible.

Ahead and to the left, battles raged on several hilltops. Probably in the valleys between also, Uncle thought. Beyond that, and slightly to their right, lay the long valley where the Queen's forces bivouacked. Uncle saw the river sparkling just beyond the camp. He judged the distance at perhaps ninety minutes to two hours away. He looked at his watch.

Two hours and twelve minutes.

"Contact!" Zombie yelled.

Uncle spun, raising his weapon to his shoulder. There, on top of the next hill over, stood a figure all in red armor. He looked like those knights one sees in museums, plate armor covering every inch, with the visor of the helmet pulled down. Some sort of symbol or device was etched into the breastplate, but Uncle could not make it out at that distance.

As Uncle drew aim on the armored man, the knight took a step backwards and vanished. Literally vanished. There was a slight shimmer in the air and then the man was simply gone.

"Oh for fuck's sake," Zombie grumbled. "This is just getting ridiculous."

"I didn't see a pocket-watch," Rider said.

"However he did it, he's gone now." Uncle stood. He motioned towards the Queen's camp. "Two hours, gentlemen. Haul ass."

They jogged for another twenty minutes, crossing between hills and splashing over little creeks. Vodka slowed, one hand to tapping his ear.

Battle, somewhere just ahead. Uncle nodded at the point man. They moved cautiously but deliberately. The sounds grew closer.

Around an outcropping of stone, the skirmish raged. A group of the Queen's men, surrounded by Metalmen. Two of the little men were down already, and not one of the other seven remained uninjured. The Metalmen sported gashes in their copper bodies here and there, but they were all operational. In another few moments, Uncle knew, the robots would finish off this group of the Queen's men. As he watched, a Metalman poked a blade at one of the soldiers. The soldier parried, but received a small nick on his upper arm for his efforts.

Uncle didn't see a human controller.

"Take down the robots," Uncle ordered.

Bullets tore through brightly polished copper, shredded gears and pulleys, tore apart struts. Two of the Metalmen managed to turn to face the team before they were reduced to so much scrap. The rest didn't even get that far.

The Queen's men watched with wide eyes, cowering in a defensive circle. When the last of the Metalmen had fallen, the soldiers turned frightened eyes to Uncle and his men.

"Please, don't kill us," begged one soldier, a short, fat man with a huge pug nose, shoulder-length brown hair, and mutton-chop whiskers.

"We're not going to hurt you," Uncle replaced his magazine. He had two spares left. "We're on a mission from your Queen, and we need you to lead us back to camp. These damned hills are confusing."

"Uh," said the soldier. "I uh... well, I mean... okay." He tugged at the neckline of his uniform tabard. "If you insist, I mean. I guess we can do that. We're supposed to be scouting but this takes priority, right?"

"Right," Uncle nodded firmly. The soldiers wanted to return to the (relative) safety of the camp, and Uncle wanted guides. The arrangement was mutually beneficial. "Lead on. Oh, and we're in a hurry, so don't dawdle."

"Why did we save these guys?" Zombie asked as he followed the departing Queen's men.

"It never hurts to generate a little good will," Uncle said. "Besides, they're people, not robots. Whichever side we feel sympathy towards, robots can be rebuilt. People are less recyclable."

Zombie's lips curled in a sneer that spoke volumes of his opinion about that.

The soldiers were good for one thing; they knew the shortest route back to the Queen's camp. Twenty-five minutes after meeting them, the team emerged into the wide river valley. The pickets and ramshackle defenses that marked the outer edge of the camp stood less than a quarter mile away across the flat mud.

They were going to make it in time.

I really need to stop thinking things like that, Uncle scolded himself a moment later.

A black cat the size of a horse appeared right in front of them. The Queen's scouts scattered, throwing themselves to the ground in terror. Vodka and Zombie pulled up short.

"No trees to hide behind," said the Cat in a malicious purr. "No-where for you to run. What ever will you do now, little mice?" It bared its long, sharp teeth at them in a sinister grin.

"It talks?" Texas cocked his head.

"I'm getting so tired of things appearing and vanishing so suddenly," Zombie snarled. "It gives me a headache."

"We don't have time for this," Uncle told the Cat. "We have no quarrel with you. Just go away, and we won't have to kill you."

"Kill me?" the Cat lowered its shoulders as it laughed. Its tail lashed back and forth. It grinned wider. "If you could do that, you'd have done so when first we met. No, it is I who shall kill you. But first; you're human. Why do you bow before the Queen?"

"You're a local," Texas said. It was a guess, but Uncle let him run with it. The new guy was demonstrating a pretty good track record so far. "Why do you serve the Queen who invaded and took over your land?"

The Cat swiveled its head to look at Texas. A little of the tension went out of the back and leg. A brief reprieve while it cleared up some misunderstandings.

"I do not serve the Queen," said the Cat. "I serve the Duchess. She serves the Queen currently, but not always." It licked its chops, then scratched its muzzle with a hind leg. "She found me when I was but a kitten, and raised me. She gives me pigs to eat, and allows me to devour the occasional trespasser. What is your excuse?"

"The Queen captured one of our people," Uncle wiped his right hand on the hip of his pants, then returned the hand to the grip of his M4. "A civilian, a little girl. The Queen made us do this one mission in exchange for the girl. We get the girl, we leave. It's that simple."

The Cat swung its great head back towards Uncle. It stared at him without blinking for a moment. "I understand," said the creature. "I can even respect that. To rescue a kitten is a noble deed." It dropped, swiftly and suddenly, back into a crouch. "Unfortunately for you, I never fail a hunt!" it roared as it sprang.

The damned thing was fast, Uncle had to give it that. Even though every one of his men had been expecting this outcome, the Cat still managed to bowl Zombie over and rake Uncle's thigh with its claws.

The rest of the team fanned out. Vodka took a shot, putting three rounds into the monstrosity's side. The Cat hissed in pain. It curled around, one claw tearing open Zombie's left bicep almost in afterthought. Texas and Vodka both drew aim and fired.

The bullets smacked into the dirt, tossing up mud. The Cat had vanished, only to re-appear behind Parrot. It lashed out with one heavy paw, hitting the medic in the back.

Parrot's scream almost drowned out the sound of bones snapping. He collapsed in a heap.

The cat charged forward, trampling Parrot in the process and ripping open several long, deep gashes.

Rider fired. A heavy fifty-cal round ripped across the Cat's cheek, taking a several whiskers and a piece of its ear. The Cat screamed and vanished.

"Wounded down!" Vodka yelled. "Texas, Rider, back to back with me! Shoot anything that moves!"

Uncle saw the wisdom of this. The Cat was far larger than a man lying down in the mud; the trio would be able to shoot without risk of hitting their own people. He threw himself down on his back. He kept his M4 free, in case the Cat appeared right in front of him.

It appeared right in front of Texas. Texas didn't hesitate. He fired point-blank into the Cat's shoulder even as the creature slammed into him. The impact knocked Rider sideways. The Cat screamed in pain again and vanished.

Rider and Texas resumed their positions. The trio knelt down on one leg, making a smaller target for the Cat.

It reappeared above Zombie, one claw raised to disembowel the man. Zombie pushed Overbite up, tangling the Cat's paw. He yelled, "Contact!"

Vodka and Rider both fired. A trio of rounds smashed into the Cat's ribs, while the single, larger ball from the sniper rifle impacted the side of the Cat's neck. Blood sprayed.

The Cat vanished, taking Overbite with it.

"Contact left," Texas yelled.

The Cat stood a dozen paces away, shaking its paw and trying to dislodge Zombie's weapon. The strap was caught on one of the wickedly curved claws.

All three uninjured men took advantage of the distraction.

Shots slammed into the Cat's legs, its chest, its head. Uncle rolled to his knees and added his own fire, walking a series of bursts from the hindquarters to the front shoulder.

The Cat screamed again. It tried to turn and run, but its left foreleg was too badly injured and would not support the monster's considerable weight. It stumbled.

Rider put one into the side of the Cat's head, behind the right eye and below the ear. The Cat jerked, staggered forward one step, then collapsed. Vodka walked forward, firing burst after burst into the Cat's head until his magazine was empty.

Uncle forced himself to his feet and limped/ran to where Parrot lay whimpering.

"You," Rider pointed at the leader of the Queen's men. "Run, and I mean but fast, to camp and fetch a stretcher. NOW!"

The man jumped to his feet and ran.

Texas and Rider joined Uncle. Parrot was holding his guts in with his hands, both of which were soaked in blood. The claws had torn him open across the belly from side to side. There is a word for this type of injury: evisceration. An ugly word for an ugly wound.

Working together, Uncle, Rider, and Texas managed to get a bandage around Parrot's abdomen. It would hold his intestines in, for a while, but Parrot was losing blood fast. The Medic kept trying to sit up, to see what was happening to him. Texas had to hold him down.

"I can't feel my legs," Parrot said.

"Where's that Goddamn stretcher?" Uncle yelled.

Rider wiped sweat from his eyes and smeared blood across his forehead. "It's coming," he said, soft and low.

Uncle knew that tone of voice. Doctors use it when they caution you not to get your hopes up.

"Stay with me, Parrot," Uncle urged. He noticed that his vision was blurring for some reason. He wiped his eyes on the sleeve of his jacket. That cleared up the blur for a couple dozen seconds.

Vodka and Zombie stood watch while the rest of the team dealt with Parrot. Zombie's arm dripped blood, but his grip on Overbite was secure. Uncle noticed that Zombie had recovered his beloved machine gun from the wreckage of the Cat at some point.

"Your leg," Rider murmured, pointing at Uncle's thigh. Uncle looked down and blinked in surprise. He'd forgotten about his own injury.

"It's nothing," he said.

"Yeah, all the same," Texas began bandaging Uncle's leg. "We've already got one macho man over there pretending he's not leaking."

"Be different," Rider said. "You're gonna get a Purple Durple for it anyways, you may as well recognize that it's there now."

He was trying to lighten the moment, Uncle knew, but the ribbing still annoyed. Parrot was, at the very least, paralyzed, and this asshole is cracking jokes? No wonder he never gets promoted, Uncle thought.

"Incoming," Vodka was looking towards the Queen's camp.

Uncle followed his gaze. A group of the Queen's soldiers, a dozen or so, were running towards them. Uncle noticed that two of them carried between them a stretcher.

Uncle looked down at Parrot. "You just hang in there, amigo. Help's on the way."

"I've seen... their version... of help," Parrot wheezed. "Might... be better off... alone."

The soldiers laid the stretcher down. Uncle, Rider, Texas, and one of the Queen's men lifted Parrot onto it. They hustled towards the camp, moving as fast as they dared. Uncle glanced back once at the dead Cat.

On a hill top in the distance, a figure all in red armor watched them. Uncle gave him a one-fingered salute, then turned and limped as fast as he could to camp.

213

CHAPTER XI
WHO STOLE THE QUEEN?

———◆◆◆———

Were we expecting it? Of course we were, sir. The Queen had all but told us that she planned to double-cross us. But we kept hoping that maybe, somehow, it wouldn't happen.

When we realized just how badly we were screwed, all I could think of was to get away from all those soldiers, and sort it out later. I knew there had to be another way home. We just had to find it.

It turned out to be far easier than I expected, all things considered.

> -CSM Daniel "Uncle" Beckworth, official de-brief, Operation Rabbit Hole

T HE CAMP WAS PRACTICALLY deserted. Only a skeleton force remained. No more than one hundred soldiers had been left behind, many of them injured. On the picket at the front of the camp, a half-dozen giant lizards napped in the sun. Uncle eyed them warily, but the lizards paid him and his team no attention.

The Queen, General Klahb, the Duchess, Rabbix, and a score of courtiers waited at the edge of camp for the team's return. The Queen sat on her throne, which rested atop a sedan chair. Ten soldiers sweated and grunted, faces red, as they held the chair aloft. The rest of her court stood in the mud like commoners.

Rabbix held the great hourglass rigidly in front of him. Uncle could see sweat pouring down Rabbix's face, and the man's arms trembled with the strain. A small amount of sand still remained in the top. Uncle glanced at his watch. Thirty-seven minutes.

"Why have you returned?" screeched the Queen. Her face, also, was red, although not, Uncle suspected, from physical exertion. "The enemy's supplies remain unburned. Our men die to provide you with a distraction, and for what? You accomplished nothing! Bring the girl and—"

Uncle held up his remote detonator. "The supplies are taken care of," he said through gritted teeth. "My man needs medical attention. Now!"

"He shall get it," said the Queen, "after you have finished the task We assigned you!"

"Not your normal shitty medical help either," Uncle continued as if the Queen had not spoken. "We have seen magic healing done here. I'm sure you save that for yourself and other 'important' people, not the common soldiers. But you will give it to him."

"What you speak of is rare, and valuable," said the Queen. "Why should We—"

Uncle pushed the button.

In the enemy camp, six bricks of C4 exploded simultaneously. The roar could be heard all the way across the hills and the battlefield. A row of fireballs bloomed on a distant hilltop. Black smoke curled and danced in the air above the destruction of Ironhand's grain supply.

The locals gasped and cringed back. Klahb gazed at Uncle in fear, warily eying the detonator. The soldiers holding up the Queen very nearly broke ranks, and her sedan chair dipped precariously.

The sounds of battle faded as human lieutenants ordered Metalmen back to camp to investigate and protect against any further threat to their supply line. The Queen's soldiers in the field let out a ragged cheer. Legs dragging and arms limp with exhaustion, the soldiers began looking for injured survivors among the bodies.

Uncle never took his eyes off the Queen during all this. "Healing for my man," he said. "Now."

The Queen shook her head to banish the shock. "Yes, yes of course," said the Queen, looking at Klahb. "Take the human to Our physicker. Go." She waved her hand dismissively.

Klahb pointed at two of his soldiers. "Bring him," said the General. They hurried off.

"We will hear your report now," said the Queen. "Yours too," she pointed at the leader of the group Uncle and his men had rescued.

"We flew to the LZ, sneaked in, did our thing, sneaked out," Uncle said. "When we came out, the soldiers guarding the gryphons were dead, and the gryphons gone."

"Yes," nodded the one of the Queen's courtiers, a large-head with a long, droopy nose, clad all in red and gold, "They returned to their pen hours ago. We assumed you had either died, or betrayed us."

"We did neither," Uncle's reply was short, clipped. There was more he wanted to say; so much more, but the Queen still had Fiona hostage. He bit his tongue, took a deep breath, then let it out in a long, soft hiss. "We circled around the enemy forces, trying to make our way back. That's when we ran into your scouting party here."

"We were surrounded," said the leader of that squad. "Metalmen killed two of my men, and would have killed the rest of us if these people hadn't arrived. It was amazing, Your Majesty. They pointed their staves at the Metalmen, and with a sound louder than thunder, the Metalmen began to fall apart. Then this one," he gestured at Uncle, "said they were working for you, and we needed to bring them back to camp right away. So we did."

The Queen's eyes bored into the soldier until the later began to squirm. "We do not know you," said the Queen. "You were not present at Our privy council earlier. Correct?"

"Quite correct, Your Majesty," said the soldier with a low bow. "I am but a humble—"

"TRAITOR!" screamed the Queen. "You did not know that these humans worked for Us! You simply took their word for it? They could have been assassins, come to kill Us!"

Klahb returned during this tirade, just in time to see the Queen point at the soldier and scream, "Off with his head!"

Klahb's lips thinned as he tried to hold back a sigh. "Of course, Your Majesty," said the General. He turned to the soldier and held out his hand. "Come along, old chap. Best to just be done with it swiftly. Dragging it out won't help."

Out of the corner of his eye, Uncle saw Zombie take Vodka's shoulder in a vice-like grip. "Stand down," Zombie whispered.

Vodka tried to shrug off the hand, but Zombie's hold was too strong.

"Stand down," Zombie repeated.

Vodka swallowed hard, his face flushed with anger. He followed orders.

Uncle's shoulders sagged in relief.

The soldier's face was pale, stricken, as he glanced back once over his shoulder. Uncle's fist clenched at his side, but all he could do was mouth, 'sorry,' to the man as the General lead the unfortunate fellow to his death.

Once the doomed soldier was out of sight, Uncle returned his gaze to the Queen's face. His eyes were cold as ice. His voice was flat, monotonous as he said, "We've completed our side of the bargain. Give us the girl."

"Oh, We think not," said the Queen with a malicious smirk. "We're only just beginning to find uses for you."

"We completed our side of the bargain," Uncle repeated. Behind him, he heard the click of Zombie thumbing off the safety on his machine gun. "We're going home now."

"No, you are not," said the Queen. "You shall work for Us for one year and one day. Payment for the food you stole. You really should have known better than to steal from Us!"

"We stole nothing," Uncle said. "That food was freely offered by General Klahb."

The Queen's laugh was brittle crystal and the howl of wolves baying at the full moon. "No," said she, "We mean the food you stole from Our palace. Oh yes, Jack told Us about that. He probably thought nothing of it, for he is Our son. But you: you are humans, outsiders. And the punishment for eating Our food is one year and one day of service." She clapped her hands together and rubbed them. "With your weapons, We shall drive this vermin, Ironhand, back to whatever cesspool birthed him in about half of no time at all!"

"Fuck this," Uncle said in the same cool, flat voice.

Zombie lifted Overbite and covered the soldiers not burdened with the Queen's sedan chair. Texas covered the courtiers and Rabbix. Rider, carrying Parrot's M4, turned to watch their six. Vodka sprinted forward, slamming bodily into the soldiers carrying the palanquin. The first two fell, and the weight of the heavy throne and the Queen atop it destabilized the entire group. The chair fell.

The Queen tumbled to the ground, rolling to her feet in an instant. "Off with–" she began to cry, but Vodka cut her off.

Coming in from behind, Vodka wrapped one arm around the Queen's throat. His other hand pushed forward against the back of her head. The Queen gurgled as the iron bar of Vodka's arm cut off her air.

Uncle walked towards her, drawing his sidearm. The Queen made an arcane gesture with her hand.

Take a thunder clap, then remove the sound and leave only the impact and the silence that comes after. That was the closest Uncle could come to explaining the results of that gesture.

Vodka flew backwards, landing on his back a good ten or twelve feet from the Queen.

Uncle darted forward. He unleashed a sharp kick to the Queen's side, catching her just under the armpit. It was like kicking a tree, but the Queen staggered off balance. Uncle shoved her, hard, and she went over. Without waiting to see how she dealt with being knocked on her ass, he fell to his knees on top of her and pressed the barrel of his M1911 to her forehead. "If you so much as—"

The Queen let out an ear-shattering scream, equal parts the pain of the damned in hell, and the terror of one who sees the reaper coming for him. The scream went on for a second that felt like eternity, or vice versa. Then, abruptly, it cut off.

The Queen was unconscious. A wisp of smoke curled up from her forehead.

"What the heck?" Uncle pulled his sidearm back just a little. On the Queen's head, an angry red burn the exact size and shape of the opening of his M1911's barrel sizzled. Little crooked black lines radiated away from the main burn, as if someone had introduced black dye into her capillaries.

"Vodka, you okay?" Uncle yelled.

Vodka sat up, cradling his left arm against his side. "Yeah," he said. "Broken arm, I think, but I'll be okay." He stood with a groan. "What hit me?"

"Magic," Texas hazarded.

"Fair enough," Vodka slung his M4 behind him and drew his sidearm. The carbine wasn't something anyone wanted to try firing with only one arm. If he accidentally killed one of his own people, Zombie would never let him live it down.

"Ah ah!" Zombie said. Uncle looked over his shoulder. Klahb had returned and was staring at them in shock. "Why don't you join us, General?" Zombie offered. "Over there with the rest of your men."

"No," Uncle stood, still covering the Queen with his sidearm, in case she was faking it somehow. "Rider, come carry this bitch. Klahb, you're coming with us."

"Whuh, wuh, uh, where are we going?" asked the General.

"You're taking us to Parrot," Uncle stepped aside as Rider came to collect the Queen.

"Oof, she's heavy," Rider grunted as he slung her over his shoulders.

"Who?" asked the General.

"Our man!" Uncle snapped. "The one you just took to be looked at!"

"Uh, okay," said Klahb. "Th.. this way,"

"I notice that your accent goes away when you're about to piss yourself in fear," Zombie commented. "You might want to watch that."

Klahb lead, with Uncle covering him. Next came Rider, then Vodka. Texas and Zombie pulled up the rear, covering the rest of the soldiers.

If Uncle had to be honest, none of the Queen's men looked particularly eager to rush to her rescue. Some of them even looked relieved. All the same, Uncle wasn't taking any more chances.

Their destination turned out to be the Queen's tent. Klahb took the team into a part they'd never seen before. There, they found a tiny old man with a huge head and a fringe of wispy blond hair standing beside a low table.

On the table was Parrot's body.

Uncle kicked the backs of General Klahb's knees and forced him to kneel. "What the hell happened?" Uncle demanded, turning his sidearm on the small man that, he assumed, was the Queen's physician.

"I... I'm sorry!" said the man, crossing his arms in front of his head and turning his face away. "He lost too much blood! I gave him a potion, but rather than going into a healing trance he just... slipped away. I'm sorry! I tried! Please don't cut off my head!"

The world spun. Uncle grabbed the edge of the table to keep from falling over. The doctor wasn't making any sense. Of course Parrot wasn't really dead. That was absurd, like saying that the sun wouldn't rise tomorrow.

Of course, the sun wouldn't rise tomorrow, not on this back-assswards fucked-up shit-hole of a world.

"G—" Uncle shook his head and cleared his throat. Parrot wasn't just any other soldier. He was a friend, a pal, someone Uncle could always count on to be there, calming and diffusing tense situations. His wife invited Uncle and his girlfriend over for tamales every few weekends.

He couldn't be gone.

But he was.

Uncle wanted to melt down, to go on a killing spree, or perhaps just curl up under the table and cry. He wanted to scream and hurl cruel words at the God that he didn't even believe in, but that Parrot had. He wanted make someone else hurt as terribly as he hurt, and to ignore everything else until this happened.

But he had a team. Other men who relied on him to lead them.

And there was the girl. Uncle remembered Parrot kneeling before her, trying to reassure the terrified child, stroking her arm soothingly. Parrot would never forgive Uncle if he didn't get the girl back home.

He cleared his throat again. "Gather his gear," he ordered. Texas and Zombie did so.

Uncle turned to Klahb. "Get the girl. If you try to mount a rescue, you'll be the second one to die, right after your Queen. If you betray us, I will hunt you with every last breath in my body, and I will make you suffer. Bring us the girl, without delay and without getting 'clever.'"

Klahb nodded jerkily. He turned to leave when Uncle spoke again. "Oh, and Jack. Fetch him also." Klahb swallowed hard, nodded, and left.

The wait passed in silence; the team was giving Uncle space. Later, he would appreciate that. Right at that moment, he was too numb to notice.

Rider set the Queen down on another table, then took up a position beside her, his sidearm aimed at her head. Uncle joined him, and together they both pointed weapons at the Queen.

A clap outside the section of the tent announced a visitor. "Enter," Uncle said.

A pair of soldiers pulled back the curtain and stepped in, dragging Jack. They stopped when they saw the situation.

One of the soldiers instinctively started to reach for his sword. "Don't do it," Rider shook his head. He pointed to the side of the curtain flap where Texas and Zombie knelt, weapons aimed at the two locals. "That thing won't even clear your scabbard before you're dead," Rider added.

While Uncle had been zoned out, Rider had arranged the team in defensive positions.

The two guards looked at each other. As one, they turned and ran back out of the tent, leaving Jack behind.

The thief-cum-prince's hands were bound behind his back. His shirt was torn. His face and body were bruised and bloodied. He had a black eye and a split lip. Someone had worked him over.

Uncle nodded to Vodka. Vodka cut Jack free.

Jack, in the meanwhile, had taken in the situation. He saw the Queen, weapons pointed at her. He saw Parrot's body. He straightened his shoulders and lifted his head. "I'll not beg," said Jack. "You may kill me, but I'll not beg."

"Kill you?" That caught Uncle off-guard. He frowned, shook his head. "No, you misunderstand. You're the only person... the only humanoid around here who has dealt straight with us. You're the only one we like. I'm offering you a ride out of here. You can come back to our world, leave the Queen and this war behind."

Jack blinked. He hadn't been expecting that. His spine relaxed slightly. "Oh, uh. Um." He pointed at the Queen, "May I?"

Uncle nodded. "No tricks." He didn't expect any from Jack, but it was becoming second nature to give the warning.

Jack approached his mother and looked closely at the wound on her head. He nodded as if this confirmed something he suspected. "That's what I thought," said the prince. "Iron poisoning. Not a huge amount; she'll recover in time although she will bear your scar forever." He stepped back. "I thank you for the offer, but I'm afraid if I went to your world, I would die within weeks. There's too much iron in human worlds."

Uncle nodded slowly. "I wasn't sure it would affect you," he said, "since I'm pretty sure you're half human."

Rider looked sharply at Uncle. "What makes you say that?"

"He's taller, his head isn't as big," Uncle shrugged. "Oh, and his father is the source of Klahb's British accent, remember?"

"Also, his name is 'Jack,'" Zombie piped up. "Come on. In a world full of 'Klahbs' and 'Rabbixes' and 'Thormases', his name is 'Jack'? Dad named him."

Jack chuckled. He spread his hands wide. "You're all very clever," admitted the prince. "These things you say are all true. Unfortunately, begin even one quarter faerie is enough that your world is a death sentence, and I'm fully half. Again, I thank you for the offer, but I must decline."

"All right," Uncle nodded. "What about being King? Wanna rule the world?"

Jack's smile was flat and humorless. "I'm afraid I can't do that either. Men don't rule, at least not among our branch. To be a King simply means to be married to the Queen. My father held no power at all."

Uncle nodded again. "Someone mentioned that men don't rule," he said. "I just thought I would make the offer. Since you can't come with us, and you can't run the place, how about this; We'll give you a head start. Take off. Make a run for it. You've got a good pair of legs on you, I'll bet you can get yourself nice and lost before Mommy Dearest wakes up and remembers that she wants you dead."

Jack's face lit up. He smiled and nodded with enthusiasm. "That offer I can, and do, accept!"

Before he could make good on it, however, there came another clap and, without waiting to be acknowledged, Klahb and the Duchess entered, dragging Fiona between them.

The girl was tied the same way Jack had been, although she had not suffered his beatings. Her eyes were wide in terror, and she shook like a leaf, but she seemed physically unharmed.

Texas pushed the locals aside and crouched next to the girl. "Hey there," he said, his voice low and soothing. "It's okay now. We're going to get you out of here." He untied the knots securing her hands, murmuring reassurances all the while.

"Go," Uncle said to Jack. "Oh, and if you find a group of men named Hayer, Thormas, and Hadda, they have a pocket-watch that might interest you."

Jack inclined his head in respect, grinning like a madman. He slipped past Klahb and the Duchess, and in a heartbeat, was gone.

"Come with me," Texas said gently. He escorted Fiona to the table where Uncle and Rider waited. Vodka and Zombie joined them, then Texas and Zombie picked up Parrot's stretcher.

The Duchess and the General watched: he blankly, her with burning, hate-filled eyes.

"'You're all just a pack of cards,'" Uncle quoted.

Awkward silence greeted this extraordinary proclamation.

"Excuse me?" asked the Duchess. "We're what now?"

"Damn it!" Uncle kicked the table upon which the Queen rested so hard he almost broke a toe. "That's how Alice did it."

The Duchess began to laugh. It was a long, loud, cruel laugh, the laugh of someone delighting in the misfortune of others, the sort of laugh the Marquis de Sade had almost surely possessed. It went on long enough that Vodka aimed his sidearm at the Duchess.

"Explain," Uncle ordered.

225

"Alice didn't do anything," said the Duchess. "The Queen sent that self-absorbed little brat home. And you, you've gone and poisoned the Queen. Who knows how long it will be before she wakes up? When she does, will she want to send you home, or just kill you?" She laughed again, sneering and mocking the team.

"Permission to cap a bitch," Zombie requested.

Uncle was tempted. Sorely tempted. But he shook his head. "Negative," he said. "We may need her alive later. Who knows." He chewed on his lip for a moment. Then, "All right. Klahb, you're going to escort us to the edge of camp and let us go. We're taking you and your Queen with us, so don't think about pulling a fast one. Rider, carry the Queen. I've got the General."

The trip through the camp was uneventful. Word had spread of the situation, and the rank-and-file soldiers and servants avoided the team like the plague. The Queen was all too fond of executing people for failures beyond their ability to control. The safest course of action was to not be present in the first place.

The lull ended when the team approached the river that marked the boundary of the camp on this side. "Contact," Zombie said softly. He was in front, carrying half of Parrot's stretcher, so he saw the situation first.

A cluster of mog turei waited at the edge of the river. Uncle thought he recognized one of them from the conversation earlier; not the leader but a slightly smaller creature with a chip missing from his left tusk.

"Easy," Uncle cautioned. "We don't know they're hostile." Better safe than sorry, however. "Put Parrot down." That freed up two more guns in case things turned ugly.

The chipped-tusked mog turei, whom Uncle mentally dubbed Chipped Tusk, lumbered out of the water. "We have been watching you," said Chipped Tusk in the kind of throaty contralto that normally only exists in dreams just before a lonely man awakens. "As you crossed the camp, we watched you," said she. With a voice like that, Uncle could not think of the creature as male. "Is this the hatchling you came here to rescue?"

Uncle nodded. "Her name is Fiona."

"Greetings, Fiona," said the mog turei. She looked at Uncle once more, "Do you intend to leave?"

"Yes," Uncle said. There was no sense denying it.

"We will help you," said Chipped Tusk. She waved an arm at the others, who sank into the water. "The ofyo tari wishes to speak with you. He requests that you bring the Queen."

Uncle nodded. "All right," he said.

"Hey, now wait a moment," said Klahb.

Uncle shook the General by the scruff of his neck. "Maybe it hasn't fully dawned on you yet, General," Uncle said, "but we no longer really care what you want, or what you think is or is not appropriate. We have no deals; you people only break them anyways. We never said we were giving the Queen back when we left camp. If we choose not to, that's our choice."

"Ah, right," said the General, swallowing nervously. "Perfectly reasonable."

"You were saying?" Uncle asked Chipped Tusk. "Where does the ofya tari want this meeting?"

"He did not tell us that," said the mog turei. "He said you would know the meaning of this; he wishes to meet you in the place where you met the second of his kind. I do not understand. I thought there was only one left of his kind."

"There is," Uncle said. He motioned for Zombie and Texas to lift the stretcher again. "Thank you," he said to Chipped Tusk. "Good luck, to you and all your people. Oh, and if you come across one of these faeries named Jack, he's a decent sort. He might be able to help you."

"Jack, son of Harzt," said Chipped Tusk, weaving her huge head in a figure-eight which seemed to pass for a nod. "His name is known to us. He is a bit of a... what is the word?"

"Scoundrel?" Texas suggested.

"Scoundrel. Yes, a good word," said the mog turei. "We will go now. Thank you, humans. Good luck."

The team crossed the river on mog turei back. On the far shore, Uncle turned Klahb to face him. "I'm going to let you go," he said. "But if you send any men after us, we will kill them. And then, we will come for you. Do I make myself clear?"

"Perfectly clear," said Klahb. "Quite."

"His accent is back," Zombie noted.

"Go," Uncle pushed Klahb back onto the nearest mog turei. The little man scampered across the living bridge as fast as he could waddle. Once he was on the other side, the mog turei sank below the surface and vanished from sight.

"So," Rider hefted the Queen again. "The castle?"

"Yep," Uncle said. "Let's roll."

They made several false starts before finding the palace. The landmarks looked different coming the other direction. Uncle spelled first Zombie, then Texas, on stretcher duty. After a time, they grew accustomed to navigating 'towards' or 'away from' the sun. That helped. They made no attempt at stealth. Each of them almost hoped for an encounter, a chance for cathartic violence. That chance never came.

The Queen stirred from time to time. Whenever she did, Rider would touch her wound with the tip of his combat knife. She would stiffen, groan, and lapse back into unconsciousness each time he did this. The black veins in her forehead ebbed and surged to the rhythm of this treatment.

After several hours of walking, they came to a ridge of low hills. In the flat land beyond, the palace squatted and sprawled like a great, cancerous, fungal infection.

Uncle had to admit that his personal feelings of the Queen might, just possibly, be affecting his aesthetic judgment of the castle architecture.

They crossed the battle-damaged and corpse-strewn lawn to the front gate that continued to hang askew. Just inside, the dismembered bodies of several Metalmen choked the foyer. The copper had been rent asunder, as if by long, incredibly strong claws.

"That's new," Vodka said.

"How the fuck did a seven-year-old girl survive this place?" Zombie inspected the carnage. It was his turn to be the one not carrying anyone.

"I don't think they were at war when she came here," Texas replied. "Also: language." He looked down significantly at Fiona, who trailed along in his shadow, eyes wide and frightened.

"Oh. Right," Zombie muttered. "Uh, sorry."

Fiona gave no indication that she had heard him. She merely clung to the back of Texas' belt. Her steps dragged and her grip was weak from exhaustion.

Uncle couldn't blame her. She'd been through hell, and that before the three-and-some-change hour march.

And now, they had no way home. He forced himself to admit the grim truth he had been avoiding. There was no way the Queen was going to send them home, and he doubted even he could climb back up the Rabbit Hole, even assuming they could find it again. If he were to be honest, he brought the team, the girl, and the Queen to the palace simply because it was a direction, any direction, that took them away from the Queen's army.

He intended to turn the Queen over to the Long Man out of spite.

Uncle drew a deep, shuddering breath. He forced those thoughts back down into the corner of his mind. For now, the important thing was to keep everyone distracted. And that meant finding the Long Man.

"What do you think?" Uncle looked at the rest of his team. "Queen's bedroom? That's where we found the head."

"I say we try the throne room first," Rider suggested.

"Oh? Why?"

Rider pointed to the pile of copper parts with his chin. "The carnage seems to head that direction."

Uncle shrugged, then nodded. "All right. Zombie, take point. Vodka, watch our six."

Other than the difficulty of navigating a corridor strewn with sharp little bits of metal while carrying two bodies, they found the throne room without incident. More Metalman bodies lay in pieces in the great hall. Curled around and draped over the back of the throne was the ofya tari, the Long Man. On the dais at the feet of the throne rested the severed head with the crown on it.

"You drug me again," Zombie aimed his machine gun at the Long Man, "and I will find a way to kill you."

The creature laughed, a low, melodious sound. "That's fair," said the Long Man. "But I have no need to drug you now. Your mission here is complete."

Uncle had the uncomfortable feeling that the ofya tari didn't mean Fiona.

"The mog turei said you wanted to see us," Uncle set his end of the stretcher down. Texas followed suit a second later. "Given what you did to us, why exactly should we even listen to you?"

"You are angry," said the Long Man. He lifted his pipe to his lips and took a languid pull. The smoke he breathed out was the normal gray color of tobacco, and he made a point of turning his head to blow it away from the team. "I understand this. What I did was necessary, and even helped you in ways you do not fully understand yet. I used you as pawns in my war, and one of you was lost as a result. I regret that, deeply, and apologize. That it needed to be done is scant consolation to you. And yet, now I have the temerity to ask you one last task." He held up a long talon as if asking for a moment's grace. "But this final task is no arduous one, and I offer a reward in return."

Uncle clenched his fists at his sides. It took an effort of will not to look down at Parrot's body. "What. Do. You. Want?" he asked, emphasizing each word with elaborate precision.

"The Queen," said the Long Man. "That is all. Leave her here with me, and go. In return, I will tell you how to get home, and even provide you with some things that will help you to do so."

"You're going to kill her," Zombie guessed.

"No," said the Long Man. He gestured at the head on the dias below him. "I am going to make her remove the curse she placed on my father. He has been punished enough, it is time he was allowed to die. I am going to allow him to rest, at last. That is all."

Uncle opened his mouth, then closed it. He stood, blinking, for a moment.

"That was unexpected," Rider's voice was quiet. The response had caught him by surprise also.

"That was the point of all of it, wasn't it?" Texas asked. "You took our guns and told the Queen what they did so she would make us use them, so that she would want to keep us, so she would betray us, so we would have to take her hostage, so we could bring her here."

The Long Man inclined his head towards Texas. "That is correct," said the creature. "Your befriending the mog turei and convincing them to rebel against the Queen was... unanticipated. Unanticipated, but welcome."

"How can we get home?" Uncle dragged the conversation back on topic. Texas allowed himself to be distracted too easily.

"Do we have a deal then?" asked the Long Man. Then he held up his talon again. "No, not a deal. You're right. No more deals. An act of faith on my part then." He sucked down another mouthful of smoke, savored it, and released it slowly. "The door in the Queen's garden is still open. The only problem is, you cannot fit through it. So, I will give you a potion that will shrink you, as I did when you came here first. Then, you will be in the Hall Between Worlds."

He paused in order to breathe more of his smoke. Uncle noticed that there was a thin haze of the stuff clinging to the ceiling. He wondered how long the ofya tari had been here, waiting for them. Since they left, maybe?

"From there," continued the Long Man, "you need but walk to the base of the Pit. There, you will drink a second potion that I will provide you, and you will ascend up, through the shaft, back to your own world."

"And how exactly do we get back to our normal size?" Zombie growled. "You're trying to trick us again."

"Not in the slightest," said the Long Man. "It is magic that will cause you to shrink. Magic does not work in your world. Therefore, the moment you arrive, you will return to your normal size."

"How do we know we can trust you?" Rider asked.

The Long Man considered him for a moment, sucking on his pipe. At last, the creature made a gesture similar to a shrug. "You cannot, I suppose. But what do you have to lose? If I am lying, all you have lost is the heavy burden of the Queen. You will still be here, hunted, alone, cut off from your world and your family and friends. In short, you will be no worse off than you are now. But if I am telling the truth, you can go home." Suck, savor, blow. "Also, I have never lied to you. I have been unhelpful and uncooperative, yes. I have used you and drugged you, yes. But I have never lied." He made the shrugging gesture again. "For what that's worth."

Uncle thought about it. There was, he decided, no flaw in the ofya tari's logic. If he was lying, the team really wasn't any worse off than they already were. The Queen was a weak bargaining chip at best, given how many people in this land seemed to hate her. So far, threats to her safety had kept Klahb at bay, but how long would it be until the Duchess made a power-grab for herself?

The ofya tari waited in silence, smoking. Giving them time to think, to come around to his way of thinking. Knowing that they would.

They had no choice.

"Fine," Uncle nodded. "Rider, drop the bitch."

Rider took him literally. He shrugged the Queen off his shoulder and let her fall to the floor with a 'Thump'. From the evil smirk on his lips, he had enjoyed that far too much.

"Now, get us out of here," Uncle said.

The Long Man pointed to the door with his pipe. "You remember where the Door is in the garden, yes? Beside it, you will find two bottles, under the rose bush. Drink the red one to grow small. Drink the green one to go home once you're under the Pit. Do not drink it before then," warned the Long Man. "Or it will be wasted. I will remain here until the curse is broken. If something should go wrong, find me here and I will do what I can. But hurry. Once the Queen wakes and removes the curse, once my father is at rest, I shall leave and it will be impossible to find me again."

Uncle tapped Zombie on the uninjured shoulder, then gestured towards the door. Zombie nodded and walked back across the hall to the door. "Clear," he called back after a moment.

Uncle turned his flat gaze to the Long Man one last time. "Very well," he said. "I... wish your father peace." That was as close to 'polite' as he could force himself to come, all things considered. He picked up his half of the stretcher.

"Good luck, humans," said the Long Man.

Texas picked up his burden, and with Rider in front and Vodka in back, they rejoined Zombie.

The garden was quiet except for the occasional rustle of vulture feathers as the birds feasted on the unburied corpses. Fiona staggered, almost fell into a pool of bloody mud. Zombie slung Overbite behind him, then picked her up. She tucked her head into the crook of his neck to avoid looking at the gore. Uncle noticed that the girl's body was shaking. She was crying.

Zombie blushed a little when he saw people looking at him. "Blo—" he cut himself off, glancing at the girl. "Just... shut up. Go."

The bottles were right where the Long Man had promised, under the rose bush near the little door. One red, one green. Uncle waited for the obligatory 'Christmas' joke, but it never came. He glanced at Rider to make sure the man was still with them.

"Uh," Texas glanced over his shoulder at Uncle. "A thought... how do we get Parrot to drink?"

"FU—dge," Zombie almost-swore. "I knew we were missing something."

"Calm down," Uncle ordered. He was exhausted, angry, emotionally wrecked. He was not in the mood for Zombie's normal theatrics, even if it was funny watching him self-censor. "We'll try pouring some on his lips. If that doesn't work, then we go back and deal with the Long Man."

234

"His lips?" Zombie raised his eyebrows.

"It's magic," Uncle said. "Who knows?"

"... Point," Zombie acknowledged.

Rider scooped up the bottles. He put the green one in the hip pocket of his fatigues. Looking to Uncle and Texas, he said, "You might want to put him down. If the entire stretcher shrinks, you might fumble him."

"The stretcher? I don't think..." Uncle trailed off.

"Magic," Rider said.

"Right."

Uncle and Texas lay the stretcher on the ground. Rider knelt above Parrot and dribbled a few drops from the red bottle onto his lips.

The effect was instant. Parrot shrunk.

The stretcher did not.

"Well, that's going to create a problem," Texas said. "Try—"

Rider was ahead of him. The sniper spilled two drops on the stretcher. Two wet spots appeared on the canvas, but otherwise, nothing happened.

"Well cra—b apples," Rider muttered.

"Okay," Uncle said. "Distribute Parrot's gear. We leave nothing behind for these vultures." He glanced over at a pair of vultures who were taking a break from feasting to watch them. "Not you. You're fine," Uncle muttered. The vultures resumed eating.

They divvied the gear. One by one, the group took sips from the red bottle. Zombie went last, coaxing Fiona to look up long enough for her sip. He drank immediately after her. They shrank together.

They stacked up on the door. At a nod from Uncle, they filed through.

*   *   *   *

 *   *   *

*   *   *   *

The hall of doors was immense when seen from the perspective of someone a foot tall. The glass table was three times their size. The lamps that hung from the ceiling were huge, but far away. The doors, except the one they had just stepped through, were built for titans.

"Looks like it was built by Dwarves," Texas said.

Vodka cocked his head and said, "What?"

"You know," Texas gestured expansively at the scaled-up architecture. "That movie about the ring. Dwarves, always building to over-compensate."

"Can we go now?" Zombie asked.

"Yeah," Uncle nodded. "Roll out."

They slowly picked their way up the hall, which was a good six times longer than it had been the first time.

Perspective. Go figure.

They reached the corner, Rider slightly in front of the others.

Combat-trained reflexes saved his life.

A shoe only marginally smaller than Rider's entire body flashed out of the darkness. Rider threw himself to the side and rolled. The shoe crashed to the ground where Rider had been half a second ago.

Uncle looked up, and up, and up. The shoe belonged to Rabbix, who was lifting his foot for a second go at crushing Rider.

"NO!" Uncle yelled. He raised his M4 and fired. Beside him, he heard Texas and Vodka doing the same.

The bullets seemed to have little, if any, effect on Rabbix. The reduced mass and the slower objective muzzle velocity meant they were little more deadly than rubber bands.

"Cease fire!" Uncle yelled. "Scatter! Make for the Pit! Rabbix, stop! We're leaving!"

Again and again Rabbix tried to crush Rider. Rider rolled to his feet, narrowly avoiding the giant foot. He sprinted this way, then that. Soon, however, Rabbix had him pinned into a corner.

"You stole my pocket-watch!" bellowed Rabbix, his voice deep and low. "You hurt Bill!"

"We don't have your watch," Uncle yelled, running towards Rabbix. He wasn't sure what he was going to do when he got there. It was instinct. "And Bill attacked us first! It was self defense!"

"Uncle!" Vodka threw something at him.

Uncle caught it mid-stride. It was a lump of something soft and spongy.

"Eat it!" Vodka yelled.

Uncle shoved the lump into his mouth and swallowed hard. It tasted like portabello. As he ran towards Rabbix, Uncle noticed that the other man was shrinking.

No, that was wrong. Uncle was growing.

What the hell? No time to worry about it right then. Rabbix bent down and scooped up Rider, who struggled and strained but could not break free.

Uncle was his normal size now. He grabbed Rabbix from behind, wrapping one arm around his throat. With his other hand, Uncle drew his combat knife. He held it poised above Rabbix's chest.

All he had to do was slam the blade home. Even if the initial thrust didn't kill Rabbix, the iron content of the knife was sure to do the trick.

He remembered the way the Queen screamed when the barrel of his sidearm touched her. He remembered the way Texas had screamed when the fire had burned him. He remembered Rider's back, clawed open by the Cat. Vodka' arm, and Zombie's. His own thigh, which still burned. Parrot, dead. He remembered fields of bodies and a room full of skulls. He remembered a severed head that screamed, and Jack saying that it was 'one' of the ones that still lived in eternal pain. He remembered the Duchess saying she turned her children into pigs before they learned to talk. He remembered betrayals and double-crosses. He remembered hunger, and exhaustion, and terror at every turn.

He remembered the Cat saying that the Duchess raised him from a kitten. He remembered the Long Man arranging everything in order to free his father from torment. He remembered the pain in the mog turei leader's voice as he spoke of the fate of his species. He remembered a farmer with splinters in his hands digging a grave for his dead grandchildren.

He remembered Rabbix, Pat, and Pat's Twin trying to save an injured lizard.

"Let him go," Uncle said softly. "Rabbix. Please. No more. Let the violence end. I don't want to hurt you. I'm sorry about Bill, but he needs you to help him recover. He needs you, Rabbix. Please don't make me kill you."

With a trembling arm, Rabbix lifted Rider and loosened his grip a little, holding the sniper up in surrender. Uncle released Rabbix' throat and took Rider gently from him. Uncle backed away, covering Rabbix with his knife.

He needn't have bothered. Rabbix put his back to the wall and slumped down. He covered his face with his hands. "Oh dear, oh dear," said Rabbix, his body shaking with sobs. "Whatever did I do to deserve this? I just wanted to be left alone."

Uncle glanced behind him. His men were running for the bottom of the shaft, Texas and Zombie carrying Parrot between them. Uncle backed up two steps, then sheathed his knife. He turned his back on the weeping local and hurried to rejoin his people at the bottom of the shaft.

Uncle set Rider on the his feet, then gently took Parrot's body from the others. "I'll go last," he said. "See you on the other side."

Rider withdrew the green bottle which, thankfully, remained intact. He took a swig, then passed the bottle to Zombie.

As Zombie lifted the bottle to his lips, Rider began to ascend, his arms pinwheeling for a second. It looked, Uncle thought, as if he were falling upwards.

Zombie drank, passed the bottle to Texas. Texas did the same for Fiona, who did it for Vodka. Vodka saluted Uncle, drank, and set the bottle on the ground.

Uncle watched his men 'fall' up the shaft until they vanished. He looked down at the body in his hand. "I'm so sorry, buddy," he whispered. Carefully, he stooped and picked up the tiny bottle. He wondered briefly if there would be enough of the potion to lift him at his current size.

Only one way to find out. He tipped the bottle. A single drop fall onto his tongue. The sky dropped out from under him, and, clutching Parrot, he fell up and up.

*   *   *   *

*   *   *

*   *   *   *

CHAPTER XII
UNCLE'S DE-BRIEF

———◆———

After that, it was the normal hurry-up-and-wait you learn to expect when dealing with cross-service and international logistics.

Yes sir, I'm going to see Mrs. Fernandez as soon as you cut me loose.

Yes sir, I'll tell her. And thank you sir.

-CSM Daniel "Uncle" Beckworth, official de-brief, Operation Rabbit Hole

"SERGEANT? SERGEANT, WAKE UP."

Beckworth didn't want to. The dream was so nice. He and his girlfriend were visiting Fernandez. The family dog, a big shaggy mutt named El Perro del Diablo, was resting across his legs while he sipped a Corona and smelled tamales cooking. He knew, somehow, that if he woke up, something terrible would happen. He sipped his beer again and tried to ignore the voice until it went away.

It didn't go away. "Sergeant! Wake up!" The world trembled. Earthquake? No, someone was shaking him.

Beckworth groaned as the dream world fragmented around him. He opened his eyes.

He was laying in the shade under a big, spreading oak tree. To his right, sunlight sparkled off a lazy river. Bees hummed in the distance. He was warm, comfortable, and there was a pleasant weight on his legs. "El Diablo?" he asked, tilting his head to look.

It was Fernandez' backpack.

The dream vanished, and reality came crashing back down around him. His chest tightened. Something burned his eyes. He would not weep. Not yet. Not in front of the men.

Beckworth looked up. Captain Park was kneeling above him, gently shaking him. "Are you awake, Sergeant?" Park asked. His voice was mellow, sympathetic.

The sergeant grunted, leaned himself up on one arm. "Yeah," he said. "I'm awake. Where are... where is the girl? Did she..."

"She's fine," Park said. "She's with her dad right now. You're the last to wake up. Come on." Park stood and offered a hand.

Beckworth kicked the pack off his legs, took the hand, and climbed to his feet. The rest of his team stood a few feet away, surrounding Fernandez' body. Beyond them, a slender man with dignified gray hair and an expensive navy blue suit knelt in the mud, hugging a sobbing little girl in his arms tightly. The other VIPs stood nearby, expressions of relief mingled with joy. Allowing an ambassador's daughter to be kidnapped on your property was probably not an awesome political move.

"I've sent for a stretcher for Sergeant Fernandez," Park said, gently taking Beckworth's arm and steering him to the rest of his group.

"How long," Beckworth looked up at the sun. "Two days? Three?"

"Hours," Park shook his head. "You were gone just under three hours."

"Bullshit," Beckworth blurted. He swallowed hard, blushing. "Uh, sorry Sir. What I mean is..."

"I understand," Park gave him a tight little smile of grim sympathy. "It's confusing for me too. Sergeant Adams said the same thing. He showed me his watch. I assume you didn't all set your watches ahead just to mess with me. Also, the sheer number of injuries you all have, and Marquez' scars... there's no way you were gone only three hours. But that's how long it's been." He held up a hand to forestall any further protests. "You can all give a full debrief once you're back home. For now, let's just concentrate on getting you there. One last thing, tho. The British Government wanted me to ask; did you ever find their missing policewoman?"

"Negative, sir," Beckworth shook his head. "We never saw any signs of her at all, I'm afraid, and none of the locals indicated having seen her."

Park nodded, shrugged, clapped Beckworth on the shoulder.

Across the lawn, the butler who had offered Beckworth tea so very long ago escorted two pairs of EMTs, pointing them towards the group. They hustled over, wheeling a stretcher between them. One pair went to check on Fiona, the others came to Beckworth's group.

Beckworth waved them off when they tried to pick up Fernandez. "We have this," he said.

In silence, Halsford, Adams, Marquez, and Beckworth lifted Fernandez onto the stretcher. Jones, his broken arm dangling loosely, saluted with his other hand. Park joined him.

The EMTs waited in respectful silence until it was over. Then, one began inspecting Jones' arm while the other wanted to take a look at Beckworth's leg.

The slender man in the expensive suit walked slowly, timidly, to the group. "I uh," he cleared his throat. "I cannot thank you enough for bringing my girl back to me." Ambassador McGinney's eyes, Beckworth noticed, were still red and puffy. He'd been crying the entire time they were gone. "I'm so, so very sorry for the loss of your man. I... I understand if you hate me."

"What?" Beckworth blinked in surprise at the man. "Why would we hate you?"

"Well, your man died rescuing my daughter..."

"That wasn't your fault," Adams said.

"You didn't ask for her to be kidnapped, and you didn't kill Fernandez," Beckworth nodded in agreement with Adams' sentiment. "The blame for his death lies squarely on the people who did this. I'm glad we were able to bring your girl back. She's very brave."

"I... thank you," the Ambassador said, wiping away tears with the back of his coat sleeve. "Thank you." He fumbled for something else to say, could think of nothing. He nodded at Beckworth and Park, then turned and walked back to where the other EMTs were finishing looking over his daughter.

"Can we go home now?" Halsford asked.

It took almost two hours before they were able to leave. Vehicles had to be sent from RAF Alconbury, and there was, they were told when the Humvees finally arrived, traffic on the orbital. That gave the local EMTs plenty of time to splint and sling Jones' arm, clean and re-bandage Beckworth's leg, patch up Zombie's arm, and in general inspect the others. Beckworth took advantage of the delay to pull Jones aside.

"What was that?" he asked.

"Sir?" Jones cocked his head in confusion.

"The thing you threw at me. That made me grow. What was it?"

"Oh," Jones chuckled softly. "Well, remember when we first met the Long Man? I grabbed some of his mushroom?"

Beckworth blinked. He had forgotten all about that. "How did you know it was the right one? Wasn't one supposed to make

243

us smaller?"

"I had a fifty-fifty chance," Jones nodded. "But I figured what the hell. You couldn't be less effective going up against Rabbix than you were."

Beckworth narrowed his eyes. "I should shoot you," he growled.

"Yes sir," Jones nodded, grinning. "But you won't."

In time, the Humvees arrived. The team was transported to the closest RAF base on loan to the USAFE. A few hours later, they boarded a C-17 for America.

They slept most of the way home.

Department of Defense

JSOC

US Army

AFO Spectre

MEMORANDUM FOR: Lieutenant General Carl W. Wilson.

FROM: Colonel Ajay Hastings

SUBJECT: Summary of events and reports for Operation Rabbit Hole.

This Comprehensive Report of Operation JSFPIIAD-002, code named, "Rabbit Hole," was compiled using recordings from individual de-briefing interviews, after action reviews, and recovered helmet-camera footage from the following individuals:

Command Sergeant Major Daniel "Uncle" Beckworth

Master Sergeant James "Zombie" Halsford

Master Sergeant Jamal "Vodka" Jones

Sergeant First Class Matthew "Rider" Adams

Staff Sergeant William "Texas" Marquez

Additional information was provided by the recovered helmet-camera footage, only, of:

First Sergeant Roberto "Parrot" Fernandez (Parrot) – KIA

Original materials are on record with the DOD and JSOC command.

Col. Ajay Hastings

JSOC

Fort Bragg

*   *   *   *
  *   *   *
*   *   *   *

THE FIRES SMOLDERED STILL, but the main blaze had flickered and died. The man who studied the wreckage of the crates was tall and slender with handsome features. His long, wavy hair was pulled back in a loose tail, and his beard was full and thick. He wore a long overcoat that may have once been blue, but had long since been bleached by sun and spray to a dull medium gray. His trousers were of newer stock, homespun and close fitting. He wore a heavy black leather glove on his left hand. With his right, he scratched at his chin whiskers.

As he surveyed the destruction, another man approached. This fellow was shorter, stockier. He had the look of a man who would, if given enough leisure, become portly but constant work kept his corpulence in check. His hair was a dull, sandy blonde, sticking out in patches here and there from under a faded red-and-white knit wool cap.

The newcomer waited a pace behind and to the left of the

first man. After a time, the shorter fellow cleared his throat.

The tall man turned his back to the destruction. "Were you able to salvage anything?" His voice was deep, cultured, and strong. The voice of a man used to giving orders, often at high volume.

"Little, sir," said the other man. His voice was meek, obsequious. It often made the taller man think of the squeaking of a mouse. "Perhaps five crates worth of assorted foods. Call it thirty or thirty-five man-days."

The taller man nodded, his deep-set eyes brooding. "Very well," sighed he. "When next you go Through, order production to continue. We need to replenish our stores 'fore we sally deeper into these lands."

"Aye aye, Captain," saluted the smaller man.

"And of the ones who did this?"

"Gone, sir."

"We are sure?"

"Fairly sure," said the smaller man. "Scouts reported seeing them returning to the Queen's palace. Long has it been rumored that there is a Portal there somewhere. They have not been seen since."

"And we are sure they are the ones who did... this?" The Captain left off stroking his beard to gesture at the smoking ruin behind him.

"Aye, sir," said the other. "A patrol of Tik-Tok Men saw the ones who did it as they were leaving. Of course, the Tik-Tok Men had no idea that this would happen."

"And the Tik-Tok Men didn't attack, because the Queen's allies were human," nodded the Captain with a sigh.

"I am not sure they are allies; not exactly, sir," said the smaller man. "They showed some evidence of acting under duress. One of our informants in the Queens' army claims they even took the Queen captive for a short time, when she attempted to renege on some sort of deal."

"Did they now? Did they indeed?" the Captain's smile was both grim and pleased. "Well then, if that is the case, I wish them bon voyage and hope that we never see them again. Where is the Queen now?"

"Unknown, sir," said the lieutenant. "Our informant said that the outlanders took her hostage and fled the camp with her. The scouting party that saw them near the palace thinks they saw the Queen with them still. It is possible they took her back home with them, or maybe killed her at the castle. Unfortunately, none of our forces have been able to penetrate the palace and return in almost a day."

"If the outlanders took her back to their world, she'll be dead in hours of iron poisoning," said the Captain. His underling shuddered. It was not a pleasant death, even for one's enemies. Better the clean death of the sword or club or axe. "Who leads the enemy now?"

"Our man inside says that the Duchess and General Klahb hold a loose alliance for the moment."

"Good," smiled the Captain. "They are both fools. If they are in charge, it can only work in our favor." He shook his head, marveling at the bad decision making of some people. "This is what happens when you execute everyone smart enough to ever pose a threat to you: you end up surrounded by morons."

"'Tis a good thing you don't do that then, sir," said the lieutenant.

The Captain chuckled in the back of his throat. "Indeed, Smee. Indeed. Now, tell me of the rebel from the Other Side? Has he been seen again, this knight clad all in red?"

"Aye sir," said Smee. "He was seen from afar, but our forces could not close with him. Starkey says he believes the knight made a run for the Glass, and probably made it."

"Unfortunate," the Captain rubbed his neck with his hand. "They are a thorn in our side, those knights. Well, no matter. Once we have succeeded in our goals, they will not matter anymore."

The watched the smoke in companionable silence for a minute or two. Then the Captain spoke again. "How goes the Mark II model?"

"Very well, sir," said Smee with a slight grimace. "The first one is being dis-assembled on the Other Side for transport through the Glass. The Gentleman says he has successfully instructed the Tik-Tok Men in how to assemble the Mark II on this side of the fog. It should be ready in two or three days."

"One could wish they were more mobile, but alas. One cannot have everything."

"Indeed not, sir. Where would one put it?"

The Captain joined Smee in a chuckle at the old joke.

"Sir, if I may be so bold as to ask a question?"

"You just did, Smee. But yes, you may ask another," teased the Captain with a sly grin.

Smee smiled for a moment to show he appreciated the effort. "The destruction of all this food sets us back weeks, if not months. The ones who did it also destroyed several Tik-Tok Men and slew Fast Rabbit Eddie. Why did you order us not to attempt to capture the outlanders?"

The Captain ran the fingers of his right hand through his beard again, fluffing it. He was silent for a time, choosing his words. When at last he spoke, it was with heavy gravitas. "I could tell you that I wanted to prevent them destroying more of our copper machines. I could say that I wished to prevent risk to any more of you, my valuable and loyal men. I could say that what was done was done, and spending resources on revenge would accomplish little. And all of these things are true, to a point."

He heaved a sigh and shrugged his shoulders. "All of these things are true, to a point," repeated the Captain, "but the truth is, I let them go because they were humans. Duped or coerced by the Queen as they may have been, they were... are... still human, just like you and I, my old friend. And it is for them, and their world, which was our world once, that we are doing all this. I could not bring myself to harm they whom we are trying to save."

He stretched then, lifting onto his toes and reaching his arms towards the sky. A sound came from his gloved left hand. He frowned at it. "It is squeaking again," said the Captain.

"We can't have that, now can we, Captain? I'll fetch the oil right away."

"Good form, Smee old man. Good form," smiled Captain Ironhand.

GLOSSARY

1SG: First Sergeant

AFO: Advanced Force Operations. A JSOC command encompassing personnel from Delta Force, the Navy Seals, and Army Intelligence.

AK-47: Avtomat Kalashnikova, model 1947. A Russian-made assault rifle.

Alpha: The letter "A" in the NATO phonetic alphabet.

AQ: Al-Qaeda

Banana Mag: Short for banana magazine: a long, slightly curved ammunition magazine, primarily for automatic weapons.

Black/Blue or **White/Blue:** Spectre's personal method of naming walls in a building whose compass orientation is unknown. The wall facing the team at the time of discussion is "red." Clockwise, the other walls are white, blue, and black. Therefore, white/blue would be the far back left corner of the building.

Blue: Friendly. A warning that the approaching person, unit, or force is friendly.

C4: Composition 4. A plastic explosive.

C-17: Boeing C-17 Globemaster III. A four-engine turbofan transport airplane.

C-130: Lockheed C-130 Hercules. A four-engine turboprop transport airplane.

CIA: The Central Intelligence Agency. The primary non-domestic intelligence gathering agency of the U.S. Government.

CSM: Command Sergeant Major.

DD 256: An Honorable Discharge form.

DARPA: The Defense Advanced Research Projects Agency. An agency and think-tank responsible for developing new technologies for use by the U.S. military.

DERPA: A portmanteau of DARPA and derp. A mocking way of referring to DARPA.

DFAC: Dining Facility. The more modern name for a 'mess hall.'

DOD: The Department of Defense.

E-9: The highest Enlisted pay grade in the U.S. military.

E-tool: Entrenching tool. A collapsible spade or shovel.

Echo: The letter "E" in the NATO phonetic alphabet.

EMT: Emergency Medical Technician.

Entrenching tool: A collapsible spade or shovel.

Flashbang: A hand grenade that produces a bright light and a loud noise in order to stun enemies, rather than injure them permanently.

FNG: Fucking New Guy.

Fort Bragg: A U.S. Army installation, home of JSOC and SFOD-D.

Fort Meade: A U.S. Army installation, main headquarters of the NSA.

HMMWV: High Mobility Multipurpose Wheeled Vehicle. A rugged workhorse truck used by the military.

Hotel: The letter "H" in the NATO phonetic alphabet.

Hua: A general-purpose response. Depending on context, it might mean 'yes,' 'no,' 'what the heck?' or just about any number of other things. Commonly believed to be a backronym of Heard, Understood, Acknowledged.

Huah: Alternate spelling of Hua.

HUMINT: Human Intelligence. The gathering of information through interpersonal means, rather than via electronic or long-distance surveillance.

Humvee: An informal way of saying HMMWV.

INSCOM: The U.S. Army Intelligence and Security Command. Otherwise known as Army Intelligence.

JSOC: Joint Special Operations Command.

KIA: Killed In Action.

M1911: A .45 caliber sidearm. Not normally issued to U.S. Army forces, but popular with AFO Spectre.

M249: A 5.56mm light machine gun.

M4: A 5.56mm carbine based on the venerable M16 assault rifle. The M4 is shorter and lighter than the M16.

MDR-TB: Multi-Drug-Resistant Tuberculosis. A strain of tuberculosis that is resistant to most, if not all, first-line drug treatments.

MRE: Meal, Ready to Eat. A pre-packaged meal used by the U.S. military. Also called, variously, Meals, Rejected by Everyone, Materials Resembling Edibles, Morale Reducing Elements, and a host of other mocking nicknames.

MSG: Master Sergeant.

Muj: Derived from the word mujahideen, muj is a pejorative used to describe any of a number of various insurgent groups in the Middle East.

NOD: Night Observation Device. A low-light amplification system.

NSA: National Security Agency. The main United States intelligence agency tasked with developing and maintaining signals intelligence (SIGINT). Also sometimes called the No Such Agency, or Not Socially Acceptable.

Overbite: The name of MSG James "Zombie" Halsford's M249 light machine gun.

Parrot: The call-sign of 1SG Roberto Fernandez.

PHR: Preliminary HUMINT Report. A briefing report derived from reports or interviews with people. In this case, it refers to Alice's Adventures in Wonderland.

Purple Durple: A mocking name for the Purple Heart medal awarded to those members of the U.S. military killed or wounded in service.

QRF: Quick Reaction Force. A rescue party.

RAF: Royal Air Force. The British Air Force.

RAF Alconbury: A RAF airbase in England on long-term loan to the U.S. Air Force.

Rider: The call-sign of SFC Matthew Adams.

SCC: Special Circumstances Command. A command component of the U.S. Special Operations Command (USSOCOM) tasked with dealing with threats of an otherworldly nature.

SFC: Sergeant First Class.

SFOD-D: The 1st Special Forces Operational Detatchment-Delta. More commonly known as Delta Force.

Shahi-Kot: A high mountain valley in Afghanistan, and the sight of the disastrous Operation Anaconda.

Six: Behind or in back of. Referring to 'Six o'Clock' on an imaginary clock where Twelve is directly in front of the speaker. So 'Watch your six,' means to watch behind you.

SNAFU: Situation Normal: All Fucked Up.

SSG: Staff Sergeant.

Tac-50: A 50 caliber sniper rifle.

Tango: The letter "T" in the NATO phonetic alphabet.

Texas: The call-sign of SSG William Marquez.

The Truck: The name of SFC Matthew "Rider" Adams' Tac-50 sniper rifle.

Twin Huey: The Bell UH-1N Twin Huey is a workhorse transport helicopter. Still in occasional service by the U.S. Air Force.

Uncle: The call-sign of CSM Daniel Beckworth.

USAFE: United States Air Force in Europe.

VIP: Very Important Person.

Vodka: The call-sign of MSG Jamal Jones.

Zombie: The call-sign of MSG James Halsford.

ABOUT THE AUTHOR'S CAT

Ozymandius, Cat of Cats, was discovered working his second job, escorting people to their cars in a Denny's parking lot for tips. He was taken in by the Author and his Wife, given a shower and a new job: being as cute and distracting as possible at all times.

Ozzy has since doubled in size, and he lives with the Author in a suburb of Atlanta, GA. where they moved after having lived in Los Angeles for most of their lives. Ozzy puts up with the Author's insomnia and need to write, as well as the Author's Wife's Cat.

Ozzy also likes to sack out on the couch while the Author plays video games (a rare occurrence these days) or table-top RPGs (even more rare). He is aware that the Author's favorite drink is Iced Tea (unsweet), and his favorite alcohol is Gin (St. George's Terroir, if you're curious).

www.ingramcontent.com/pod-product-compliance
Lightning Source LLC
Chambersburg PA
CBHW070859250626
47159CB00003B/1125